D0209365

THE ORGANS OF SENSE

ADAM EHRLICH SACHS

the Organs of Sense

)

FARRAR, STRAUS AND GIROUX | NEW YORK

Farrar, Straus and Giroux
175 Varick Street, New York 10014

Copyright © 2019 by Adam Ehrlich Sachs
All rights reserved
Printed in the United States of America
First edition, 2019

Library of Congress Cataloging-in-Publication Data
Names: Sachs, Adam Ehrlich, author.
Title: The organs of sense / Adam Ehrlich Sachs.
Description: First edition. | New York : Farrar, Straus and Giroux, 2019.
Identifiers: LCCN 2018044051 | ISBN 9780374227371 (hardcover)
Classification: LCC PS3619.A278 O74 2019 | DDC 813/.6—dc23
LC record available at https://lccn.loc.gov/2018044051

Designed by Richard Oriolo

Our books may be purchased in bulk for promotional,
educational, or business use. Please contact your local
bookseller or the Macmillan Corporate and Premium Sales
Department at 1-800-221-7945, extension 5442, or by e-mail
at MacmillanSpecialMarkets@macmillan.com.

www.fsgbooks.com
www.twitter.com/fsgbooks • www.facebook.com/fsgbooks

1 3 5 7 9 10 8 6 4 2

Thank you to Molly Atlas, Jeremy M. Davies, Lauren Roberts, Maris Dyer,
Claire Nozieres, Enrichetta Frezzato, Karolina Sutton, the
Rohr family and the Jewish Book Council, the National
Endowment for the Arts, and Nina and Tatyana.

For my mother

And in memory of my grandfather,
Walter Ehrlich

Look out at and look into.

—Giambattista della Porta, *Magia naturalis*

THE ORGANS OF SENSE

ONE

*I*N AN ACCOUNT sent to the *Philosophical Transactions* but for some reason never published there, or anywhere else, a young G. W. Leibniz, who throughout his life was an assiduous inquirer into miracles and other aberrations of nature, related the odd and troubling encounter he had with a certain astronomer who'd predicted that at noon on the last day of June 1666, the brightest time of day at nearly the brightest time of year, the Moon would pass very briefly, but very precisely, between the Sun and the Earth, casting all of Europe for one instant in absolute darkness, "a darkness without equal in our history, but lasting no longer than four seconds," the astronomer predicted, according to Leibniz, an eclipse that no other astronomer in Europe was predicting, and which, Leibniz explained, drew his notice in part because the astronomer in question, whose observations of the planets and the fixed stars were supposedly among the most accurate and the most precise ever made, superior to Tycho's, was blind, and "not merely completely blind," Leibniz wrote (in my translation from the Latin), "but in fact entirely without eyes."

There could be no question of his *feigning* blindness because his sockets, and this much was known, were empty, wrote Leibniz, for whom this encounter seems to have both hastened and brought to a close the sole significant intellectual crisis of a philosophical career otherwise dominated by the sanguine rationalism for which it is now known, and for which, at least since the time of Voltaire, it has periodically been ridiculed.

Now, this astronomer had built, it was rumored, the longest telescope known to man, and therefore the most powerful, a telescope said to stretch nearly two hundred feet, reported Leibniz; but according to all known laws of optics the true power of a telescope is a function also of the power of the eye that peers into it, left or right, and the power of the eye is of course a function of the existence of the eye, and in this case neither eye existed, "neither the left nor the right." Hence in mid-June when Leibniz set out from Leipzig for Bohemia—first by carriage, down sun-dappled forest lanes, then, upon reaching the foothills, by horse, past the black mouths of salt mines, and finally, in the high mountains, by foot, along muddy paths forged by goats, over passes still deep in snow, a journey it would be all but impossible to imagine him making in his big curly wig and expensive silk stockings if we did not have this textual evidence that he indeed made it, although the absurd image of the Leibnizian wig poking through a snowdrift, or of Leibniz himself stepping around a goat, has been sufficient in some quarters to cast doubt on the authenticity of the whole document—he knew that he was dealing most likely with a mystic, a madman, or a cunning fraud. But there was, as he explained to the *Philosophical Transactions*, a fourth and presumably final possibility, a possibility as intriguing as it was improbable: that he would encounter up there in the snowy mountains of Bohemia a man of reason, a man of science, whose prophesied flash of darkness would actually come to pass, who in other words stared up at the sky with his empty sockets and saw somehow what no other astronomer in the world could see, foresaw with no eyes what they could not foresee with two. If that were the case, Leibniz concluded, then when the light went on again four seconds later it would find the laws of optics in a shambles, knowledge in ruins, the human mind in an intimate embrace with the world, and the human eye in a state of disgrace.

He intended to reach the observatory by sunrise on the twenty-eighth, to stay there two days and two nights in order to "rigorously but surreptitiously assess the astronomer's sanity" through "a series of subtly stringent interviews proceeding from the political to the theological," i.e., from the lowest to the highest, "by way of the ethical, the logical, the astronomical, and the metaphysical," and finally at noon on the third day, i.e., the thirtieth, to observe by the astronomer's side the Moon's predicted occultation of the Sun, the foretold four seconds of darkness on Earth, "the assessment sine qua non of his sanity."

He could pass my assessment without passing God's, Leibniz wrote.

We are actually always passing each other's sanity assessments but failing God's, he wrote. I'm always passing your assessment and you're always passing mine, always with flying colors, this is what a conversation is, an alternating series of not-very-stringent sanity assessments, though in God's eyes presumably we're frequently mad.

Still we never increase the stringency of our assessments!

Of course, even the most stringent human assessment is ridiculous in light of even the laxest assessment administered by God, Leibniz wrote.

It is worth noting that two weeks earlier, for reasons that remain obscure some three and a half centuries later, Leibniz had been denied his doctorate in law by the faculty of the University of Leipzig, despite having recently published his first book, *On the Art of Combinations*. Upon hearing the verdict he had gone for a walk on the outskirts of town, in the Rosental woods, where, while staring at the trunk of a tree, he was struck for the first time—as he recalled decades afterward in a letter to the French skeptic Simon Foucher—by the "calamitous" implications of the philosophy of Descartes, who had severed the mind from the world, transformed the world into a gargantuan machine, and made the mind doubt everything but its own existence. For a brief moment in his nineteenth year Leibniz lost his faith in reason. The next fortnight finds him en route to

Bohemia. I imagine him trudging through that summer snow in search not only of material for publication but of a happier and more harmonious relationship between mind and world.

In any case, something must have gone wrong, his calculations, his cartography, for it was not until after sunrise on the thirtieth, more than two full days behind schedule and only a few hours before the predicted eclipse, that Leibniz reached the observatory, and almost without realizing it, for he was at that point, as he recounts, suffering from hunger, dehydration, and hypothermia ("I have nearly completed a treatise on some remarkable properties of mountains," he reports to the *Philosophical Transactions*), and had hallucinated, over the course of the night prior, while staggering from one peak to the next under the lash of a freezing rain, a vast number of astronomical observatories "of every conceivable and inconceivable geometry," not only triangular observatories and pentagonal observatories but observatories of hundreds of sides and in fact even thousands of sides, "in short, a night of pure polygonal unease." "Observatories were constantly popping out of the mist, and only after I ran up to them in relief did I realize they were in my head." So, when the Sun rose and he saw right in front of him a small, perfectly circular tower of red brick, crumbling in parts, perched on the edge of a high cliff well above the clouds, with an immense telescope, even longer than rumored, protruding from it at an angle over the void, he assumed at first ("not unreasonably!") that this circular observatory was just another illusion produced by his bedeviled mind, the final illusion, the observatory toward which last night's distressing sequence was inexorably tending, and which, knowing his mind, his mind would not rest until it had produced. ("In the astronomer's mind I would soon encounter a similar, but of course not identical, since no two things in nature are identical, sort of mind.") It was only when he heard the telescope creak ("animalistically") in the wind that Leibniz realized he had actually found it, "it was not inside my head, it was actually out there in the snow on the edge of the cliff."

On the next page of his account he depicts with a draftsman's hand the intricate system of pulleys and poles that held the heavy iron instrument aloft, marking lengths and angles with terrific precision. It is an impressive diagram, a marvel of its kind, far more detailed than the diagrams most instrument-makers of the time drew or commissioned for their own contraptions. The caption reads: "It was not inside my head."

)

THE TOWER HAD FEW WINDOWS, and the few that it did have were small, and shuttered tight, but after several circumnavigations of the structure Leibniz found a slat that was slightly askew and permitted him, if he stood on his toes, to peer inside. Outside it was bright and clear but inside the observatory it was dark apart from the light of a single candle, which dimly illuminated a very old man sitting on a three-legged stool, pressing one of his two empty eye sockets to the brass eyepiece of that colossal telescope. He neither wore glass eyes nor covered his sockets with patches; where the eyes are usually found "he merely had two uncanny voids." Obviously someone at some point had simply gone ahead and plucked them out. Every so often the astronomer would suddenly pick up his quill and write something down with considerable urgency, and although Leibniz could not make out from his vantage point what it was the astronomer was writing, "he gave off at such moments the distinct impression of someone who has really seen something." If this was a sort of performance, it was not clear for whom he might be performing, since there was no one else save a fat slumbering cat in the observatory, and as far as Leibniz could tell, he, Leibniz, had not yet been detected. If this was a performance for God, God, the being that need only be possible to be actual, and Who therefore is actual, because He is possible, and Who as a consequence of His actuality perceives at every instant an infinity of perceptions, would, no doubt, not be fooled, a fact of which reason itself, if it functioned rightly in him, would inform the astronomer. And if it is a performance for himself, he is, as I will prove, mad, Leibniz wrote, for it is part of the essence of a performance that one stages it for others, so anyone who performs for himself acts as if he has within him another being, who might be performed for—an evident absurdity; and if he believes this absurdity, then he is mad, and if he acts this way without believing it, then he is also mad. Hence, Leibniz reasoned, if this "ceremony of sight" (my translation) is performed for himself, then he is mad; if it is performed for God, then he is also mad; and if it is performed for others, there being no one else here besides me, whom as far as I can tell he has not detected, then he is also mad. So, if he is sane, and he has not detected me, then this is not a performance, and either he really sees, or he thinks he really sees.

)

AS FOR HIS PHYSICAL APPEARANCE, apart from his missing eyes, Leibniz reported to the *Philosophical Transactions*, the old astronomer was shriveled-up and bony and hunched over, and had some white hair on his head but not a lot of it (though each strand was long, there were not many strands), and the skin of his neck sagged below his chin, and his nose was big, the big bent nose perhaps of an Israelite, though altogether his face emanated an aura of "amiability and intelligence." Whenever the astronomer bowed his head to peer into the telescope, his head, from Leibniz's vantage point, vanished completely behind the high jutting ridge of his shoulders; "his spinal column had probably deformed with age." The astronomer wore the rags and furs of the goatherds Leibniz had passed on the ascent. "Nothing on his feet, nothing on his head." "The possibility that he actually *was* a goatherd, who had lost his eyes, and his mind, and strolled into this observatory, and began calling himself 'the astronomer,' was of course not lost on me." From the moment he first saw him, Leibniz was well aware that what the old man herded might be something quite other than "flocks of truth and falsity through the pastures of the kingdom of reason."

On the next page: a drawing of the old man hunched over on his stool, at the eyepiece of the telescope, the lengths of his limbs and the angle at which he held his head marked with precision as though the man himself were part of his instrument. The caption reads: "*Was* he a goatherd?"

If the solar eclipse took place, Leibniz noted, that was sufficient proof that he was, in fact, an astronomer, because the probability of someone who is not an astronomer predicting, eyes or no eyes, an eclipse that no other astronomer in the world has predicted is negligible. But if the solar eclipse failed to take place, it was no proof that he was *not* an astronomer, since it is not only nonastronomers who mispredict eclipses but also astronomers, eyes or no eyes, though of course especially no eyes. The probability of someone who *is* an astronomer, even a sighted one, mispredicting a solar eclipse is actually quite high, as any induction over past solar eclipse mispredictions will indicate, since astronomers, even the sighted ones, are constantly mispredicting eclipses. "If the eclipse does occur we can deduce that he is actually an astronomer and actually sane, but if the eclipse fails to occur we can deduce nothing at all—not that he is not an astronomer, not that he is a fraud, not that he is not sane: nothing!" Leibniz suddenly realized the *one-sidedness* of the sanity assessment that would shortly, for it was now almost nine o'clock in the morning, be administered by God in the form of a solar eclipse occurring or failing to occur. If the old man passed the test he was indeed sane, but if he failed the test it was no proof that he was not sane.

He could fail God's assessment without failing mine, Leibniz wrote.

It is straightforward to prove that someone is an astronomer, or is sane, but how do you prove that someone is *not* an astronomer, or is *in*sane? The first proof is trivial, the second perhaps impossible, Leibniz explained. How in general do you prove that someone is insane? What would such a proof even look like? Natural phenomena are of no help here. God, who, of course, as a consequence of His nature, has infinite knowledge of the universe, including the universe inside the human head, knows the answer, but the limitations of man prevent man from receiving that knowledge from Him. "I hazard to suggest that man is, in this respect, on his own." There were now exactly three hours until the predicted eclipse. Leibniz would, in that time, he wrote, rap on the window, gain entry to the observatory, ask the old man simply, How did you come to lose your eyes and how do you claim to see the stars without them?, and then at the stroke of noon incline his head toward the heavens. If Leibniz deemed the man's story sane, and the solar eclipse furthermore occurred, then the old man was certainly sane. If Leibniz deemed the man's story insane, yet the eclipse occurred, then, too, the old man was certainly sane. If Leibniz deemed the man's story insane, and the eclipse furthermore failed to occur, then the old man was probably, but only probably, as it would be no demonstration, insane. And if Leibniz deemed the man's story sane, but the eclipse failed to occur, then the old man was possibly (but only possibly!) sane, although, in truth, in that case, at once the thorniest case and the most common, and, added Leibniz, actually even the quintessential case here on Earth, we would know more or less nothing at all.

"At that moment," Leibniz wrote, "I rapped on the window."

)

ONE EVENING, a long time ago, in fact a *very* long time ago, specifically in the last year of the last century, that is, in 1599, "back when I still had my eyes!," as the astronomer told Leibniz and the latter reported to the *Philosophical Transactions*, a new object appeared in the heavens over Bohemia. Never before had such a thing happened. It seemed to pop into existence from one moment to the next. "The existence of things until then had operated quite differently!" In a corner of the sky that had been ink-black since the time of the ancients there was now something irrefutably twinkling, a twinkling that stood in total contradiction to the doctrine of Aristotle positing the eternal perfection and perfect fixity of the celestial spheres. Yes, in the fifty-five spheres by which we were ostensibly bound nothing new was supposed to take place, nothing was ever to die, and nothing was to be born, either! That doctrine, as is well-known, the astronomer said, had long been preached by the Aristotelians of Prague on every street corner and in every lecture hall and even right into the Emperor's ear. Now, perhaps you could claim that this twinkling had always been there and man had missed it, or that it bloomed into being only in the sublunary sphere, not so much higher really than the clouds, or even that it was a shared delusion, that it twinkled in reality on the surfaces of our retinas or on the insides of our heads, but you could not deny that something was twinkling. *Something*, in short, twinkled, the old astronomer told Leibniz, pausing briefly to peer into his telescope, pick up his quill, and write something down. Even in disputing *what* twinkled or *where* it twinkled you were admitting *that* it twinkled. That it twinkled was certain. "Simply put, it twinkled!" the astronomer cried. Not even the Aristotelians could deny that it twinkled, and the astronomer—though he had no formal training in mathematics or metaphysics, being the son of a sculptor who had whisked him into his workshop the moment he could speak and expected him from then on to hammer rather than ponder, to chisel rather than calculate, to sand and polish rather than observe and explain, who in general preached the virtues of the hand over those of the eye and mind and who even announced more than once that he could go on living if his eyes were plucked out but if his hands were cut off not—recalled dashing around Prague all night the night the new object appeared, forcing dogmatic Aristotelians of the prior generation to admit that something new was twinkling up there, and then tying those rigid old Aristotelians in philosophical knots. He would come upon an old Aristotelian and immediately tie him in knots. "No sooner had I happened upon another Aristotelian than I had tied him in some of the tightest possible philosophical knots, all on the basis of what he could see with his very own eyes," Leibniz quoted the astronomer as saying. It wasn't only he of course—all over Prague elderly Aristotelians were being set upon, made to look at the twinkling thing, and then tied in knots, simply scooped up out of their academic pens or snatched from their academic roosts and tied unceremoniously in knots—but he himself, even though probably not one person in Prague would so much as remember his name now (Kepler's name they would remember, of course, but not his!), "tied at least ten or eleven Aristotelians in knots that night, *tight* knots, truly tight cosmological knots," he said, "the kind of knots they would forever struggle to get out of, but would never be able to get out of as long as they lived because I'd actually used their own eyes to tie them. If you use *your* eyes, they'll always squirm out of it, but if you use *their* eyes then they're trapped, and in this case I used what their eyes had indubitably seen of that incontrovertibly twinkling object," a heavenly object which, as Leibniz noted in a parenthetical addressed to the editor of the *Philosophical Transactions*, may correspond, if we permit for the possibility of the old man mixing up his years, to the supernova of 1604, what is now known, needless to say, he added, as Kepler's Supernova. "The secret," the astronomer told Leibniz, "is to tie a person up using his own retinal impressions, so the more he sees, the tighter he's tied."

)

KEPLER, BY THE WAY, as the astronomer knew for a fact, according to Leibniz, had eaten a heavy dinner of bread dumplings that night and fallen asleep early, before the new object had even appeared in the sky. By the time he woke up and looked out the window, the Prague Aristotelians were already completely tied in knots; perhaps there were a few stray Aristotelians whom Kepler could claim to have tied in knots with his *De Stella Nova*, but essentially that book entered a Prague in which the Aristotelians were mostly already totally tied in knots. It was, incidentally, Kepler's well-known hankering for bread dumplings, and the fatigue those dumplings inevitably induced, that caused him to miss untold astronomical phenomena throughout his life; it is accurate to say that throughout his entire life Kepler never actually saw anything for the first time, he only observed what other people observed first, so filled was he with soporific bread dumplings—the optical nerve, said the astronomer, is directly connected, as Vesalius showed, not only to the brain but also to the stomach and extremities—which is why in place of his eyes, always half-closed in a dumpling-induced stupor, Kepler had to substitute his notorious mathematical prowess. But mathematical reasoning as a means of accessing reality can only go so far in replacing vision. For this reason, "I myself have never eaten a bread dumpling after four o'clock in the afternoon, even though there's nothing in the world I'd like to eat more in the evening hours, and by the time seven or eight rolls around my mind is often screaming for bread dumplings, just as Kepler's mind was always screaming for bread dumplings. But unlike Kepler I have always denied myself." He likewise, unlike Kepler, had always denied himself all goulash and all roasted meats served after the hour of four o'clock in the afternoon, and as a result of this lifelong self-denial was always "preternaturally crisp in the head" by the time the stars began to shine. The astronomer's firm conviction was that anyone who eats foods like goulash or bread dumplings after about four in the afternoon, or five at the latest, cannot (unless we're dealing with a ludicrously light dumpling, a dumpling you hardly feel in your belly, the kind of divinely light bread dumpling we could theorize about forever but that in practice we never actually encounter anywhere on Earth, much less in Prague) call himself an "astronomer," perhaps he can call himself a "mathematician" or a "philosopher," but he cannot in good faith call himself an "astronomer," and that includes the gastronome Tycho Brahe. "You simply cannot eat such a meal at such an hour and afterward expect to see," the astronomer told Leibniz. "I mean truly see."

When he said the words "truly see" he pointed at his empty eye sockets.

As a result of never eating a bread dumpling after four, or even after three, or two, or, if he anticipated a specific astronomical event that night, one, or noon, or even eleven in the morning, or even after ten, the astronomer had seen a great deal of the night sky, "more of the night sky than anyone in history," though of course seeing so much was a consequence not only of his evening diet but of his instrument, too, the observational instrument that he himself, as he would shortly explain, the old astronomer told Leibniz, all competing priority claims notwithstanding since they were all uniformly lies, pure and utter lies, had conceived, designed, and wrestled into being in the wake of the emergence in the night sky of the new object. "I have seen a great deal with the aid, as I shall explain, of this splendid instrument," said the astronomer, patting the telescope, in Leibniz's account, "and I continue to see a great deal." As if to prove it he peered into his telescope, picked up his quill, and wrote something down in his large ledger.

)

YES, HE *CONTINUED*, the astronomer repeated, now putting special stress on that word, or so it seemed to Leibniz, to see a great deal, a repetition and a stress in which Leibniz said he detected for the first time in their conversation a note of provocation: Prove that I cannot see what I claim to see! And, indeed, Leibniz's inability thus far to prove or disprove the astronomer's claim was already at this early stage starting to vex or even torment him, since the truth of it resided in a head less than one and a half feet from his own. The problem of entering a human head—a problem that hitherto had not even struck him as a problem at all, and which afterward would never strike him as a problem again, because before that day, and again after that day, but not *on* that day, Leibniz had absolute faith in the power of rational discourse to lay bare for us the contents of a human head—now struck him, only a few minutes into his exchange with the astronomer, as potentially insoluble, horrifically so. As the astronomer's head talked, Leibniz half listened to it talk and half tried to figure out how to get inside it. It is rare, Leibniz noted, that we can pinpoint the precise geographical location of a truth, in this case a little less than a foot and a half away, in a quasi sphere (a head) whose circumference was itself a little more than a foot and a half, and yet have no idea what that truth actually *is*! He could cradle that head in his hands without getting an iota closer to the truth within it, and if, merely as a thought experiment, he were to reach over all of a sudden and crack that head open, the truth, "far from being freed from its shell like a walnut," would simply perish along with the conditions that gave rise to it, i.e., the astronomer's head, since we are dealing here with a contingent rather than a necessary truth, the-astronomer-without-eyes-can-see implying perhaps an absurdity but not a contradiction, as it hinges, Leibniz noted, on empirical rather than logical properties of eyes and sight.

This, incidentally, is the earliest appearance in the Leibniz corpus of the distinction between absurdity and contradiction, which in mature works like his *Critical Remarks Concerning the General Part of Descartes' Principles* (1692) would serve to safeguard the possibility of the doubtful and the absurd, not to say the insane, from the Cartesian dictum that "what is doubtful should be considered false."

"How can I get in this head?" Leibniz reports thinking over and over again. "How? How? How? How can I get in this head? How can I get in this head? How? How can I get inside this head?" The problem of getting inside another head, and seeing what that head was seeing (or not seeing) and what it was thinking (or not thinking), now struck Leibniz as a profoundly philosophical problem. Neither cradling it nor cracking it open would do it, for the barrier involved not only bone but also a thick layer of philosophy. The human skull consists, one might say, Leibniz wrote, of a quarter-inch-thick layer of bone and a quarter-inch-thick layer of philosophy. Of course the brain is also cushioned by various membranes and fluids. A skilled doctor can penetrate the skull with a drill, and he can cut through the membranes with a knife, and he can drain the cerebral fluids with a pump, but his instruments are utterly useless for penetrating that solid, condensed layer of philosophy. "Even the most state-of-the-art medical instrument wielded by the best doctor in Paris will simply bounce off the cerebral-philosophical membrane," Leibniz wrote. That left language. "Never had I been so reliant on words to expose to me the innards of another head, and never had words seemed so unequal to the task," Leibniz wrote, noting that the astronomer, who had never once stopped talking while Leibniz entertained these troubled thoughts, had returned to the topic of Kepler and bread dumplings, and Tycho and meat. "These words were supposed to illuminate for me this old man's mind? Words like 'Kepler' and 'dumplings' and 'four o'clock' and 'five o'clock' and 'Tycho' and 'venison' and 'five o'clock' and 'six o'clock' and words like 'Kepler' and 'goulash' and 'seven o'clock' and 'no astronomer' and 'Tycho' and 'goose' and 'eight o'clock' and 'no astronomer,' and also, for the first time, words like 'Galileo' and 'fettuccine' and 'nine o'clock' and 'no astronomer'?" From these words was he really supposed to be able to determine what the astronomer saw, and whether he saw, as well as whether and what the astronomer thought?

Leibniz angled his pocket watch toward the light of the half-melted candle. It was now ten past nine. Through the warped slat he could see a small slice of the bright blue sky.

)

THE ASTRAL TUBE, which others call the telescope, was invented not, as is commonly claimed, in 1608, but in 1599, according to the astronomer, by which Leibniz notes he presumably meant 1604, nor was it invented by a Dutch spectacle-maker, nor by a Florentine mathematician, nor again by a Neapolitan magus, to which figures history conspires to give credit because it does not want to admit that the person who first extended one of man's senses was merely the self-taught son of a Prague sculptor. The astronomer had penetrated the secrets of nature on his own, outside of any institution, e.g., the spectacle-maker guilds, the mathematical faculties, the esoteric circles of magi, and for that reason history had always been suspicious of him and had always conspired against him. "Yet this tube is no more Galileo's tube than that star is Kepler's star, and this I shall prove to you, Herr Leibniz," he said. "You asked how I lost my eyes, and you asked how I can see without my eyes, but you failed to ask, How did you discover your tube? If wisdom consists, as the saying goes, in asking the right questions, it would have been wiser to ask not only the two eye questions but also the one tube question. Yet you shall know the answer to all three before the eclipse plunges us into darkness.

"And at the moment we are plunged into darkness, you shall see that these three questions are really one question," he added, peering into the telescope, picking up his quill, and writing something down—a long string of numbers, or so it seemed to Leibniz in the faint flickering candlelight.

"You because you're still young probably believe that the things you invent and the things you discover will be named after you, whereas the things invented by others and the things discovered by others will be named after others. It is not so. For example, I had nothing whatsoever to do with a certain mechanism for the very rapid and ostensibly painless plucking of feathers from a duck. And yet it is named after me. There is a contraption for hoisting the curtains of a theater with the press of a pedal not the crank of a winch—I've never touched it! But of course they attribute that curtain contraption to me. I did not discover the rodent that bears my name. There is in the Americas a fungus . . . in short, I have never laid eyes on that fungus. And so on. Yet the telescope, which is mine, they give to others."

Then the astronomer said: "Of course, whether the telescope is attributed to me or someone else doesn't really matter, I'm even a little bit ashamed to harp on it, because when I die, which by my calculations will happen not long after the eclipse that will take place some two and three-quarters hours from now, I will be taking the telescope with me, and I will be taking Galileo and Kepler with me, and I'll be taking Tycho with me, too, they're all dead of course but nevertheless I'll be taking them all with me, and anyone who credits the telescope to anyone else I'll be taking with me, as well as the people they credit, as well as everyone else, and actually I'll be taking the whole world with me, and even you, Herr Leibniz, I will be taking you with me, too, you probably didn't know that! You because you're young probably think that *you'll* take the world with *you* when *you* die, deep down every young person thinks that he will take the world with him when he dies, that's the canonical young person's belief, because deep down young people don't really believe in the reality of other people, they haven't had the sheer reality of other people drummed into them yet by the schools, but what I have discovered through the most rigorous astronomical research is that *I* will actually take the world with *me* when *I* die. As a child I stupidly believed that I would take the world with me when I died, which belief was fortunately drummed out of me during the few years of schooling I had before my father whisked me into his workshop. The reality of other people was drummed into me and my belief that I would take the world with me when I died was accordingly drummed out of me. I learned next to nothing in school, but the sheer reality of other people *was* drummed into me. Elementary school is mostly useless, of course, but as a social mechanism for drumming into people the sheer reality of other people it is probably unsurpassed. I'm actually grateful for school, because by the time my father yanked me out of it by the ears I genuinely believed in the sheer reality of other people! Which, needless to say, is an extremely useful belief for going about life. There's no more practical belief for going about life, and through life, than a belief in the reality of other people. Almost no one succeeds in the world without that belief, and all art and science flows out of that extremely expedient and uniquely advantageous belief, without which the stock market, too, would actually immediately shut down. And as a consequence of that belief being drummed into me, my childish, self-indulgent belief that I would take the world with me when I died was, thankfully, drummed out of me. Of course I eventually found my way back to that belief and realized it was perfectly true, but now it was true for the most rigorous and quantitative astronomical reasons," the astronomer said, patting the telescope. "Every great thinker, by the way, has always without exception found his way *back* to his earliest childhood beliefs; right at the end he realizes that his whole intellectual life has been nothing more than a putting-on-firm-foundations of what he thought right at the start. Bad thinkers, I include incidentally Kepler and Tycho and Galileo in this category, and also Copernicus, start over *here* and end up over *there*, and the farther apart *here* and *there* are the better they think they've thought, and the louder the world claps, as if they're children in a jumping competition, because the world thinks thinking is a kind of jumping, and in fact the kind of thinking Kepler did *was* a kind of jumping, but true thinking is actually an elaborate standing-still, or at most a going-over-there followed by a coming-back-here. While the world applauds the thinkers who choose to participate in the children's jumping competition, the true thinkers are standing utterly still in a very complicated way. And since nonthinkers also tend to stand quite still, and nonthinkers vastly outnumber true thinkers, the world assumes that anyone standing still is a nonthinker and therefore does not applaud these standing-still types; but if you look very closely at a nonthinker and a true thinker you'll notice that they're actually standing still in completely different ways. So I came to realize that I really *would* take the world with me when I died, the fixed stars and the erratic ones and the Earth and the Sun and everything else, just as I had once thought, *I* would, not *you*, and not anyone else, either, but for entirely different reasons than I had once thought," the astronomer said, patting the telescope. The content of the belief was the same but the armature around it and supporting it from underneath had gone from "pure childishness" to "extreme scientificity."

"This probably sounds obscure but what I mean will become perfectly clear," the astronomer told Leibniz. He pressed an empty socket to his telescope, picked up his quill, and wrote down a long string of numbers.

Since this belief turned out to be true, it didn't matter, according to the astronomer, who got credit for inventing the telescope, it was petty and absurd to go on and on about the credit he deserved but did not get, he said. Who cares! Let Galileo have credit, or Lipperhey, or Kepler, or Della Porta, or whomever else, "Seriously, who cares?" cried the astronomer. Who cares! Who cares! Who cares! Who cares! Still, it was slightly better, he supposed, for the last two-odd hours of the world to possess a smidgen more truth and a smidgen less falsity, and, in any case, the young man had asked what happened to his eyes, and how he could see the firmament without them, questions that were of course intimately connected to the question of the development of the telescope, which was of course a variant of the question of who truly invented the telescope, i.e., me, the astronomer said, these three questions are really one question, so here, he said, in Leibniz's written account, is the fact of the matter.

TWO

SHORTLY AFTER THE appearance in the heavens of the new object, the astronomer's father, who didn't show the slightest interest in it, because, as he once put it to his son, "that's up there and we're down here," a point of view that wounded the son but which he could not after all disprove, "I could not tie him in knots as I had the Aristotelians because he simply didn't *care* about the twinkling thing, not what it was, not where it was, not even *that* it was," decided, in an attempt to reverse his fortunes, which according to the astronomer had plunged from great heights into an abyss, to present Emperor Rudolf, who as it was known had an insatiable appetite for the monstrous and the esoteric and was a fanatical enthusiast of any mechanism that mimicked nature, with a perfect simulacrum of the human head. This mechanical human head would be capable not only of blinking its eyes and chomping its teeth but also of imitating the human voice through an astoundingly intricate system of tubes modeled in part on the apparatus by which the brazen bull of Phalaris had transformed the shrieks of the criminals roasted to death within it into eerily realistic bullish bellowing. For it to be a genuine automaton, the head, of course, could have no one inside it, it had to be void of everything but toothed wheels turning one another, so the initial sound would have to be produced by mechanical means rather than the yelps of the damned, the astronomer told Leibniz; but the apparatus that converted that first sound into something ostensibly human would be based, his father explained, on the principle of Phalaris's bull. "We shall invent the modern bull of Phalaris!" his father told him. To the son the idea of a mechanical human head was abominable even though it was actually he who, in the course of the furtive studies he pursued each night, had first come across it, in a book called *On the Sense of Things and on Magic*, written by the heretical Dominican friar Tommaso Campanella just before his arrest by the Inquisition in 1594; in this book, the astronomer told Leibniz (who reported the claim to the *Philosophical Transactions* "although," as he noted, "it cannot possibly be true, since that book was not published until 1620," and suggested that the astronomer may have meant Campanella's earlier *Philosophy Demonstrated by the Senses*),

Campanella writes of coming across a passage in a book by William of Paris in which William claims that Albertus Magnus had built in Cologne around 1250 out of pure matter a mechanical head that could speak in a human voice. Campanella himself did not believe that such a head was possible, in fact he adduced this head precisely as an example of what it was that natural magic could *not* bring about, "I do not hold to be true that which William of Paris writes," wrote Campanella, as the astronomer told Leibniz, Leibniz wrote, but the astronomer's father—who had been racking his brain for a marvel he could make that would astonish the Emperor and thus restore the astronomer's father to his former stature, even to his former title, for if the astronomer was not lying to Leibniz his father had at one time been the Imperial Sculptor to Rudolf's father and predecessor, Emperor Maximilian—believed that not only was such a head possible, it would actually be quite simple. "I can make that head!" he cried, according to the astronomer, when the astronomer mentioned the idea to his father as though it had occurred to him ex nihilo. The idea was abominable to the astronomer but he knew that his father, whom besides fearing, admiring, resenting, and loving, he now pitied, would take to it. "Every sentiment a boy can feel toward his father I felt toward my father and every sentiment an artist can feel toward his art my father felt toward that mechanical human head," the astronomer told Leibniz. He distinctly recalled the first moment of sheer elation, the cries of "I can make that head! I can make that head! I can actually make that head!" He really thought he could make that head! the astronomer recalled. He was confident he could make that head and that that head would flabbergast the

Emperor. With a sweep of his arm his father cast into the trash decades of labor, including the almost infinitely mirrored microcosm of the cosmos that had been his first gambit to get into the Emperor's good graces, but in which his father had quite recently, and rather traumatically, lost faith. For years, indeed for much of the astronomer's adolescence, his father had been gluing thousands or tens of thousands of tiny mirrors to the inside walls of a box, but one day, not long before that new object appeared in the heavens, "he peered into the peephole of the box and immediately started weeping." Never before had the astronomer seen his father weep. It was horrible to see, "horrific!" "The cause of his weeping of course was the realization that he had devoted a sizable chunk of his life to a many-mirrored box." Whenever we devote such a sizable chunk of our lives to such a box, gluing mirrors in it and so forth, and then realize rather far along that it has not magically metamorphosed into a microcosm of the cosmos, we weep—that's natural. "We weep upon realizing that it has remained a mere box, I understand that now." At the time, though, it was extremely upsetting, the astronomer said. "I often wish I hadn't seen it." To see your father peer into a little box he has made and begin weeping remains upsetting no matter how much you claim to comprehend it in retrospect. Imagine, he put so much faith into that little box, he truly believed in the box, and then one day he peers into the box and begins weeping! He had really believed in that box, but from the moment he peered into the box, he could no longer sustain his belief in the box. "His faith in that box could not withstand what he now saw in it, which was basically just a lot of mirrors." Though he saw himself as the most practical and skeptical of sculptors, and sculpting as the most practical and skeptical of art forms, he was in truth driven by a faith even more fervent than that which drove penitents to wander the streets of Prague thrashing themselves bloody with iron-studded whips, for he believed without question that the incremental addition of a particular mirror, one of thousands, who knew which one, would suddenly transform that object from a mere many-mirrored box into a microcosm of the cosmos. For years he glued in mirror after mirror, awaiting with a conviction that in retrospect seemed to the astronomer uncanny the marginal mirror that would effect that metamorphosis and give him a box worthy of bestowing on the Emperor. Leibniz comments: "His father seems to have believed that the qualitative problem of transmuting a many-mirrored box into a microcosm of the cosmos could be reduced to the quantitative problem of pasting in, e.g., the three hundred and forty-fourth mirror, or the three hundred and forty-fifth mirror." The astronomer said: "No one should have to see his father put so much faith in such a small box and then all of a sudden lose that faith in that box." That day the astronomer wept, too, and so did his mother; the fact of the matter is that they, too, had had faith in that box; they, too, had believed (probably based on the uncanny conviction of their father and husband) that it would at some point transfigure itself from a mere many-mirrored box into a microcosm of the cosmos, rescuing its maker from the commercial, artistic, and psychological abyss into which he'd been plunged when Emperor Rudolf dismissed him as Imperial Sculptor and transferred the imperial capital from Vienna to Prague. "Father begged us, weeping, Look inside, tell me what you see when you look inside! What do you see? *What do you see?* And Mother peered in and said, I see a microcosm, and I peered in and said, I see a many-mirrored box. And Father knew of course that Mother was lying and that I was telling the truth."

The astronomer paused to peer into the telescope. Then he said:

"All day long we took turns peering into the peephole and weeping." It was the end of his childhood. "When you peer into your father's mirrored box and tell him point-blank that it's not a microcosm of anything, least of all the cosmos, you are needless to say no longer a child." A teardrop had formed in the corner of one of the astronomer's sockets, a fact to which the latter drew Leibniz's attention and which Leibniz confirmed in his letter. Just as he could still see, he could still weep, the astronomer explained, since his faculty of sentimentality like his faculty of sight had not been damaged in the slightest when he lost his eyes. And Leibniz noted parenthetically that a failed assassin of John the Fearless of Burgundy was likewise seen to weep soon after his eyes had been cut out, and that an anatomist at Montpellier who examined the corpse reported that the tear ducts remained intact. The astronomer said: "I've always been interested in sentimentality, never scorned it, never feared it, always adopted a scrupulously scientific attitude toward it, so I'm actually glad you got the chance to verify this teardrop. You see it, yes? You confirm it? This is, needless to say, a most sentimental subject matter for me." His father, like all fathers, had once been all-powerful, and his father had been even more all-powerful than most. He had once been the most powerful sculptor in the whole world. In Vienna not only the Hofburg Palace but the entire city had basically burst at the seams with his father's busts, friezes, fountains, and columns. As a boy born in a city decorated to his father's exact specifications, the astronomer often had the peculiar feeling, upon turning a corner and stumbling across another of his father's columns or fountains or friezes or busts, that he had actually been born inside his father's head. "The cityscape conformed to his concepts." Sometimes as a boy the astronomer strutted down the streets of Vienna "with tremendous conceit, for this was none other than my father's head we were all walking through!" and sometimes he skulked through the alleys with his back pressed to the high walls, woozy, bewildered, hyperventilating, looking in every direction for a way out of his father's big black-bearded head—"forgetting of course that the very exit for which I was searching would also be built by him, as were the very walls against which my back was pressed." His conceit turned into claustrophobia, his claustrophobia into conceit, these sensations were utterly inextricable or possibly even the same sensation, the astronomer told Leibniz.

He added: "You have to understand all of this to understand the telescope."

And: "I want you to see what I'm seeing when I peer through the telescope."

And also: "By no means is the telescope merely an *optical* instrument!"

Then one morning Emperor Maximilian died. By noontime that same day Rudolf had boxed his father up in a marble sarcophagus sculpted by the astronomer's father and by nightfall messengers were streaming forth from the Hofburg Palace toward the homes of Maximilian's former ministers. Their services were no longer needed. First the new Emperor sacked his father's Imperial Secretary, then the old Imperial Physician, after that the Imperial Mathematician, and then, at the stroke of midnight, the Imperial Botanist, a man who had grown "outstanding plants" to "outrageous heights," who had introduced the persimmon and the pomegranate both to Europe north of the Alps, whose orchards erupted with "red apples the size of children's heads." If he's sacking the botanist he's sacking everyone, the astronomer remembered his mother saying; she stayed up all night waiting for the knock at the door. But the sculptor, then at the pinnacle of his powers, inhabiting an opulent stone mansion in the dead center of a city that hewed to the very contours of his head, atop which sat a black velvet cap with the phenomenal feather of some exotic bird, said: "He would never dismiss me, not in a million years!" the astronomer recalled, pausing now to peer into the telescope, pick up his quill, and write something down. That night his father slept soundly in his madness—for that's what it was, madness. Whenever you refashion your physical surroundings to reflect on the outside the insides of your head you run the risk of going crazy, which is precisely what happened to his father in Vienna, a place that rather than resisting him, and thereby preserving his sanity, proved all too pliable in his fists. So he was stunned, stupefied, when as the Sun rose the knock that his wife had been expecting and that he thought unthinkable sounded at the door. That knock woke him from one form of madness only to plunge him into another. For shortly thereafter the Emperor moved his court from Vienna to Prague, from gilded Hofburg to grim Hradčany, and the astronomer's family followed him north, leaving their stone mansion on the finest street in the center of Vienna for a drafty wooden house on the periphery of Prague so that his father could try to reclaim the title of Imperial Sculptor. His entire life was now oriented around reclaiming that title. How his father wanted that title back! He claimed he didn't need it back, he actually *wanted* to not want it back, he probably wanted to be the kind of person who neither needed it back nor wanted it back, who thought that such things were meaningless, but everything he did, including transplanting the family to Prague, indicated, in contrast to everything he said, that he both needed it back and wanted it back, that it was for whatever reason meaningful to him, and the astronomer could tell even at his age that his father would never be happy again until he had it back. But Emperor Rudolf was no Maximilian, and Prague no Vienna. If Vienna resisted him too little, Prague resisted him too much, "also obviously a recipe for madness." In Vienna he met too little resistance and went crazy, while in Prague he met too much resistance and went insane. Sculptures that made sense in Vienna made no sense at all in Prague. Vienna is famously a city of golden facades, Prague famously one of black spires emerging from the mist and penetrating the sky. Vienna under Maximilian was enamored of surfaces, Prague under Rudolf enamored of depths, and therefore his father, a sculptor of surfaces not depths, flourished in Vienna, to the point of madness, but failed in Prague, to the point of madness. "I myself, incidentally," the astronomer said, "have had a lifelong affinity for depths and no interest in the surfaces of things," while his own son, a tapestry-weaver "who will enter this tale later on, and in a most disturbing fashion," was, like his grandfather the sculptor, interested only in surfaces, so the astronomer, a lifelong investigator of depths, was basically "bound on both sides by surface-lovers," Leibniz quotes him as saying. In Vienna he had seen his father mold the whole world and emboss it with gold, while in Prague he watched him glue thousands of mirrors into a little box, peer into a peephole, and weep. Times had changed. "Probably for me it was a presentiment of his mortality," noted the astronomer, bending over arthritically on his stool to stroke the head of his sleeping cat, whom he now identified to Leibniz as Linus and who still had not once in Leibniz's presence opened his eyes. "Not only had this virtuoso of appearances pandered to the local taste for essences, and not only had he failed," the astronomer went on, "but I myself told him he'd failed." From that moment on he felt like the father to his own father, hence his bringing to his father the idea for the mechanical human head, abominable though he thought it was, "the way one brings home for one's son a toy or trinket one cannot oneself see the value in."

There is pathos, of course, in seeing one's son seize with enormous delight upon something one knows oneself to be worthless.

And how his father seized upon that head!

All the faith he had put in the box now went into the head, right into that head. "He put all of his faith in that mechanical human head." The few new commissions that still came in he declined. "Everything now depended on that head," the astronomer told Leibniz. His father called it the Head of Phalaris. If his father knew that the sculptor who had presented Phalaris with the brazen bull wound up being burned to death by Phalaris inside that selfsame bull he did not let on. The astronomer began to have dreadful premonitions. Of course his father "could not *actually* be stuffed inside of his own head," the head having a circumference like the mean adult male of just over one and a half feet, "a body cannot be stuffed inside a head, that's clear," and since moreover it was to serve as an instrument of simulation and entertainment rather than persecution and execution it seemed unlikely that the Emperor, even if he were not amused by it, would consign its inventor to death. "The question of the Emperor's amusement was, however, not a minor one, as you shall see," the astronomer said, "and the foreboding I had about the head almost as soon as my father began building it, and in particular the peculiar foreboding I had about the eventual presentation of that head to the Emperor, was not, in fact, without foundation, for as you shall see, Herr Leibniz, something very terrible did come to pass, something very terrible indeed! Even though that terrible thing was intertwined in a way I could never have foreseen with something very great."

The astronomer put one empty socket to his telescope, picked up his quill, and wrote something down. There were two and a half hours till noon. Leibniz reported seeing a sliver of the Moon through the slightly warped slat, but where the Sun was at that moment he did not know. "And I might have been mistaken about the Moon."

)

ALL DAY LONG the astronomer and his father hammered together that mechanical human head. Then his father went to sleep and he stayed up all night conducting his clandestine investigations into optics, reading Euclid and Ptolemy and Grosseteste and peering at the firmament through a glass, or in the reflection of a curved mirror. During the day he and his father scavenged lead scraps, which they melted down and sculpted into the shell of the head, elegant and lifelike, and topped with a shock of thick brown hair donated to them gratis by an attendant of the anatomical theater at Charles University where a week before a young thief had been dissected. Then his father went to bed and the astronomer—by the light of a single candle lit only after he heard his father's sixth snore, for one snore could of course be faked, as could two snores or three, even four simulated snores is not unthinkable if his father had suspicions, and the idea of feigning five snores to catch your son in some verboten act is, if absurd, not impossible, whereas after six snores his father was probably asleep—read, for example, the portions of Friar Bacon's *Opus Majus* concerning the physiology of vision or his *Letter on the Secret Workings of Art and Nature* with its depictions of those ingenious devices of antiquity that according to legend made distant things seem near or near things distant, such as the fabled glasses with which Julius Caesar is said to have seen the cliffs of Great Britain from the beaches of Gaul, or the gigantic mirror atop the Pharos of Alexandria with which one could not only spot enemy ships at a distance of six hundred miles but by concentrating the rays of the Sun on them just so even set them ablaze. Naturally with all this reading the astronomer's eyes began deteriorating, "the eye always deteriorates when it focuses on something so near at hand, in so weak a light," so he had to purchase spectacles, first thin ones, and then thicker and thicker ones, until eventually he wore the thickest spectacles in Prague, but "for some reason my father never inferred from the thickness of my spectacles my contempt for his values." Each morning when his father's snores subsided it was time to return from the realm of contemplation to that of fabrication. For weeks the astronomer did not sleep. If he wasn't peering into his father's mechanical human head, he was peering out of his own head. One head was to be looked into: the mechanical head. The other was to be looked out from: his own organismic head. The former head had to speak, blink, and chomp, the latter head to think and see. But in his mounting exhaustion it did not take long of course to descend into complete head confusion, "utter head chaos." Everything got mixed up! Which head was for looking at, and which head was for looking? One night he spent all night observing his head, instead of using his head to observe. "Obviously I had to use my own head to observe my own head, so in a sense I was still using my head to observe, but what I was observing *with* my head *was* my head, rather than the new twinkling object in the heavens." He actually observed his head observing his head being observed by his head: a complete waste of time. That whole night was a waste, "particularly since the sky was perfectly cloudless." He ought to have spent that time observing the firmament in the reflection of a rounded mirror. Not to mention that the head doing the observing was never quite the same head as the head being observed, even if it had the illusion that it was observing itself, so his data besides being worthless were meaningless. A head "no matter how sensitive" cannot catch itself in the act of observing itself, that much he did determine. "The observer head and the observed head are two wholly different heads, even if they sprout from one and the same neck." Thus amid the confusion of heads, there was a multiplication of heads. The next day he spent all day tinkering with the cogwheels in his father's mechanical head in hopes of inducing it to think, if not to reflect. Only toward the end of the day after hours of failing to make the head think, much less reflect, did he suddenly remember, prompted by his father's asking him, So how's the blinking coming along?, that this was actually *not* the thinking head, it was the blinking and chomping head! "Wrong head once again!" He was supposed to be contriving the flapping of the eyelids, not the churning of thought, the tingling of sentiment, or the synthesis of concepts. The eyes were to open and close, that's all. So this whole day, too, was a waste. And then that night, as his father slept, the astronomer while looking at the heavens through a lens realized that he could see nothing, nothing at all, not a single star all night either fixed or wandering, the sky was cloudless once again and filled presumably with phenomena—indeed he would learn the next morning that Venus in the course of the night had transited Jupiter—but there might as well have been a curtain drawn across it for he found himself attending exclusively and involuntarily to his own blinks, scrutinizing his own blinks with an absorption that actually entirely occluded the world outside him and above. He said: "That night though I knew very well which head I had on my shoulders I still could not stop devoting my attention exclusively to my blinks, noticing each of my blinks, feeling and registering each of my blinks, counting my blinks well into the thousands, analyzing my blinks into their constituent parts, to the point where I could actually no longer blink, I basically forgot how to blink, or rather I suddenly understood blinking too well now to do it, I saw *through* what it means to blink, to experience an infinitesimal flash of darkness between two prolonged exposures to the external world, My God, I thought, *that's what a blink is?*, my thinking you see had made my blinking impossible, I could still chomp, as I determined, oh, I could speak and chomp perfectly well, but I could no longer blink no matter how dry my eyes, I had utterly dismantled my blinking machine, it lay, as it were, in pieces, which I now had to put back together using only the most fundamental physical principles, I had to teach myself from scratch *how* to blink again, how to do this very simple thing, this very simple blinking thing, that hitherto I had done instinctively and in fact continuously from birth."

In short, the astronomer told Leibniz, he had entered a period of madness.

When he emerged from it the next morning, he emerged with the principle of the telescope.

There was no eureka moment, he said. "There was only madness, and then incredible vision."

The astronomer put an eye socket to his telescope, picked up his quill, and wrote something down.

Of course, his inability to furnish that eureka moment, to retrace precisely the route by which he had arrived at the notion that two convex lenses placed one behind the other would magnify, albeit invert, the world—the foundation, Leibniz noted, of what is now called the Keplerian telescope—rendered him suspect in the eyes of the world, and especially in the eyes of the chroniclers of the world, who, in devoting their lives to carving from the infinitely extended, infinitely dense glob of absolute nonsense known as reality numerous little globules of nonsense, then compressing these globules of nonsense into beads of pure nonsense, and finally stringing together these nonsensical fact-beads into handsome glittering concatenations of seeming sense, i.e., their history books, practice sanity, promulgate sanity, and privilege, in selecting what and especially whom to preserve and parade about for posterity, a species of sanity. Now, sanity has, no doubt, accomplished a great deal throughout European history, the astronomer told Leibniz. Sanity is important, too! But in all of the hoopla over sanity, we ought not to neglect the contributions of madness. "Of course, it is true, if I might anticipate your objection, Herr Leibniz," the astronomer said, "that these sane chroniclers sometimes pay lip service to the merits of madness, or more than sometimes, perpetually, actually these staunchly sane chroniclers are almost always completely obsessed with madness, the saner the more obsessed, probably precisely because they sense the strictures imposed on their thoughts by their sanity, and they fill their histories with hymns to madness and its fruits: with painters who painted their greatest paintings with their left hand, in the dark, while chained by the right to a wall in a Fool's Tower, with philosophers who lived in filth but spoke the truth, with mystics who walked into the desert and lived for forty years atop a pillar before returning to the city bearing the word of God. Their histories, you will object, Herr Leibniz, are in fact nothing *but* histories of madness, fairy tales and fables of madness, odes to madness as the supreme mechanism of art and science, histories of the world as the handiwork of the mad! And I reply: Whatever it is these sane chroniclers are chronicling, it is not madness. The painter is locked up in a Fool's Tower . . . but he paints a painting the sane see as beautiful. The philosopher lives in his filth . . . but he says things the sane see as true. The mystic climbs up his pillar . . . but he climbs back down it with what the sane see as the word of God. This isn't madness," he told Leibniz, "it is only the portion of madness recognizable to the sane, expressible in the tongue of the sane, and is ipso facto the sane portion of madness: This is sanitized madness! The portion of insanity that can be put in the language of the sane is obviously the sane portion. It is the untranslatable residue that constitutes true madness. Notice how in the history books you never come across a man or indeed a woman who climbs up a pillar for no reason, and never comes down. Where is the history of this pointless pillar person? Whose bones are picked clean by the birds? Where is the historian who will write the history of this person who climbs up a pillar for no reason, reports nothing from God, and is ultimately devoured by birds? Where is the history of the philosopher who lives in his own filth, subsists on garbage, grunts incessantly, like a beast, brutalizes himself, and has never once been heard to utter anything even remotely intelligible, not a single word, much less a syllogism? Where is the historian who will write the history of this philosopher? I will tell you where he is: He's nowhere! He does not exist! He does not and cannot *by definition* exist," the astronomer said, according to Leibniz. "For the instant a historian writes a stupendously long history of a person who climbs a pillar for no reason and is devoured up there by desert birds, or of a bestial philosopher who cannot speak and eats garbage, the historian ceases to be a historian and becomes, himself, a madman. In the eyes of the world and in his own eyes also he has climbed his own pillar, ceased speaking intelligibly.

41

"So it is that any book that tells the truth about the telescope is regarded as nonsense, including my own *On the True Nature of the Astral Tube*, which I had printed in Frankfurt at my own expense, and distributed for free at the fair there, one thousand copies, all of which vanished immediately and without a trace," said the astronomer.

His words were not even admitted as evidence, let alone taken as proof.

"And so I resigned myself to vanishing, likewise, without a trace."

After all, most people simply vanish without a trace when they die, and so, he thought, would he.

Then, lifting a crooked forefinger and issuing a crooked grin, he said:

"Until, that is, I foresaw the solar eclipse.

"I," he added, "and no one else!"

An eclipse was actually better than words. The same words mean different things to different people, but a solar eclipse looks the same to everyone standing in the same place at the same time.

"And so, Herr Leibniz, as long as *you* see the eclipse, too . . ."

If Leibniz saw the eclipse, too, the astronomer "would not vanish after all!"

The astronomer pulled a pocket watch out of his rags, either glanced at it or perhaps felt the angle of its hands with his fingers, rammed it back in his rags, and turned again to Leibniz.

"But you are still wondering, But how in the world did this crazy old fool lose his eyes? Who plucked them out, and why? For I am revealing nothing you haven't intuited already when I tell you that they did not simply fall out on their own . . ."

THE TRUTH IS THAT he himself did not understand right away the actual nature of his invention, nor, although it required considerable fortitude to resist the temptation, did he construct right away a prototype—for it so happened that the very morning on which his madness receded, leaving in its wake the concept of this remarkable distance-eradicating tube, his father rushed into his bedroom "not realizing that he was rushing into the birthing chamber of an epochal idea" and proclaimed with palpable pride that their mechanical human head was complete. Come! Look! See for yourself! His eyes shone. An impromptu demonstration was arranged. His father, wearing the black velvet cap he had not worn since his days at Emperor Maximilian's court at Hofburg, but which even as the family slid into destitution no one dared to suggest he sell, and he did not propose it either, stood behind the Head of Phalaris. Then, with a legerdemain he had rehearsed fanatically so that like an illusionist he would be able to operate the automaton at the Castle without the Emperor's apprehending its mechanism, he turned a small crank buried in the copious curls at the nape of the thief's neck, which powered in turn a tiny rotary fan with three blades, which impelled air into a byzantine network of tubes, which produced from the head's mouth in a wheezy, staccato, oddly high-pitched, vaguely unearthly, but basically comprehensible voice a very popular Bohemian folk song, then a poem commemorating the total annihilation of the Turkish fleet at the Battle of Lepanto in 1571, and lastly a short selection from the catechism composed by the illustrious Dutch Jesuit Peter

Canisius and ratified for use across the realm by Rudolf's grandfather, Emperor Ferdinand the First. All the while the teeth chomped and the eyes blinked. The head asked itself one final question from the catechism, "What is understood by the name of Faith?," answered it, "A gift of God, and a light wherewith man being illuminated doth firmly assent and cleave unto those things which are revealed by God," and the performance was over.

The workshop was silent now. When he could stand the silence no longer, his father tugged at his graying beard and said: "Well? So?" And he stood there, awaiting his son's judgment. The feather in his black velvet cap, which in Vienna had always stood straight as a steeple, now drooped, pointing if not quite at the floor then nevertheless no longer at the heavens. It was astonishing how old, how visibly old, he had become, "less old than I must look to you now," the astronomer told Leibniz, "but still old, old, truly old!" He added: "Possibly the sole aspect of the essence of a head expressed permanently on its surface, i.e., on its skin, is its age." How could he tell this old man the truth? That he'd made an amusing parlor trick? That however high he had elevated this mechanical head, it still languished as far below man, as infinitely far below man, as man languished below God? That in point of fact it did not even rise to the level of an abomination? "Watch it again!" cried his father, and again albeit more frantically he spun the crank, and again the folk song started up, and the whole routine repeated itself. And again it went silent and again he plucked at his beard and again said, "Well? So?"

The next word I say will shatter this old man into a million pieces, the astronomer thought.

Now the folk song started up a third time, and the astronomer, losing patience, was about to utter something quite cruel—something terribly cruel—when he realized that his father's hands were still, and the mechanical head was silent. The singing now was coming from outside. The astronomer flung open the window, stuck his head out, and "it was only then that I grasped the enormity of my father's accomplishment." For there in the stinking alleyway behind the workshop was a man with a head on his shoulders that was likewise singing, chomping, and blinking, "and actually nothing else." He enticed the man into the workshop with the promise of something more to chomp on, "something sweet, I promised." He positioned the real head beside the mechanical head and cranked the mechanical head and told the real head, Be yourself. Now there were two heads singing, two heads chomping, and two heads blinking, "one of the heads was ostensibly also thinking but if you couldn't see the crank you would be excused for thinking that the thinking one was the lead head with the thief's hair." Until this moment the astronomer had conceived of the human head as primarily a thinking thing; he now realized that it was first and foremost a singing thing, a chomping thing, and a blinking thing. "We create all kinds of scholastic perplexities for ourselves by thinking of the human head as a thing for thinking that are eliminated when we think of it as a thing for chomping," the astronomer said. This was a critical juncture in his philosophical development. His prejudice against the mechanical head was rooted (he realized as he watched the flesh head sing and chomp) in a sentimental rather than a scientific conception of the human head. Campanella had written, sentimentally, that

45

"pneumatic apparatuses can never capture a human soul," but that assertion at once vastly overestimated the soul and hugely underestimated pneumatics, the astronomer realized as he looked back and forth between the head of lead and the head of flesh, which was now asking, Where was its sweet thing, where was its sweet thing? It is true that his father had not elevated the mechanical head to the level of the human head, as he thought he had, but what he had done instead, and it amounted to the same thing, or more strictly speaking to its polar opposite, was grab the human head by both ears and yank it down to the level of the mechanical head. He was not a bad artist, really, he had just drastically misconstrued his own medium. In trying to breathe life into the mechanical head he had actually sucked life out of the human head, the more life he thought he was breathing into one the more life he was sucking out of the other, and he kept breathing into the first (but actually: sucking out of the second) and breathing into the first (sucking out of the second) until "both heads were sucked astoundingly free of life and thought." The mechanical head was worthless, a curio, an aristocratic gewgaw, but his father without knowing it had created the modern human head, the seventeenth-century human head, the astronomer said, the head that every learned man in Europe would soon want to be seen wearing on top of his body. Women, too; the Marquise Catherine de Vivonne apparently caused a sensation in Paris when she wore that head to the literary salon she hosted in the *chambre bleue* of the Hôtel de Rambouillet. Of course, the astronomer himself later contrived an even newer head, an eighteenth-century head, "a head that will actually be everywhere in the eighteenth century and

46

will probably even endure into the nineteenth century, to the extent, obviously, that our particular world persists after the eclipse," but that is getting ahead of ourselves, the astronomer told Leibniz, and (rapping on his skull with his knuckles) "what you and I carry around on our shoulders is still to a considerable degree the head chiseled, unbeknownst to him, by my father."

"Well?" said his father a third time, tugging frenetically at his beard. "So?"

And the astronomer replied: "It is your masterpiece."

He had one suggestion only. Observe how a lit candle held near the eyes of the real head caused the pupils to contract. The mechanical head lacked of course any such so-called pupillary reflex. His father thought this a minor matter but the astronomer insisted it was an omission that could doom the whole work, for since the time of Galen, if not before him, the widening and narrowing of the pupils has been seen as a sign not only of operative vision but of the presence of inner life. If it was true, as it was said, that the Emperor incorporated only ostensibly "perfect" objects into the exquisite collection of naturalia and artificialia that he kept under lock and key in the North Wing of his Castle, that even the monstrosities preserved there in jars were perfect monstrosities, that he scrutinized prospective instruments, ivories, tapestries, gems, bezoars, sculptures, and automata with the fervor of a lunatic, that he had rejected an astonishing portrait of his great-great-great-grandfather Frederick by Dürer due to an unstipulated "issue with the lips," that a bump on the surface of an ostrich egg troubled him intensely, that he spent weeks on end wandering the North Wing pensively rearranging his mirabilia into ever more auspicious orders, ever more truthful orders, orders purportedly ever more reflective of the cosmos, only to command his servants in a burst of sudden staggering wrath that everything be put back just as it was: if all this was true, the astronomer told his father, as he recalled to Leibniz with a rueful laugh, then there was no doubt he would discover the mechanical head's lone empirical lapse, the flaw in its eyes, and not only discover it but fixate on it, "for an individual like the Emperor the tiniest of flaws will occasion the most fevered of fixations, what seems insignificant to us will seem significant to him, I told my father," and ultimately he'd not only fixate on it but even reject the whole head on account of it. Yet it would be simple to fix. Indeed, he already had the solution! "And purely for effect I went to my room and fetched my copy of Witelo's *Perspectiva*." There is a certain black fabric known to swell—he told his father—when heated, two circles of which would serve perfectly as pupils; and to gather the light and focus it upon them, two convex lenses would serve ideally as eyes.

)

THEN THE ASTRONOMER told Leibniz: You will shortly accuse me of perfidy, if not patricide. You will perhaps be right to. Yet what I told my father about the Emperor was also probably true. Once, many years later, as the Emperor's Court Chamberlain and I stood in the Castle before Arcimboldo's *Water*, he told me the following story. He and the Emperor, he told me, had once stood before that very painting, just as he and I stood before it now, and the Emperor had said to him: I have often been indicted for fixating on the insignificant, but throughout my life I have always found that it is precisely in the insignificant that the significant lurks. And the Court Chamberlain had replied: And in the significant lurks likewise the insignificant. The Emperor: Indeed it does! The insignificant is in the significant, the significant in the insignificant. They agreed, the astronomer told Leibniz, that the significant was rarely if ever found in the significant and the insignificant almost never in the insignificant but rather the significant was in the insignificant and the insignificant in the significant. And the Emperor told his Court Chamberlain how he came to possess that spectacular painting, which as surely you know, Herr Leibniz, depicts the head of a woman by the ingenious juxtaposition of a thousand beasts and beings of the sea. The Emperor says to him: Many years ago one of my agents, a soi-disant connoisseur of the art of Italy, returned from a journey to Florence and Milan with two paintings for my consideration, each portraying the head of a woman in profile, but one which did so with perfect grace, naturalness, and simplicity, while the other did so by the juxtaposition of fish, many fish, "together the fish make a head," the agent told the Emperor. And the Emperor tells the Court Chamberlain: The instant my agent utters the phrases "juxtaposition of fish" and "together the fish make a head," I know, sight unseen, that it is that *second* head, i.e., this fish head, this head which my agent, an erudite man who'd studied for years and years in Rome and Bologna, is signaling to me with all of his words and all of his gestures is ostensibly the *in*significant head, that this head is in fact the significant head, and the simple, natural, graceful head, the ostensibly *significant* head, is worthless. Evidently, the Emperor

49

tells the Court Chamberlain, my agent was embarrassed to have even brought me this head composed of fish, he considered it beneath him, but often my agents must bring me paintings they deem beneath them because they think (and I know that they mutter as much among themselves!) that my tastes run toward what they consider the perverse, although I of course think that *their* tastes, in running toward the simple and the natural, not to mention the graceful, run precisely toward the perverse. Each side thinks that the other side's taste runs right toward the perverse, a symmetry broken only by the fact that one side is supposed to be procuring art for the other side, i.e., they for me, not I for them, I am quoting the Emperor here, the Court Chamberlain said, the astronomer told Leibniz. In any case I decide to toy a little with my agent, to torture him just a little bit, in hopes perhaps of making him see that all of his Bologna-bought erudition and all of his Rome-bought erudition put together was useless to him in the ultimate task of divining the significance which lurks in the insignificant, the task facing us all, the Emperor says. *Possibly* a good educational institution can help one see how the seemingly significant is, in truth, insignificant, but in seeing the significance within the seemingly insignificant one is always alone. In the first half of life we ruthlessly flush out the insignificance of the seemingly significant, for which an education might come in handy, but in the second half we must divine the significance within the seemingly insignificant, for which task an academic institution is not merely impotent but actually detrimental, notice how my agent's learning blinded him to the value of the head made up of various fishes. You will note, by the way, Herr Leibniz, how this man who stood at the center of the most formidable institution in the whole world outside of the Catholic Church apparently shared my ambivalence not to say my antipathy toward institutions! One discovers allies not to say duplicates of oneself in the most unexpected places. Here the astronomer peered into his telescope. Then he said: So, the Emperor and his Italian agent go into the Castle's so-called Artwork-Viewing Chamber, where these two quite different women's heads (and actually these two quite different approaches to art and existence) are hanging on the wall opposite each other, one by Bronzino, the other, of course, by Arcimboldo. And the agent starts going on and on in his professorial fashion about Bronzino's brushstrokes and mastery of perspective and treatment of light, all in the service of this perfectly competent and even technically virtuosic but patently pointless painting, with its elegant surface concealing a void, a painting incidentally that his father the former Emperor would have adored, while on the opposite wall, totally ignored by the art agent, who obviously considered it beneath him, was this perfectly ridiculous painting whose utterly *in*elegant surface of juxtaposed fish concealed within it an entire world, and which incidentally his father the former Emperor would have abhorred. So the Emperor interrupts the agent and says, Tell me about the composition of the head made of fish. And the agent says, Of course, My Lord, and he launches into a disquisition on Arcimboldo's brushstrokes and Arcimboldo's perspectival technique and Arcimboldo's treatment of light. And it occurs to me, the Emperor tells his Court Chamberlain, that there's one word he's not uttering, and that word is "fish." I keep expecting him to say the word "fish," or "fishes," and he keeps saying almost every word *except* "fish" and "fishes." At any moment I think he'll finally say the word "fish," finally relent and say the word "fish," at last surrender and say the word "fish," or "fishes," but so far he has *not* said the word "fish," and he's almost summarized the formal properties of the entire painting! And I realize: My agent wants to synopsize the formal properties of the woman's whole head without even mentioning the fact that it's made up of fish! That aspect, for him, is insignificant! It was an amazing feat, actually, to hold forth on this painting at length without using the words "fish" or "sea creatures," nothing about "oceanic organisms," no reference to "beasts of the deep." By ignoring the fact that the head is composed of fish he is, intentionally or not, trying to coerce the painting into the categories familiar to him from his books, that's why I'm hearing so much about brushstrokes, perspective, and light, but not a word about aquatic critters, a great deal about the color palette, nothing about a world beneath the waves. The Emperor tells the Court Chamberlain: My agent, I realize, has only looked at this painting through the lens of his books, or in the reflection of his books, never directly with his own eyes. He hasn't actually gazed at this painting with his own two eyes, unmediated by his books, and since his books erase the fish he erases the fish. His eyes actually are not his own.

You know a great deal about this painting, the Emperor told his agent, the astronomer said.

And the agent, bowing his head just a touch, replied: Thank you, My Lord.

You know everything there is to know about this painting! Truly!

And the agent said: I would never bring an artwork to His Majesty without having studied it extensively.

Studied it. Yes. *Looked* at it, the Emperor said.

And the agent, after a moment, bowed his head just a touch.

You have *looked* at the painting, then, said the Emperor.

The agent took one of his hands in the other. Of course, My Lord.

Excellent, good. So you have *looked* at the painting with your *eyes*, said the Emperor, according to the astronomer. And your *eyes* have seen the *fish*.

And the agent said: Yes, My Lord.

And since you have studied the painting, a painting composed primarily of fish, you have, therefore, naturally, studied the fish.

The agent squeezed his own hand. Naturally, My Lord.

And the Emperor said: Please identify for me all of the fish.

And the agent went ashen, according to the Emperor, the astronomer told Leibniz. And in a quavering voice he had managed to say, This is an eel, when the Emperor raised his hand to stop him and said, You know who would enjoy this is the Imperial Fish Specialist. Now of course, the Court Chamberlain told the astronomer, there's no such thing as an imperial fish specialist! But the Emperor summons one of his valets and instructs him in a whisper to send in a servant clad in academic finery who is to nod *yes* after the first twelve fish named by the agent but after the thirteenth fish to shake his head almost imperceptibly *no*. My Imperial Fish Specialist knows all about fish, he will enjoy this, he will enjoy this, the Emperor kept telling his agent. Soon this fictitious fish expert entered the Chamber accompanied by two imperial guards whom the Emperor had sent for also and who took up their positions on each side of the agent, where they stood impassively with their immense swords in front of them balanced by their sharp tips on the silk rug. Please identify the fish, the Emperor said. And I am thinking to myself, the Emperor tells me, the Court Chamberlain told the astronomer, This is a lesson in proper vision. I am teaching him how to see. The relationship between surfaces and essences. The significance and insignificance of certain surfaces, the attendant presence and absence of certain essences. The difference between books and the Book of Nature, between the self-serving writers and the ambitious publishers of his beloved books and the writer and publisher of the Book of Nature, the *self*-publisher of the Book of Nature, i.e., God. After this, I'm thinking, the Emperor told his Court Chamberlain, my agent will never again rely on his books when his eyes will do! Never again on the opinions of his forefathers when his eyes will do! The fish, the fish, please identify the fish, the Emperor said, and his art agent, in a now thoroughly strangulated voice, began by naming the more recognizable creatures, first the eel again, then the lobster, then the octopus, and then the crab. After each one the Emperor glanced at his Imperial Fish Specialist, who nodded. Tortoise, stingray, sea horse, shrimp: all correct, indicated the ersatz fish specialist. Swordfish? Nod. Pike? Nod. Flounder? Carp? Nod! Nod! The agent was gaining confidence. He must have learned a thing or two from those nauseating Mediterranean fish markets he had to pass through en route from one gallery to another, one library to the next! the agent must have thought, said the Emperor. A mind such as mine is actually always absorbing the world! Now he pointed at the creature that constitutes the eye of Arcimboldo's woman and said: Sunfish. Ironically, the Emperor would later learn, as he told the Court Chamberlain, the Court Chamberlain the astronomer, and the astronomer Leibniz, that this was quite correct: The eye of the woman *was*, in fact, the eye of a sunfish. But the agent obviously did not know that, and when he and the Emperor looked over at the Imperial Fish Specialist—who pursed his lips and shook his head—the blood that little by little had returned to the art agent's face now drained from it once more, and the Emperor murmured, Take him to the dungeon and gouge out his eyes, they aren't his anyway and he knows not how to use them, and the two guards had hauled the agent halfway across the Castle complex before the Emperor ran up, almost speechless with mirth, and revealed that all this was just a little joke, a little joke, that's all!—albeit a little joke with a dead-serious lesson in it. Via humor, I am honing your eye, the Emperor told his agent. Arcimboldo, you see, the Emperor told his agent, began with fishes, but out of fishes he made the most magnificent face, whereas Bronzino began with a face and ended up with nothing. You cannot aim right at the face! The *goal* of course is a human face, not fish, but one arrives at human faces only through the roundabout route of fishes. (The Emperor added: I am saying something fundamentally philosophical when I say: The Bronzino is boring.) The true artist walks straight toward the insignificant, while slyly keeping an eye on the significant, and moving at all times away from the gorgeous, he instructed his art agent, the Emperor recalled. The Emperor had a lot more to say on the subject of significance and insignificance, but he noticed at that point that his art agent had urinated down one of his pant legs, so he thanked him graciously for both paintings—which can now be found in adjacent galleries at the Kunsthistorisches Museum in Vienna—and sent him on his way. The astronomer told Leibniz: It was a nasty little joke, the Emperor told his Court Chamberlain, but from then on he brought me the most marvelous art. Peering into his telescope, the astronomer added: One wants above all to understand the Sun, but one cannot aim one's telescope right at the Sun!

)

THIS, THEN, WAS THE MAN whom his father had to amuse with his mechanical head. Now, it so happens that the frigid winter morning on which the astronomer and his father set out to obtain an audience with the Emperor was the sixteenth morning of an interminable astronomical disputation the latter had convened at the Castle for the purpose of determining whether the new twinkling thing which had recently appeared in the heavens dwelled above or below the sphere of the Moon, and therefore deserved or did not deserve to be called a star. At once intrigued and tormented by that object's inexplicable emergence and enigmatic meaning, the Emperor had summoned not merely every astronomer in the realm ("minus of course myself!") but also freethinkers from the Low Countries, Oxford theologians, Jesuit mathematicians from the Collegio Romano, and Peripatetic schoolmen from Padua, who came north on horseback or sailed south up the Elbe or in one case scrambled ("just as you scrambled!") over these very mountains on foot. From the far-flung window of their workshop the astronomer and his father could see the skylights of the Castle's Great Hall pop open and a slew of astronomical contraptions emerge into the Prague sky, where they were whipped about by the crazed winter winds. A big brass something-or-other groaned over the city. It is said, the astronomer said, that Emperor Maximilian, upon learning that Rudolf intended to abandon the Hofburg and all that he'd accomplished there and move the imperial capital to Prague, had decreed on his deathbed that nothing in Prague rise higher than the steeple of the Cathedral of Saint Vitus—"Nothing higher!" At that moment, the tale went, he had a stroke that robbed from him for the final forty-eight hours of his life all of his language except the words "no," "higher," "steeple," and "Vitus," with which he emphatically filled the silence. In his last hour he retained only the word "no," but "everyone understood the gist of what he was saying," the astronomer told Leibniz. It was not as though the dying Emperor had constructed that steeple, the steeple was centuries old, no, this was "a pure posthumous filial constriction." "The gratuitousness of it amazes me still." But some of these contraptions soared higher than the steeple, and some even soared much higher. Our search for truth inevitably makes a mockery of our fathers' deathbed decrees, not as an empirical matter but as a logical one, since what we mean by truth and where we look for it are obviously defined, in negative, by nothing other than what our fathers decree on their deathbeds, construed loosely to include their decades of decline. "Is your father dead?" the astronomer asked Leibniz, and Leibniz said yes.

"Then this isn't news to you," the astronomer said, and Leibniz said no, it was not, although as he noted parenthetically to the *Philosophical Transactions* he was merely appeasing the astronomer on this point since he had nothing but the fondest memories of his father, a professor of moral philosophy at Leipzig who had died when Leibniz was six years old and with whose beliefs Leibniz's own were in "perfect accord." (Two years before his death half a century later, in an often-quoted 1714 letter to Nicolas Remond, Chief Counselor to the Duke of Orleans, in which he provides a brief polished account of his own philosophical development, Leibniz would claim to "possess no memories of my father," and deem his father's philosophy to be "of no especial interest.") Now, the astronomer went on, hoisting onto his lap his plump cat, who without opening his eyes began to purr, some of these contraptions were quite sophisticated, and some were quite large, and one, the big groaning brass one, was both sophisticated and large, but all of them, as anyone could plainly see, were nothing but naked-eye astronomical contraptions, contraptions only as powerful as the eyes that peered into them, contraptions which in no way transcended us.

In the Castle, brought there by the invited astronomers, were contraptions that left us as blind as before, or basically as blind, the astronomer thought, while in my head—the head of a *non*-invited astronomer!—was a contraption that would permit us to see, I mean truly to see.

Now it was merely a matter of getting this head into that Castle.

This head, containing that contraption, or the concept of that contraption, into that Castle.

Under the guise of helping his father get his father's mechanical head into that Castle.

"Tomorrow, I told my father," the astronomer told Leibniz, "we get this head into that Castle! Purposefully ambiguous of course about *whose* head, *which* head. I mean, of course: Let's get *my* head into that Castle! but my father hears: Let's get *your*, or *our*, head, the head we built together, into that Castle! And he, his beard now basically completely white, his mouth more or less toothless, on his head his prized plumed cap, breaks into one of those infinitely creased old-person grins that evoke the beatitude of an infant.

"You see this tear, yes?" the astronomer asked Leibniz. "You verify it? The interesting thing is that I weep most not when I ponder my feelings for my father but when I ponder my father's feelings for his cap, or his feelings for his box. Not my feelings for him, not his feelings for me, not his feelings for my mother, or my mother's feelings for him—though all of these feelings like all family feelings were perfectly potent—but rather his feelings for his cap and his feelings for his box, as well as my mother's feelings for his cap, for she was always trying to keep that cap clean for him even in the years he wasn't wearing it, that black cap my father loved so much collected dust like crazy and it's not too much to say that my mother, who was actually an extremely literate and intelligent woman, the daughter of a renowned jurist and humanist from Regensburg, wound up locked in a life-long battle with the dust-collecting-qualities of my father's black velvet cap. It is not the relationship between subjects and subjects that makes one weep most but the relationship between subjects and objects, that's insufficiently understood! When I picture my mother trying to keep my father's cap dust-free I can produce a teardrop almost at will."

He peered into his telescope.

"Sentimentality remains radically understudied. The scientific study of the sentiments is still utterly in its nascence. Only in the last year or two, in Delft, has a teardrop finally been put under the microscope. Sentiments can be investigated only to a certain extent by introspection, i.e., in the absence of a microscope. Delft is the undisputed capital of teardrop microscopy."

He peered into his telescope.

"The microscope has made its way to Amsterdam and The Hague, but in Amsterdam they put only sputum and spermatozoa under their microscopes, in The Hague similarly only sputum and spermatozoa, whereas in Delft, sperm yes and sputum yes, but also teardrops. The result is that eroticism and the respiratory system are totally devoid of mystery throughout the Dutch Republic, but the sentiments, insofar as they are understood at all, are understood only in Delft."

He peered into his telescope.

"And even in Delft not well."

He peered into his telescope and wrote something down.

They set out early one morning, his father bent low beneath a knapsack containing the Head of Phalaris, which he insisted upon carrying himself. It was snowing. The Sun rose dimly in front of them, behind a tangle of tree limbs lined with white. As they passed the midpoint of the Old Stone Bridge, where centuries before the martyr John of Nepomuk had been flung into the Vltava on the orders of Wenceslaus, King of Bohemia, and which now was presided over by a statue of Emperor Maximilian on his steed, the winds, which were already crazed, grew positively demented, howling, as the astronomer recalled, over the frozen surface of the river below. Somewhere high above, hidden in swirls of snow, the big brass contraption groaned. The weather, in fact, had been worsening for weeks, the Sun had slipped behind a cloud the moment the Emperor had signaled the start of his astronomical convocation with the ringing of the bells of the Cathedral of Saint Vitus and it had not reappeared since, but only now, at the instant, as it happens, that the astronomer and his father reached the bottom of the long stone stairway that wound its way precipitously up to the Castle, did the storm intensify into a blizzard. It was well-known at that time that meteorological conditions in Prague were causally connected to conditions in the Emperor's mind, a phenomenon that certain churchmen as well as the vulgar attributed to the action of demons flitting in and out of the Emperor's head, which evidently they could, on this theory, enter at will—"anything of course can be explained by recourse to a head-entering demon!"—although the astronomer, employing a precursor of Torricelli's barometer, had been able to establish that the Emperor's head actually influenced the city of Prague through the medium of the air. So what they beheld in the skies now they would presumably behold in the Emperor's head, if indeed they reached the Emperor at all. That boded well for the astronomer, since it meant the virtuosi invited into the Castle along with their archaic contraptions had failed to put the imperial mind at ease and had even whipped it further into a fervor, but it boded ill, he thought, for his father, and his father's trinket, and did little to quell his appalling suspicion that he was deliberately escorting the old man to his doom. And as his father began dragging himself up those steep stairs, his huffing and puffing audible above the fantastic clatter of the gale, one hand outstretched for balance and the other pressed to his cap, which threatened to fly off at any moment, its feather flapping spasmodically in the wind, the astronomer felt quite certain that his father's heart was about to give out, or that his father would slip on the ice and crack his skull on the stone, and even had a vision of the mechanical head sliding out of the sack and obliterating itself and its fragile inner workings as it whacked every single step all the way down before vanishing with a realistic gurgle in the Vltava. But that did not happen. In fact, as they approached the Castle, his father seemed, somehow, to gain strength. He caught his breath, straightened his shoulders, put down firm footfalls on the icy stone, while behind him his son began to huff and puff, to curl inward against the driving snow, to slip and stumble and once very nearly stagger backward into the abyss. By the time they reached the top of the stairs, where a snowy halberdier manning a grand gate flanked by two statues of Emperor Maximilian thumped the ground with the butt of his weapon (thus bursting forth from the snow blanketing him) and ordered the two to go no farther, he saw that his father's beard, underneath the ice that now encased it, had even recovered some of its former coloring: the white was flecked with gray. This was no mere trick of memory. "He really was extracting some sort of life force from his increasing proximity to the center of the Empire and directing it toward his beard." The astronomer realized that he did not and could not comprehend the appeal to his father of proximity to power until that moment, as he watched it affect the coloration of his father's beard. "We were very different creatures, I realized, if I could not even sense this life force emanating from the center of the Empire, whereas he not only sensed it but somehow tapped into it to effect the rejuvenation of his beard." It was not merely a matter of different tastes, of valuing things differently, but of different sensory apparatuses, of sensing things differently. "Seeing his beard get grayer, first a little grayer, and then a lot grayer, I naturally felt a surge of sympathy for my father, whom I ought to have regarded not as a man with different principles but as an animal with different senses, less a shameless courtier than a bat," he told Leibniz. (One is reminded of Bertrand Russell's contention that the contradictions of Leibniz's philosophy stem from his hunger for "the smiles of princes.") With newfound vigor the astronomer's father righted his cap and in a bold voice informed the young halberdier that he was the former Imperial Sculptor to the deceased Emperor Maximilian, King of Hungary, King of Bohemia, and King of the Romans, and he, who had designed the famous Maximilian Fountains of Vienna, had come for an audience with Emperor Rudolf. And he said it in such a way that the halberdier not only swung open the gate forthwith but even saluted them as they passed. At another gate a hundred yards closer to the Castle this performance repeated itself precisely, and soon a retinue of guards, functionaries, and attendants had materialized around the astronomer and his father and conducted the two of them toward the bowels of the Castle complex, blowing through gates, doors, and checkpoints, eliciting a blur of bows, salutes, and clicked heels, while his father's barely suppressed grin beamed forth from within a beard that was by now "the formidable and frightening black of my early childhood."

At last they entered the Great Hall, a vast vaulted chamber that had hosted countless coronations, royal weddings, winter waltzes, and other scenes of official elation, including the occasional chivalrous competition, "three weeks ago horses had galloped up and down that hall to the ecstasy of the Emperor," but which now was a scene of utter despair, scored by the tick-tock of precision clocks and swarming with men of science who in their fancy black cloaks and frilly white collars twirled their well-oiled models of the cosmos or pointed their useless instruments at the gray Prague sky, and in the midst of whom, upon his throne at the head of a banquet table laden with cold cauldrons of stale goulash and littered with the bones of diverse beasts and birds, sat the Emperor himself, cradling his huge, profoundly horrified-seeming Habsburgian head in the palm of one hand. "My first glimpse of the man, and of his huge imperial head, and of the horrified expression upon the face of it, which I immediately found not only congenial but reminiscent of an expression I'd sometimes seen when, while trying to glimpse a reflection of the heavenly vault in a spherical mirror, I glimpsed instead, however fleetingly, my own face." To this horrified imperial head the astronomer of course sought to bring "intellectual relief," while beside him his father, "precisely I think because the appearance of that new twinkling object had not thrust his own head into metaphysical torment," dreamt merely of bringing artistic delight. The astronomer added: "Only someone essentially untroubled by the nature of things will go around offering delight rather than relief, as I often told my son, himself a purveyor of art delights rather than means of mental relief. Only someone whose head is rarely or never thrust into philosophistic torment would rather please the eye than relieve the intense philosophical pressure that builds up behind the eye, I often said to him," said the astronomer. One glimpse of the Emperor's head was enough to assure the astronomer that it was not only huge, it was also thrust deep into torment. Why, the astronomer recalled asking himself for the first time in his life, had such an expression of fathomless metaphysical horror never flitted across his father's face? He said: "It is only upon leaving one's father's house and workshop, and gazing upon another man's face, that one realizes, retrospectively, that there are expressions one never observed upon one's father's face, the range of expressions of which had seemed, growing up, exhaustive, i.e., definitive of all possibilities." Distinctions, and hence knowledge, and hence self-knowledge, begin with this gazing-at-another-man's-face. "There's no knowledge until there's *another* man's face." In your father's house, gazing at your father's face, the world is bright, but without definition; then you leave home, and gaze elsewhere, including at other men's faces, and your eyes begin to deteriorate, but your mind begins to discern, and the world dims, but grows more distinct; finally, your eyes are plucked out, but your mind becomes infinitely discerning, and the world goes black, but becomes fantastically well-defined, "possessed of a crispness that in fact remains shocking to me." That's the standard story of knowledge acquisition, he said, "and the standard story is *true*." This process of coming to know himself, "which only with the eclipse will come to fruition," began with that gazing-at-the-face-of-the-man-in-the-alleyway but quickened markedly with this gazing-at-the-Emperor's-face, and observing upon it an expression (of fathomless metaphysical horror) that he'd sometimes fleetingly seen in his spherical mirror but, since he'd never seen it upon his father's face, had never registered seeing until now, "I must have seen it without *seeing* it," he must have overlooked it as trivial, perverted, or an artifact of his instrument. Seeing the Emperor's face schooled him in the art of seeing his own. "I had to admit to myself the terrible truth that I already, within seconds of seeing him across the hall, felt a closer kinship to the Emperor than I ever had to my own father, simply because we, and not my father, nor later my son, were seemingly thrust into the same torment." Years later, incidentally, the astronomer had done everything in his power to introduce his son to that torment, obviously he'd felt a certain ambivalence about seizing a young person's head and thrusting it without warning deep into the philosophical torment, "Did I really have the right, I had to ask myself, to thrust this content young man's head deep into torment? For the sake of company? What are we doing, exactly, when we give a child reams of reading material for the express purpose of thrusting them into the age-old torment?," but even though he'd decided that, yes, he had that right, and even though he'd actually gone ahead and thrust his son's head deep into the torment, his son was not, in the end, tormented. He kept "bobbing up like a buoy from the philosophical depths." A head might be more or less dense than the philosophical fluid into which it is plunged. His son's head was less dense. "The deeper I thrust him into the depths, the higher, like a buoy, he bobbed." A uniquely untormented individual, for better or worse, interested above all in the delights and distractions of art. His father and son would have liked each other, "had they ever met." He added: "A logical impossibility, of course, as my son's birth was a distal effect of the same cause, this encounter with the Emperor, that more proximally brought about my father's demise." Neither could've understood how the popping into being of a point of prettily twinkling luminosity overhead could bring to the imperial face such an expression of horror, nor, for that matter, how the horses who had galloped up and down here three weeks ago could bring him such happiness, whereas the astronomer with one glance at the Emperor thought he understood him, i.e., understood both why the horses had made him so happy and why the popping into being of that new twinkling thing now horrified him so.

The astronomer stroked his cat, peered into his telescope, picked up his quill, and wrote something down. Only someone truly horrified by the heavens can derive such happiness from a horse, and, a fortiori, a cat, he said. When you see someone deriving not altogether too much happiness from a horse, or a cat, you see someone at ease in the world. "An aphorism," declared the astronomer. "A man delighted by a cat is discomfited by existence, a man delighted by existence is discomfited by a cat." A cat owner is invariably an individual not in possession of any consoling doctrines or articles of faith, just as an individual in possession of some such doctrine invariably *has no cats*. A man who believes he possesses both a cat and a consoling doctrine will discover at some dreadful moment, when his faith is put to the test, that his doctrine is not truly consoling, or, if it is, that his cat is not really a cat. In his blackest hour he discovers that the doctrine on which he has founded his life is itself without any foundation, or if it does have a foundation his cat is a dog, the astronomer said, according to Leibniz.

Leibniz wrote: "Here the notion entered my head, and I could neither dislodge it nor yet judge the truth of it, that the cat, too, was missing its eyes."

Now, the astronomer went on, the Court Chamberlain approached the Emperor—who was listening halfheartedly to a German mathematician demonstrating with obsequious gestures and honeyed words the inner workings of the largest and most sophisticated of the contraptions, the brass one whose groans sounded as far as the Jewish Quarter—and whispered into the Emperor's ear while pointing at his father's former Imperial Sculptor, who stood as broad-chested as he could at the far end of the Great Hall. The Emperor raised his head a half inch off his palm and said, just loud enough for the astronomer to hear it over the din of "zenith"s and "azimuthal"s and the whistle of the cold wind coursing through the open windows and spewing snow on the floor, "My father's what?," in a tone—was it wistfulness? disgust?—which the astronomer could not decipher, "nor, of course, owing to the strange acoustics of that vaulted hall, was the tone of those words as they reached my ears necessarily that with which they resounded in the Emperor's head." The Court Chamberlain whispered once again in his ear and the Emperor, with eyes fixed gravely on the astronomer's father, said something in response, and then let his head sink back onto his palm. The Court Chamberlain made his way toward them. "I assumed we were about to get thrown out, or locked up, or worse."

Everything depended now on the exact nature of the Emperor's attitude toward his father, and by extension his father's representatives, several decades after his father's death, and this, to his subjects, was notoriously inscrutable. On the one hand, as you know, said the astronomer, the Emperor had forsaken his father's palace in Vienna for his own Castle in Prague, but on the other hand, and this I may not have mentioned yet, he filled Prague with hundreds of statues of his father. Hundreds of statues! However, the astronomer added, each statue portrayed his father at only three-quarter size. In other words, he populated Prague with innumerable, slightly smaller-than-life representations of his father. What should one make of this? "What does it mean? Was it merely parodic?" the astronomer wondered as the Court Chamberlain approached them. But if it were merely to parody his father, why would the Emperor have chosen as the moment to memorialize his father's greatest triumph, when he rode his steed into Transylvania after conquering it from the Turks? Innumerable, slightly too-small fathers riding victoriously into Transylvania, the astronomer thought as the Court Chamberlain strode swiftly toward them, a territorial inheritance which, as it happens, Emperor Rudolf would later relinquish back to the Turks in a series of skirmishes he hardly contested. What does this mean? The statues are too small, yes, he thought, but they are triumphant, as indisputably triumphant as they are self-evidently too small. And parody, anyway, needless to say, is always implicitly reverential of what it parodies, it always takes most seriously precisely that which it mocks most ruthlessly, this paradox is well-known, so even if these statues were intended not as tribute but as parody, perhaps especially if they were intended as parody, they still reveal the high esteem in which the Emperor held his father, the astronomer thought, with the Court Chamberlain now no more than a dozen paces away. Yet how high could that esteem really be, he thought, given that the steed in these statues was full-size, not three-quarters, so that the father actually looked extra small compared to his horse? "How, Herr Leibniz, would you characterize this relationship? He commissions hundreds of statues of his father, yet each is slightly smaller than life, although also quite regal in bearing, and at a moment of military triumph, yet dwarfed by his horse? What kind of relationship is that? What is the nature of it? Which sentiments are involved?" The *number* of statues indicates one thing, the *size* of them another, the *air* of them another still, and the size of the *horse* in them quite another, "and of course that is only four of the infinite attributes of these statues!" One could not escape the conclusion that the Emperor's filial sentiments were, correspondingly, infinitely complex. On the other hand, the Emperor would either receive his father's sculptor or he would not. The most multifarious phenomena are always being boiled down to the most ridiculous dualisms, said the astronomer—"just as, tomorrow, you will remember only that the Sun was eclipsed by the Moon, or that it was not."

The Court Chamberlain was upon them.

Emperor Rudolf, he declared, with a smile that to the astronomer seemed simpering and suspicious, would be honored to receive a gift from Emperor Maximilian's illustrious former court sculptor. The latter nodded, straightened with a licked finger the refractory feather on his cap, clutched to his chest the knapsack containing the mechanical human head, shot his son a proud impish gleeful glance—eyebrows arched, lower lip bit—and then followed the Court Chamberlain across the Great Hall, past a withered old Paduan declaiming energetically from Aristotle's *On Coming-to-Be and Passing Away*, between a trio of Jesuits scribbling figures and formulas on their slates, around a rotund Oxford bishop and oculist examining in the flickering light of a waxy candelabra a human eyeball seemingly astonished at its own state (and taken as it happens from the same young thief whose thick hair now festooned the Head of Phalaris), and at last, at long last, to the foot of the Emperor's throne. And the Emperor, in whom the German mathematician's monologue on his large, infinitely sophisticated, infinitely hopeless instrument had appeared to induce a state close to death, for his chin had fallen to his chest, and his eyes had closed, now opened them again, sat bolt upright, clapped his hands, and murmured something to the Court Chamberlain, who cried out to the crowd, in a manner that filled the astronomer with filial dread, "An artistic interlude!"

The chatter stopped at once.

The wind died down also.

Even the logs in the fireplaces ceased to crackle.

The hall was silent now save for the lamentations of the instruments.

And the Court Chamberlain, as far as the astronomer could recollect, per Leibniz, declaimed: "This gentleman, who served His Majesty's father in Vienna, and fashioned that splendiferous city, as well as the Hofburg within it, so precisely according to His Majesty's father's whims and wishes that whenever he stands in the Hofburg, in Vienna, His Majesty feels, as he has often expressed it to me, that he is standing inside his father's head, inside his father's head, that is, inside his father's head twice over"—inside *his* father's head, the astronomer told Leibniz, not mine!—"has fashioned for His Majesty, we are given to understand, a marvelous self-moving art head." And the words "marvelous self-moving art head," with their farcical ring, made the astronomer tremble. He told Leibniz: "Perhaps to exact revenge on his father by means of mine, perhaps to divert himself from the seemingly insoluble problem of the nature of the new object in the night sky, the Emperor, I realized, was about to turn my father and his work of art into an object of ridicule."

The Court Chamberlain said: "Please, sir, the moving art head, the moving art head!"

The astronomer peered into his telescope.

There were titters—"genuine titters!"—as his father delicately removed the lead head from its sack and held it in his hands.

"And yet, *were* there titters?" the astronomer said. "Now, whenever I think back on this moment, I always think, Were there titters? And almost always I think, There *were* titters, I almost always think there were genuine titters! And I can almost always still hear those titters, that tittering, all of it aimed straight at my father. Whenever I wonder if in doing what I did next I did something immoral, I summon those titters, I play those titters for myself, and in hearing those titters in my head I know I did something moral, for my father I know would rather be dead than be made into an object of ridicule in the court of the Emperor. The head was intended to provoke, among other passions, laughter—but not this kind of laughter. Those titters implied delight perhaps but not the right type of delight, amusement perhaps but not the right form of amusement, everyone was probably highly entertained by the head but they were not entertained by the head for the right reasons. It's not enough to know they were entertained by the head, we must ask *why* they were entertained by the head—*why were they entertained by the head?* I can hear the Emperor tittering, at the idea that this manmade metal head could possibly provide solace to him in his mental torment, that it could even touch him in his torment at all, and I can hear that obsequious young German, who as I later learned was none other than the famous Kepler, tittering, at the contrast between my father's creation and his own, even though his own brass contraption however big and sophisticated could no more touch the Emperor in his torment than could the mechanical head—and basically I can hear everyone tittering! Hundreds of men of science tittering at my father and tittering at his art! These men who in a few short decades would all be wearing his head on their shoulders! Yet at other times, in remembering the moment my father removed his head from that sack, I *cannot* summon those titters, sometimes I think I actually hear no titters at all, not a single titter, none. And instead I think I hear silence, I think I hear a perfect and attentive and even reverent silence, and at such times I have to ask myself if I may have added those titters in retrospect, if those aren't real titters at all, if it's conceivable that I scored this memory with after-the-fact tittering in order to justify what I did next."

For when his father placed the Head of Phalaris on the banquet table before the Emperor, the astronomer saw that the clouds had parted just enough to permit a glimpse, for the first time in sixteen days, of the new twinkling thing. It shimmered and burned in the heavens behind the Emperor's head. His father lay his hand upon the crank, the laughter, if not the silence, reached its peak, the place shook with laughter or silence, and at that moment, before his father could impart life to the head, the astronomer bellowed from the back of the Great Hall: "My Lord, I have invented an instrument that brings far things near, and with it I can yank that twinkling thing down from the firmament into this very room!"

And he flew across the Great Hall, and seized his father's mechanical head, and dug his fingers into its eye sockets, and tore out the two convex lenses.

And he held one lens in front of the Emperor's eye and the other an arm's length away toward the luminous object.

And the Emperor peered through both and muttered, "My God." And then: "It is a new star."

With that, the astronomer told Leibniz, the Great Hall erupted so to speak in pandemonium. Mathematicians and theologians thronged him to shake his hand and examine the New Star through his instrument, and he was thankful that his view of his father and in particular of his father's face was, consequently, occluded. "That it would be eternally occluded"—that his father would, on his way home, heave the now mutilated Head of Phalaris onto the frozen Vltava from the midpoint of the Old Stone Bridge, and then hurl himself into the hole the head made—"I of course did not know."

He learned what his father had done only the next morning, by which time he had already been appointed the Emperor's Imperial Astronomer.

The astronomer was silent for several minutes.

Then he said: "I am tempted, on occasion, to describe the astral tube as an apparatus that allows pressure to escape from this little head of ours into which a whole world has summarily been stuffed." He added: "Though strictly speaking of course that is nonsense."

The astronomer pressed an eye socket to his telescope, picked up his quill, and wrote down a very long string of numbers. For a split second, writes Leibniz, a sunbeam happened to align precisely with the warped slat of the window blind and blasted the interior of the observatory with a brilliant light, "excruciating after such a prolonged spell of continuous quasi-darkness." Leibniz shielded his eyes. On the astronomer's lap the cat opened his eyes, which gleamed crazily in the sunlight, "and therefore existed." Then the Earth rotated a little bit and the light was gone. It was now ten o'clock "on the dot," reported Leibniz to the *Philosophical Transactions*, in my translation. One hour had gone by, and if the astronomer was right about the eclipse, there were two more still to go.

THREE

*H*IS DUTIES AS Imperial Astronomer, the Court Chamberlain informed him, were threefold, the astronomer told Leibniz. First, "and, needless to say, the only duty of any significance to me," he was to deploy his astral tube to map the starry heavens more accurately and more precisely than ever before, to compose, that is to say, a star catalogue of unprecedented accuracy and unprecedented precision, "and also, I volunteered, unprecedented prodigiousness," for he was confident, as he informed the Court Chamberlain, that with his marvelous device he would not only see all the known stars more clearly than they had yet been seen but also see unknown stars that hitherto had been too dim or distant to see. Second, he was to cast horoscopes for the Emperor, whose actions, and particularly whose thoughts, were—according to the Court Chamberlain, who claimed to be speaking on behalf of the Emperor, i.e., conveying the Emperor's thoughts on this as well as all other matters, although the astronomer would later learn there were those in the Castle who held that the Court Chamberlain, the only official with unrestricted access to the North Wing, where the Emperor dwelled all day among his monstrosities and wonders and increasingly often slept at night, was systematically misrepresenting the Emperor's thoughts and wishes in order to amass power for himself, "Nothing he tells you ought to be taken at face value!" the Imperial Antiquarian hissed once in passing after seeing the astronomer emerge from the Court Chamberlain's office—while not exactly determined by the stars, "and in this sense His Majesty's thoughts are perfectly free," nevertheless inclined by the stars, i.e., subject to their influence, "and in this sense His Majesty's thoughts are, if not quite coerced, still drawn in certain directions, or so His Majesty thinks, not constricted but still coaxed hither and thither." Of course, as the Court Numismatist once mused—and he, the astronomer, had found the argument compelling—it was in the Court Chamberlain's interest to install in their heads a picture of a sovereign not wholly in control of his own faculties, for the less power the Emperor seemed to have over his own head the more the Court Chamberlain seemed, perhaps only in their eyes but in their eyes was half the battle, or more than half, to have over it. The Court Numismatist said: "One sometimes has the sense that the Emperor's apparent madness has been filtered through, if not concocted by, an exceptionally rational mind, a calculating and conniving mind, that this is really a manipulative sane man's madman, a madman whose seeming madness is in truth serving some very ambitious sane person's purposes." It was, of course, also possible, conceded the Court Numismatist, that the Court Chamberlain was a genuinely loyal servant to a genuinely mad monarch; this was the view of the Court Cartographer. A third theory, promulgated only by the Distiller-Royal, and he only hypothetically, as a sort of amusing thought experiment, was that the Court Chamberlain was himself quite mad, and that we therefore knew very little and perhaps nothing at all about the actual state of the Emperor's mind. "And so," the Court Chamberlain went on, "if you would, each morning, and on the holy days each evening, too, determine by means of your tube the influence on His Majesty's mind of Mercury and Mars and Saturn and so on, the Emperor would be most grateful." The third and final duty of the Imperial Astronomer was to tutor the Emperor's bastard son as well as his three illegitimate daughters in the subjects of the quadrivium—"for it is the Emperor's most fervent wish" (according to the Court Chamberlain) "that each of his children and his son in particular be conversant in the mathematical arts, that is to say, in arithmetic, geometry, music, and astronomy."

He repeated: "His son in particular."

In exchange the astronomer would be granted, first, an annual salary of so many thalers; second, stewardship of the Imperial Observatory, including access to the Castle Workshop,

Castle Library, and Castle Laboratory, and carte blanche use, "within reason," of the treasury for the making of his tubes, a "carte blanche" and a "within reason" that obviously—as the astronomer was later to realize—each annulled the other, for if "carte blanche" meant anything at all, "within reason" obviously meant nothing at all, and vice versa, "within reason" meaning something meant "carte blanche" meant nothing, not to mention that if he was indeed bound by reason, who knew what reason meant, if it meant by his own reason or by the Court Chamberlain's reason or by some kind of shared reason, if such a thing existed, that is, perhaps his rights to the treasury extended only so far as the boundary set by common sense, a probably purposeful ambiguity that would intensify the Court Chamberlain's power over him, with finally dire consequences; and third, he was granted for his living quarters a stately residence no less impressive than the Viennese mansion in which he'd been born. It was perched high on Hradčany Hill not far from the Castle, just beside an old Benedictine monastery whose bronze bells were pealing merrily as the astronomer pulled up in his carriage.

)

THAT DAY, THE DAY AFTER, and the day after that, the astronomer oversaw the construction of the first telescope, a brass tube thirteen inches long fashioned for him by a crew of expert metallurgists in the Imperial Forge and fitted at both ends with a lens of fine Murano glass purchased with imperial funds and shaped to the astronomer's strict specifications by a master lens-grinder from Nuremberg along with his Augsburger apprentice, and which magnified objects two times. "In other words," said the astronomer, "a magnifying power of *two*. You'll want to write that down, Herr Leibniz, for the numbers will prove dreadfully significant in what is to come. Two, a magnifying power of two, and a length of thirteen inches."

On the night of his third day as Imperial Astronomer he began cataloguing the stars. That night, the night after, and the night after that, he trained his astral tube at the celestial meridian. When a star crossed it he gave a shout, an assistant wielding a quadrant called out the altitude, another watching a clock called out the time, a third wrote down these two spatiotemporal coordinates in a ledger, which a fourth compared to the corresponding entry, if one existed, in the famous catalogues of Piccolomini, Tycho, and Bayer. Toward dawn on the first night, throughout which the monks in the monastery kept their bells ringing continually as if in anticipation of his feat, the astronomer surpassed the 919 stars enumerated by Piccolomini.

And he thought cheerfully: I have now seen more stars than Piccolomini, if not yet Tycho or Bayer.

)

THE NEXT MORNING, having sent word to his metallurgists and lens-grinders that he desired now a tube of fifteen inches, forged not of brass but of bronze, and with the power to magnify things threefold, the astronomer, careful not to neglect his other duties, wrote and dispatched by messenger a horoscope for the Emperor "consisting of course of utter nonsense but of utterly rigorous utter nonsense, and which brought His Majesty good tidings." It is in dealing with the nonsensical, he noted, that we must be most rigorous, for sense itself is always by definition quite rigorous, the requisite rigor has already been provided by reason working hand in hand with reality, it is precisely by its stiffness and structure that we identify it *as* sense, if it's very stiff and very structured we tend to say: That is, or makes, sense, whereas nonsense must be structured and stiffened from without, i.e., given form, which is why writing the Emperor's horoscope, insofar as it entailed writing an absolutely nonsensical document, was no easy task, it was harder even than his scientific labor of the night before, a fact which, the astronomer added, might have suggested to him now what he realized only much later—namely, that there was something awry with his science. Then, with a Latin edition of Sacrobosco's *Algorismus vulgaris* in one hand and a German vernacular version in the other, he set out for the turret in which he'd been told that the bastard prince dwelled, on the southernmost corner of the Castle complex, antipodal to the North Wing and overlooking the Imperial Menagerie, where imported beasts with eccentric stripes stood shivering in the snow; but after knocking three times on the thick wooden door with no answer, and observing only blackness between the bars of its little iron-grated aperture, and extracting from the four palace guards playing cards on the floor of the corridor nothing but shrugs, smirks, sexual innuendo, and sarcastic asides, the astronomer, "without, as I realized only later, asking myself *why* Prince Heinrich if indeed he did dwell there dwelled in such a turret, behind such a thick wooden door, with such a small iron-grated aperture, minded by so many armed guards," went off to look for one of the princesses.

At length he found the youngest of them, Katharina, a girl of perhaps eight or nine, of at least seven and at most eleven, softly singing a song to herself in the so-called Music-Making Room amid the clutter of old instruments there, many of which, he saw, were glockenspiels, most of which, in fact, he realized, were glockenspiels, and actually all of which, on closer inspection, were glockenspiels, the instruments were all glockenspiels without exception, "Basically it was just a room full of glockenspiels," of various shapes and sizes and states of disrepair, all of them heaped together, piled on top of one another, there was something gruesome about this glockenspiel pile, this big heap of hundreds if not thousands of glockenspiels, the millions of metal bars of which flashed splintered reflections of little Katharina's unkempt blonde braid as it swung to and fro behind her head. She sat cross-legged on the floor. He stood outside the doorway and listened to her sing. Her voice, while untrained, was lovely, the tune lilting, but the tale it told, of a "little pink pig" trying to evade slaughter at the hands of a "big black-bearded butcher," began to perturb the astronomer. At first, as the little pink pig "pops out" of the big butcher's arms and "pops through" a hole in the fence, he thought: She's singing one of those wily-barnyard-animal songs beloved by children the world over; and he expected, needless to say, that the pig would emerge victorious from the encounter; but shortly thereafter the butcher "catches that little pink pig by her pink little leg" and "chops it off with his big shiny axe." The refrain, "appallingly, to my mind," spoke of the pig's survival: "But did she go down? No she did not go down, no she did not go down, no she did not go down!" The astronomer marveled: "The song wishes this to be heard as a message of *resilience.*" The pig escapes again, is instantly caught again. In the second, third, and fourth verses, as the astronomer eavesdropped and Katharina's braid swung to and fro, the butcher chops off the pig's second, third, and fourth legs. "But did she go down? No she did not go down, no she did not go down, no she did not go down!" By now, the astronomer noted, one was praying for the pig to go down, at last to die. Instead she escapes again, the butcher catches her again and chops off her head, then chops her in half, "But did she go down? No she did not go down, no she did not go down, no she did not go down!" The butcher chops the pig into quarters, into eighths, into sixteen pieces, into thirty-two, still the pig doesn't die, but that fact was actually becoming—as the song went on—less and less appalling and more and more abstract, his revulsion subsided, "The song," he realized, "had taken a *mathematical* turn," it seemed to be no longer about the brutality of the butcher but the perplexities of the infinite, the pig endures in sixty-four pieces, in one hundred and twenty-eight pieces, "the characters were receding, the numbers were coming to the fore," two hundred fifty-six, five hundred twelve, and at this point the astronomer realized that if he did not intervene the song would actually not come to an end, not ever, or at least not until she lost interest in singing it, "and small children as I've since established time and time again, Herr Leibniz, do not *naturally* lose interest in singing songs," it is an empirical fact, he noted, that children are instinctually drawn to infinitely long, infinitely iterative songs, we all sing such songs throughout our childhood, and it is only at a certain stage of our maturation, a stage evidently not yet reached by Katharina, that we abruptly stop singing such songs and subsequently sing only finitely long songs. One might, of course, postulate that Princess Katharina's powers of computation would impose their own limit on the length of the song, which required its singer to multiply by two larger and larger figures, but the astronomer could already intuit, and would soon confirm, that this little girl's mental abilities were of no common sort. So he tiptoed in, picked up one of the many mallets littering the floor, and at the moment she reached once again the refrain he struck on a glockenspiel the corresponding note.

She spun around, aghast, "white, as the saying goes, as a ghost," Leibniz quotes the astronomer as saying.

And she cried: "You mustn't touch that!"

And he, although he suspected, correctly, that he already knew the answer, said: "What a pretty song! Where did you learn such a pretty song?"

And she, although she wished, clearly, to continue frowning, could not suppress a small smile: "I learned it from Heinrich."

And he cried: "From Heinrich, yes, I thought so! I thought from Heinrich! And where is Prince Heinrich now?"

Her smile vanished. "Heinrich's in heaven now. You don't know that?"

When he said nothing, probably simply sat there with his mouth hanging open, she took on a look of solicitude remarkable in someone so young, inflected possibly by the joy of knowing something an adult did not, and about a matter so serious, and she patted his arm and said: "There, there." And then: "It's a shock, I know, it was a shock for everyone, that's what Father said, a terrible, terrible shock! We were all so sad, Father and

I cried and cried, we even cried more than anyone else, especially more than Margaretha who I actually don't even think cried at all, Wilhelmina cried probably the second most, but Father and I definitely cried the *most* most, Father because Heinrich was his only son and I because I was Heinrich's favorite sister, everyone knows Heinrich loved me more than Wilhelmina and Margaretha, he *tormented* me more, yes, he used to tickle me the way that hurts more than it tickles, you know how instead of stroking your skin people sometimes poke into your bones? He thought I tickled him too *gently* but what he called proper tickling I called poking into my bones! He used to tickle me way past the point where I was laughing to the point where I was screaming, but even Margaretha admits that he obviously tormented me more because he loved me more. Heinrich used to say, Wilhelmina and Margaretha prefer people, you and I prefer animals, those two are people people, we are animal people, they prefer to go to balls and interact with people, we prefer to go to the menagerie and interact with animals, they're perfectly happy to have the same conversations over and over and over again with the same small circle of people, we're perfectly happy to have the same conversations over and over and over again with the same small circle of animals, they'd always rather dance with a duke than feed a donkey, we would always rather feed a donkey than dance with a duke, wouldn't we, Ina?, and I would say, Much rather, much much *much* rather!" Katharina cried, the astronomer recalled. "He would say, We prefer cows to count palatines, and I would say, *Much* prefer!" Then she said: "But we don't have to be too sad, at least not too too *too* sad, Father says, because Heinrich is happier in heaven, a lot happier, he wasn't all that happy here, I mean here on Earth, Margaretha says he was always sighing and even though she doesn't mean that nicely it's true, he *was* always sighing, even while petting the animals he was sighing, even while petting his *favorite* animal, this big old hog of his, he would sigh. Father brought in more and more exotic animals to try to cheer him up, first a zebra, then a camel, then a lion, then an orangutan, but Heinrich never favored these exotic animals, he always favored that hog, but even while petting that hog of his, actually *especially* while petting that hog of his, he would sigh. He was always feeding that hog slices of melon from a bucket, flinging his arms around its big head, and sighing. I sigh, he told me once, precisely *because* he's my favorite creature, we're always saddest when we are *with*, not apart from, our favorite creatures, he said every single poet from Homer till now has got this completely backward, our loneliest loneliness actually occurs when we're right *beside* our most beloved loved ones, we want to be able to do *more* to our favorite creatures than pet them, this we somehow feel is not enough, for certain casts of mind at least it is not enough, for some casts of mind it may be enough but for other casts of mind it is not enough, yet no matter what cast of mind we have we can do nothing but pet these beloved creatures, we can do no more than this, this is all we can do, he said the mind wants more from other beings than it can ever obtain from them, here I'm speaking mainly but not exclusively of beasts, in other words of the human-beast relationship, that's what Heinrich said, I remember *exactly*," Katharina said, according to the astronomer, Leibniz wrote to the *Philosophical Transactions*. "And I said: But you *do* do more than pet him, you also feed him melon, and he said: I want more than *that*, too, more than melon—I want to do more than just feed him slices of melon! I want more than this exchange of melon for affection, this wretched melon-affection transaction! But when I asked him *what* he wanted to do to his hog that he could *not* do to it, he got frustrated and said: If it could be put into words, Ina, then I could do it. Anything that can be put into words one is capable of doing to anyone. But what of what cannot be said? he said. Margaretha says he was just fundamentally an unhappy person, or a fundamentally unhappy person, I forget which, she's always saying stuff like that even now that he's gone, I think she says it to make me upset, she kind of likes it when I cry, she'll say, Heinrich was never happy, and I'll say, Well, he *sometimes* was, and then she'll say, No, he never was, never! And I'll try to run off before she can see me cry but obviously I'm usually already crying a *little* bit, and she'll yell, Oh, great, that makes sense, go cry in the Music-Making Room *simply because you can't admit that Heinrich was a fundamentally unhappy person, incapable of joy!* Wilhelmina says she says that stuff not to make me upset but just because Margaretha is *also* fundamentally an unhappy person, or a fundamentally unhappy person, and the favorite topic of conversation among the fundamentally unhappy is the fundamentally unhappy, it brings them a little bit of happiness to pick apart other people's unhappiness, that's their one little joy in life and they're actually extremely extremely good at it, that's what Wilhelmina says. She says people like Margaretha can never sense their own unhappiness but they're brilliant at sensing other people's unhappiness, the unhappy she says are like bloodhounds of unhappiness, always sniffing it out, tracking it down, tearing it apart in their huge jaws, yapping with pleasure the entire time, sound like anyone we know? That's their one tiny little joy in life so you know what, fine, let them have it! That's what Wilhelmina says, anyhow," said Katharina. She lowered her voice: "She says if Margaretha weren't so upset about the wedding she would be in *heaven* there, everyone's unhappy at a wedding, even the happy couple!"

"What wedding?" the astronomer asked.

"The *wedding*!" she hissed. "Wilhelmina's marrying the Count Palatine of Zweibrücken next month, you don't know that? We're not really supposed to talk about it in front of Margaretha though, if we can help it." She whispered: "I'm on flower-petal duty!"

And the astronomer said: "When, if I may ask, did Prince Heinrich pass away, was this all very recently?"

And Katharina said: "Oh, no, it was months ago, months and months and months and months ago!"

And he said: "And *how*, if I may ask, did Prince Heinrich pass away?"

But to this she did not reply. That's all right, he said, you don't have to tell me if you don't want to. But to this, too, she did not reply. Presently she began to sway to and fro again. He assumed that she would break into song, as before, but no, this time she swayed to and fro without uttering a word, her disheveled braid reflected around the room in a million glittering bits and pieces. To sway like this while singing was one thing, to sway like this completely silently quite another. Say something, please, the astronomer said, but she would not, not one word, she would not even acknowledge his presence, no, now she would only sway, only silently sway! What, he thought, have I done? He was supposed to tutor her in the mathematical arts, but instead, in asking after the cause of death of her brother, a person who, incidentally, according to the possibly mad and probably manipulative Court Chamberlain, was very much still alive, I've somehow caused her to start swaying, I have caused her to start silently swaying, and now I cannot make her stop! Meanwhile through the window the Sun was sinking huge and red behind the black spires of the town. In some far-flung window—he imagined, why not, that it was his widowed mother's—a lantern was already lit. Within a few minutes the evening star would appear. Before long he would need to procure his new tube from his metallurgists and lens-grinders and make his way to the Imperial Observatory. "I could hardly, however, leave the Princess in such a state, such a strange, silent, swaying state." For her sake, but also for his. "Outside, in the hall, the perpetual patter of bureaucratic footfalls. At any moment, I thought, a bureaucrat will burst in here, lay eyes upon this scene, and interpret what he sees, first to himself and later to the Court Chamberlain, in the most uncharitable light imaginable." How, though, to snap her out of it, so to speak? What thoughts, if any, he wondered, were going through her mind? What inward state did this outward state signify? Or perhaps this behavior wasn't atypical of small children? How, the astronomer actually found himself asking himself, and in asking himself this question he felt that his incipient astronomical career had taken an odd turn, do small children behave, typically? What *is* a small child, does it *think*, and if so, *what* does it think? The absurdity of his predicament was not lost on him, the astronomer said, for he'd been appointed to plumb the mysteries of the heavens, yet it was the mysteries of an eight- or nine-year-old girl's head that he now found himself plumbing. "The rich, I thought to myself, may hire you under the pretense of having you plumb for them the mysteries of nature, but it is almost always their children's heads, if not their own, that they wish in the end to be plumbed," he told Leibniz. The hint of a new intuition: he'd extricated himself from one family only to find himself entangled in another family, an actually even bigger and hence more emotionally convoluted family, when what he wanted was to peer in perfect solitude at the firmament. So it was that rather than pondering questions on the order of, Which force occult or otherwise dictates the motions of the orbs?, he found himself pondering questions on the order of, How do I get this small child to stop doing whatever it is it is doing?

Now, the solution to *that*, thankfully, lay quite literally at hand, for he had not in all this time let go of the mallet and upon realizing this he brought it down loudly on one of the glockenspiels. Instantly Katharina sat quite still and clapped her hands over her mouth. "You mustn't do that, I told you!" And why mustn't I? "Because these are *Father's* glockenspiels, we aren't to touch them!" These are *all* Father's glockenspiels? "All of them! All Father's glockenspiels! All! All! All!" It doesn't appear that he uses them, he said, and he struck another note. "He might! At any moment he might! Nothing good can come from touching Father's glockenspiels, that's what Wilhelmina says!" Yet the squeal she issued when he struck a third note seemed to contain not only terror but also a mischievous delight. Obviously, the astronomer said, there was nothing in the world Princess Katharina wanted more than to make music with her father's corroding glockenspiels; why else would she sit among them? "Your turn," he declared, and he held out the mallet. She looked at it intensely, the surfaces of her eyes seemed to strain toward it, but she made no effort to take it. "Take it, you're allowed!" the astronomer cried, waggling the mallet. "In fact, your father has *asked* me to teach you music. Why do you think I'm here?" He waggled the mallet again. Tentatively she took it. "And he said we could touch the glockenspiels?" "That's what he said," he said, and in his head he heard himself murmur the words "within reason." "Promise?" "Promise." And Katharina brought the mallet down on a glockenspiel key.

The note rang out.

"I cannot describe the look on her face," the astronomer told Leibniz, peering into his telescope, "except to say that I realized only at that instant that I would one day want a child of my own." He added: "A colossal miscalculation, of course, as you'll see, Herr Leibniz; how many people exist merely because their parents happened to observe a stranger's child in an abnormally sublime moment? Such moments of abnormal sublimity among the children of strangers are probably responsible for the existence of millions. And yet, if I saw again that look on her face, I'm not sure I wouldn't want another one."

That, he told her, is a D-flat.

He taught her the notes, then the scales, then various elementary techniques, then various higher techniques, then various even higher techniques, and finally actually the very highest techniques, all of which she picked up with astonishing ease and miraculous rapidity, it was clear she was a prodigy, and by the time the Sun slipped below the horizon she had mastered

Gabrieli's *Toccata del decimo tono* as well as four of Sweelinck's most difficult fugues. "I'm sorry, I have to go now," the astronomer told her at last, "but shall we continue our lessons tomorrow morning, first thing?" and Katharina cried, "Yes, sir, thank you, sir, thank you!" and she curtsied, curtsied again even more emphatically, and ran out of the room. A moment later she ran back in, cupped her two small, hot hands around one of his ears, and whispered: "Father says he died of a broken heart, but *I* know he really fell off the tip top of a tower and broke open his head. I *heard* the thud. See you tomorrow!"

She curtsied a third time and ran out.

)

WHEN, HOWEVER, HE RETURNED the next morning, Princess Katharina wasn't there, and neither were the glockenspiels.

"Listen," the astronomer told Leibniz, peering into his telescope.

In the course of the intervening night, at the last stroke of midnight, as the two Roman automata who stood atop the astronomical clock slowly wound down their flagellations of the automaton Christ, and in the background the bells of the Benedictine monastery continued to chime wildly, ceaselessly, to the point where he began to wonder whether their liturgical calendar contained feasts and solemnities unheard of in other strains of the faith, the astronomer surpassed the 1,005 stars tallied by Tycho Brahe.

And he thought joyfully: I have now seen more stars than Piccolomini and Tycho, if not yet Bayer.

Then he thought: What will it mean for me to have seen more than Bayer?

To compose, that is, a star catalogue greater than Bayer's *Uranometria*?

The telescope is only an instrument, a means to an end—nothing in itself.

The importance of seeing more than Bayer. The necessity, the astronomer said, of seeing more than Bayer.

"Suddenly: the fear that I would *die* before having seen more than Bayer."

At dawn, as the Sun rose, after requesting from his lens-grinders and metallurgists a tube not of fifteen inches but nineteen, forged not of bronze but of silver, and with the power to magnify things not three times but four, and after dispatching to His Imperial Majesty a horoscope which prophesied, nonsensically but rigorously, i.e., on the most precise possible astronomical grounds, both tremendous obstacles and the tremendous fortitude necessary to surmount them, he hurried without a second of sleep yet with a proverbial spring in his step to the Music-Making Room. His high spirits, he was surprised to realize, derived not only from pride at his own progress ("Yes, I think I thought I was making *progress*, actual scientific progress!"), but from his anticipation of the pleasure of another music lesson.

But the room was bare now except for a single harpsichord that stood on the spot where yesterday Katharina had sat and sung.

After a moment the astronomer realized there was someone kneeling behind the harpsichord. It was the Court Chamberlain, who by means of the most infinitesimal adjustments left and right was attempting to align the harpsichord's bench with the center of its keyboard. "Symmetry, sir, symmetry!" he cried with a broad smile. The Princess, he explained in response to the astronomer's inquiry, had departed at daybreak for Madrid to visit her cherished cousins at the court of Philip the Pious. She had begged to go, all dinner she had tugged at His Majesty's doublet begging to see her Spanish cousins, and at last her softhearted father had given in. It was a shame to cut short her lessons, said the Court Chamberlain with a pained expression, but would these hours not in any case—here he peered at the astronomer pointedly—be better spent perhaps on the mathematical tutelage of the Prince?

It had the form of a question but it was not one. The astronomer returned to the turret at once, at a run, gripped the iron bars, stuck his head between them into the squalid pitch-blackness beyond, and bellowed Heinrich's name, not once or twice, and not three times or four, or even five, but altogether six times, at the top of his lungs, wondering all the while if the name he was bellowing still referred to a living being, and why the guards behind him were giggling, and if he had gotten Katharina in trouble, and whether she was really on her way to Spain, on the eve of her sister's wedding no less, or else had been spirited away to some forsaken corner of the Castle, and what the Court Chamberlain's aim was and if it was the Emperor's aim, too, and what all this had to do with him, and with the heavens.

He said: "The constant thought: We ought not to have touched her father's glockenspiels."

From the black bowels of the turret there was, once again, no answer.

He even aimed his fifteen-inch telescope into the turret, in the hope that it might concentrate and convey to his eye the few particles of light scattered within, but still he saw nothing.

He put one eye socket to his telescope, picked up his quill, and wrote down in his ledger a long string of numbers.

"Nothing," he said. "Nothing."

In a stupor, stung by guilt and seized with foreboding, he staggered up and down the corridors of the Castle calling out Princess Katharina's name until from within the Small Dining Room a voice replied and bid him enter. Here he found a woman in a very large-circumference skirt seated before an elaborate silver place setting. And she, who while not old, he said, wasn't young, smirked and said: "So, you're looking for Katharina, are you?" And, glancing up over her shoulder at the unsmiling bewhiskered old man who stood ramrod straight just behind her chair, she added: "Everyone is always looking for Katharina, aren't they, Gottfried? And if not Katharina, Wilhelmina! Yes, there is worldwide interest in the whereabouts of *those* two, of some others not so much—of the whereabouts of *some* people the world really couldn't care less, isn't that so, Gottfried?" The bewhiskered old man cleared his throat. "At table," he said, "one must have a serviette, a knife, a fork, a spoon, and a plate. It would be entirely contrary to reason to be without any of these things while eating." Margaretha went on: "Of course, it used to be Heinrich whose whereabouts were most sought after, Father was constantly asking everyone, Where is Heinrich? How is Heinrich? But *now* of course Father knows precisely *where* Heinrich is, precisely *how* Heinrich is . . ." It struck the astronomer that he ought not ask her right away where her brother was, how he was. If he was. "Our conduct at table is an outward expression of our inward essence. Proper eating is nothing less than ethics made manifest," said Gottfried, whom, Leibniz wrote, the astronomer recognized now as the acclaimed author of a thousand-page treatise—composed of a series of imagined exchanges between Epictetus, Epicurus, Plato, and Seneca the Elder—on the edification of ladies, one third of which attended to the theory and practice of dancing, another third to the theory and practice of dining, and the last third to the art of polite discourse. In the corridor, a pretty young lady tiptoed hastily past the door to the small Dining Room, pinching in each hand a piece of her long white gown. Margaretha smirked. The astronomer remembered pressing ahead: "I am, I must confess," he told her, "a bit concerned that your youngest sister did not show up for our lesson today, indeed that she seems to have vanished overnight along with your father's glockenspiels, the Court Chamberlain claims she's gone to Spain but I'm inclined to doubt that." Margaretha burst into laughter. "My *father's* glockenspiels? Is that what Katharina told you? That those glockenspiels belong to our *father*? Oh, that is marvelous. Marvelous! Father's glockenspiels. Oh, I *love* that!" She clapped her hands together and howled. "Father's glockenspiels! Father's glockenspiels! That's actually hilarious." A servant placed before her a bowl of piping-hot soup. "The spoon is intended for liquids, the fork for solids," said Gottfried. "In parts of southern Italy and Sardinia thick soups are sometimes consumed with a fork, but that is entirely contrary to reason." Margaretha continued: "You will find, sir, that my sweet little sister, bless her heart, is not the most trustworthy authority on the ins and outs of our family life, on the laws that govern our little familial cosmos. She is, after all, a relatively recent arrival! So much happened before she was even born, so much that it's actually unfair to expect her ever to wrap her mind around it . . . She popped into being, you understand, in a world that was already very much *in progress*, that's the fate allotted to younger siblings, particularly *much* younger siblings . . . Past injustices are, in the eyes of a younger sibling, and in particular in the eyes of a much younger sibling, just the furniture of the world she's born into, that's all, furniture that's always been there . . . A decade-old injustice that for the older sibling is still fresh, still raw, has for the younger sibling the inevitability of an end table, the agelessness and innocence of an armoire, the sheer implacability of a couch . . . One does not interrogate the furnishings of one's *first* bedroom . . . And so even the most well-intentioned younger sibling—which Katharina undoubtedly is!—will bridle at the efforts of her older sibling to point out to her how her whole world, her whole family, throbs with ancient obscure injustices, how it consists of these ancient obscure injustices, sedimented on top of one another. Youngsters like Katharina, I've found, have basically no interest in learning about the gradual sedimentation of very ancient, very obscure injustices that constitutes their world, their family . . . They have a vested interest in thinking the world to be fashioned by some other mechanism, but as I always ask her: *What* other mechanism! Perhaps you have some other mechanism in mind! Needless to say, she has no other mechanism in mind . . . I point out: Notice how even the most harmless words, like Father's 'Good morning,' are not harmless at all, since they are intended above all *for Heinrich*, not for us, and think about what that means—but my sensitive little sister, rather than reflecting on this fascinating feature of our family life, starts to cry and runs off to the Music-Making Room. I point out: Notice how Father's eyes betray him, notice *whom* (which child) they alight upon while he pronounces this seemingly all-inclusive morning greeting. Not Wilhelmina. Not you. Certainly not me! They alight upon Heinrich, I point out, and she runs off to the Music-Making Room. In the evenings I point out: Notice how Father's 'Good evening' is intended above all for Heinrich, not us, his eyes betray him, think about what *that* means—and she runs off to the Music-Making Room . . . I sometimes feel she has *chosen* not to see the truth of things, sometimes seeing the truth, especially about Heinrich, I tell her, and about Father, is a matter of choosing to do so . . . Plus Wilhelmina's always feeding her her Wilhelminian pap, her middle-child peacemaking pap, prepared by means of her famous Wilhelminian smoothing-everything-over techniques, *that* obviously doesn't help Katharina see the world as it truly is . . . Aha, there she goes now!" The pretty young woman in the long white gown tiptoed past the door to the Small Dining Room, going the other way this time, and casting in a quick sidelong glance as she went by. "Not to mention that our lovely little bride-to-be has never perceived the oddness of the Katharina/Heinrich relationship, which I *do* perceive, it's hard to miss if you're looking out for it . . . Yes, I fear the true nature of our family eludes both of my dear sisters completely . . . Particularly of course as it pertains to Father, and to our unhappy Heinrich . . ." "Which," asked Gottfried, "is the spoon for eating soup? Which, in other words, is the so-called soup spoon? The ethics of soup are the ethics of splattering. Eating," according to Gottfried, according to the astronomer, "is an inborn impulse buried in the mortal body after the Fall."

The astronomer peered into his telescope, picked up his quill, and wrote down a long string of numbers.

"So," he remembered saying, "when Katharina says that Heinrich fell from the top of a high tower . . ." and Margaretha had picked up a spoon, smiled with infinite forbearance into her steaming soup, and said: "Let me begin this way: If you do not understand that those are in reality *Heinrich's* glockenspiels, if you do not understand the circumstances in which he amassed such a vast and expensive collection of glockenspiels—not one of which he played more than once, you must wrap your mind around this, that he never played a single one of those exorbitant glockenspiels more than a single time!—then you cannot begin to understand our family, or our father. You cannot begin to understand how our family works. How it *functions* . . ." She began spooning up her soup. "Nor can you understand what in recent months has befallen Heinrich—or rather, what Heinrich has *done* . . ." "But," said Gottfried, "it is possible to rehabilitate this brute inborn impulse by applying at table a number of rules, a finite number of wholly rational rules." Between spoonfuls of soup, Margaretha went on: "And you cannot begin to understand his glockenspiels without first understanding my headaches, the horrible headaches I have endured almost continuously for years and years, but about which my father has always been extraordinarily skeptical." From the moment her headaches first appeared—in the middle of a minuet in her fourteenth year—her father had never believed in them. He claimed of course to believe in her headaches, You, my dear, he told her, she said, are the authority on what's happening in your own head, but it was obvious that he doubted them. "And my bodily aches, too, he disbelieves." If her soup was too hot, Gottfried advised, she ought to blow on it in the bowl, never in the spoon—"reason dictates that hot soup if it must be blown on at all be blown on in the bowl." In Spain they blow on hot soup in the spoon, "but that is contrary to reason." Such rules do not obtain, needless to say, when we eat alone, he added: "Only at table does eating rise from a matter of mere efficiency to a matter of ethics." The ethical problem of soup, *at table*, he said, is the ethical problem of splattering. "Manners presuppose others." Leibniz: The astronomer shifted Linus a little on his lap, peered into his telescope, picked up his quill, and wrote down a string of numbers. The astronomer: The Princess had slurped up about half of her soup. She said: Her horrible bodily aches began soon after her horrible headaches first struck, also (as it happens) while she was in the Great Hall learning the steps to a minuet. "A different minuet, but a minuet all the same." She had collapsed on the dance floor both times and both times was carried to her chamber. Both times the Imperial Physician had been summoned and both times he'd declared—"after the most cursory conceivable examination of in the first instance my head, and in the second my body, the first time barely palming my forehead, the second barely palpating my kidneys"—that Margaretha was in perfect health. This in spite of the fact that she could describe with precision where her pains were located, her head pain "near the exact center of my brain, midway between its two hemispheres and equidistant between front and back," and her bodily pain "most intense in each of my bones but also in all of my joints and beneath my skin, about one-eighth of an inch beneath my skin all over my entire body, concentrated in particular in the region between my knees and my neck, *including* my knees and my neck, but also around my shins, calves, feet, and face." The bodily pain was best described as an incessant itching deep in her bones. She was also always tired, she noted, and the nodes in her neck were constantly enlarged. "She suddenly seized my hand," said the astronomer, "and touched it to a node in her neck, which was perhaps slightly swollen." "You feel that, yes?" she said. "And this is nothing, they actually get a *lot* more enlarged."

She was also always cold, she added.

Leibniz writes: "However one inclines concerning the existence of the pain in the middle of Princess Margaretha's head, it is interesting to note the degree to which her description of its whereabouts corresponds to that of the famous pineal gland of Monsieur Descartes."

And from time to time, she added, her hair fell out in clumps.

Gottfried: "It is in the nature of bread to be broken by the hands, not sliced by the knife."

Once she even brought a clump of hair to her father in her fist, but it made no impression on him at all. "Perhaps he imagined I had torn it out myself."

You must understand, said Margaretha as her soup bowl was cleared, that her father is not some staunch skeptic, no Socrates reincarnate—"He is not, sir, a Bohemian Montaigne! He believes, on the contrary, everything." In the dictations Dr. Dee took from angels her father had full faith, in Mr. Kelley's trans-mutations of metals likewise, Herr Thurneysser the quack apothecary he regarded as a wonderworker, and when on warm evenings the windows in the North Wing were thrown open it was not uncommon to hear him intoning kabbalistic incantations in unison with the Jew Judah Loew. He does not doubt any of that. "But *my* pain, he doubts." A crazy old man came barefoot from Krakow, proclaimed that he had perfected the ancient lost art of divining the future by inspecting the intestines of animals, in particular of poultry, and demanded from the Emperor an outrageous sum to tell his fortune; her father paid it at once and for months afterward spoke with awe of that Polish magus's admirably accurate duck. "But *my* pain, he doubts. What a demented Krakowiak claims to perceive in a duck's liver my father believes, what his eldest daughter tells him she feels, he doubts. The maddening itching she endures in her bones and beneath her skin, the agonizing ache in the dead center of her head: *These* phenomena His Imperial Majesty sees fit to subject to withering skepticism! In *this* case the evidence, which is to say his own daughter's word, not to mention the clump of hair in her fist, is insufficient!" She burst into laughter. A platter of veal tongue was placed before her. Why, Margaretha demanded—and she seemed, according to the astronomer, genuinely bewildered—would she make up this pain? To what end? "A princess in possession of the faculty of reason will naturally serve tongue to herself using the tongs," Gottfried said. "Compare the fingers of a senseless princess, which during the course of a meal will have touched all manner of sauces and syrups, and other greasy substances, to the fingers of a sensible princess, who having served herself the tongue with the provided tongs has kept her fingers clean." Why make up this pain? Did her father imagine she *wanted* to spend her life attempting to persuade him of the reality of the itching in her bones and the ache in her head? A daughter should not have to convince her father that her bones itch, "that is not a *desirable* father-daughter relationship!" she said, and burst into laughter, and speared a tongue with her fork. "I am going to tell my father every single day that my bones itch and my head aches, even though they don't, simply to torment him and cause him pain: That is what my father must think that I must be thinking! I shall concoct a pain to cause him pain, and his pain (his concern) will give me pleasure: He must think that I'm thinking along lines like that. And to think that I am thinking along lines like *that*," she said, laughing, "is tantamount to thinking me mad." Gottfried: "The manifest senselessness of a princess whose fingertips are slathered in sauces or syrups." Her headaches grew worse and worse. The Imperial Physician continued to insist they were not real, not *really* real. To her father he said things like: I do think that *she* thinks they are real, and: The pain in her head exists in *her* world, My Lord, it just doesn't exist in ours. He spoke of her phlegm and bile and said: We ourselves are always the worst witness to what ails us. She begged her father to send another doctor, a Paracelsian, if not a demonologist, "anyone less shackled to the Galenic dogmas!" Yet he refused. He said he didn't want to undermine the authority of the Imperial Physician ("even if upholding his authority over my head meant undermining mine"), but the truth of the matter, Margaretha told the astronomer, and the latter told Leibniz, is this: that he did not want to squander a single thaler on his deluded daughter's illusory head ailment. Finally, one day, she stopped getting out of bed. The next day, it just so happens, was her mother's birthday. For her, his beloved mistress, visibly pregnant with his fourth child, whose delivery a few months later would kill her—"One cannot, of course, hold against Katharina the fact that she was a huge fetus, an abnormally huge fetus, and in the end a lethally huge fetus—the irony of this being of course that she's now exceptionally *short* for her age"—the Emperor had organized various festivities. Margaretha sent word: She could not get out of bed, her headache now was too painful, she wished her mother a most happy birthday but to her great regret would not be able to join them. Her father sent word back: You *will* join us. The palace guards who delivered that message hauled her by the armpits to the Great Hall. First there was a banquet, during which her head pounded. Next there was a concert, during which her head throbbed. To conclude there was a demonstration of the—"dubiously ennobled," she said—Balthasar von Ulm's purported perpetual motion machine, a vast canvas-covered wooden wheel some eleven and a half feet in diameter, capable of turning twenty revolutions per minute while hoisting a weight of some thirty-five pounds, and doing so, declared its impresario-inventor, indefinitely, entirely on its own, without any source of external power. The wheel started to rotate. The Emperor was delighted. "Look at that!" he cried, catching first Heinrich's eye, then Wilhelmina's eye, and only then (and only because Mother nudged him with her knee) my eye, said Margaretha, then Heinrich's eye again, then Wilhelmina's eye again, and only then (and only because Mother nudged him with her knee again) my eye again. Throughout her childhood her mother was actually constantly nudging her father to remind him to engage with *her*, too, to appreciate with his eldest daughter, too, this or that wonder, this or that marvel, this or that spectacle, like the spectacle of this wheel, "don't only enjoy it with Heinrich, enjoy it with Margaretha, too!" her mother was always reminding him by means of her knee nudges, "which were a lot less surreptitious than she seemed to think," Margaretha said. Her mother probably thought she saw none of these nudges, but the truth is she saw all of them. (She added: "As soon as Mother died, and therefore stopped nudging Father, he never again paid the slightest attention to me.") "Astonishing!" her father had cried in the Great Hall as the wheel spun. "And entirely of its own accord! Is the wheel not astonishing, Margaretha?" And Margaretha had replied, "Astonishingly astonishing, Father," but in a tone that left no doubt as to her actual feelings about the wheel. "In those days I liked nothing more than to yawn before my father's marvels and monstrosities." He would show her a three-headed beast pickled in a glass jar, she would yawn, and "that, in my childhood, was as close as I got to happiness." And yet she *was*, at least at first, astonished by this wheel. The truth is that she shared her father's zeal for mechanism almost to the degree Heinrich did, but she had always hid that zeal from them in favor of the more immediate pleasure of casting scorn on the things they loved. In their presence she feigned an interest in high fashion and fine dining, in exquisite balls and eligible bachelors, "hence," she said, bursting into laughter, "Gottfried here, a *gift* from my father, who actually imagines I'm still interested in an advantageous marriage!" when in fact, "in another life, I might have been a clockmaker." At that moment Princess Wilhelmina in her long white gown tiptoed past the door, going the same way she had been going the first time. Margaretha: It was, incidentally, supposed to be some enormous tragedy that her younger sister was getting married before her, and to a member of the redoubtable House of Wittelsbach at that, that's why the wedding was spoken of only in whispers, but "when you see the fop to whom she's betrothed you'll realize it's an enormous comedy!" This the astronomer would learn to be true. Half rising from her chair, Margaretha peered out a window overlooking the town. "Often one finds him bathing totally nude in the Vltava in plain view of all the plebs and potentates of Prague." She laughed, kept looking for a moment more, said, "Not now, but often," and sat down again. "She has been fitting that wedding dress for months now, you know. Months! She has two fitting rooms, each with a hundred full-length mirrors, and she goes back and forth between them a thousand times a day. The fitting rooms are actually identical, but she says each gives her a slightly different perspective on her figure. What *I* find curious is that the route between them always seems to pass *right by* the room in which I happen to be sitting . . . Curious, no? . . . We always speak of Willa the peacemaker, Willa the sensitive one, Willa-who-is-attuned-to-feelings—never Wilhelmina the person wholly capable of purposefully inflicting pain, all the more so because she's so attuned to feelings." Not to mention that the dress already fits her perfectly, everything always fits Willa perfectly, "She got Mother's body, I got Father's body," Heinrich and Katharina also got Mother's body, "I'm the only one who got Father's body!" Wilhelmina tiptoed past the door, going the other way again. "In short," Margaretha whispered, "everyone thinks she's doing a splendid job of not rubbing her impending wedding in my face, not pressing on what they assume is a sensitive spot for me, when in reality that's *exactly* what she's doing: rubbing her impending wedding in my face and pressing on what she assumes is a sensitive spot! What she doesn't realize is I'm not sensitive *there*. What she fails to realize is that I *want* her to marry this person, because of how ridiculous he is." She rose partway from her chair, peered out the window, then sat down again and whispered: "I would *love* to see her marry this ridiculous person, I cannot *wait* to see Wilhelmina who is such a terrific judge of character joined in holy matrimony with a fool, I am so excited to see what sort of ridiculous offspring they produce! I wish I could show you him bathing. It is impossible to imagine her loving this person, even she must know she doesn't love him, what she loves is the notion of marrying someone, *anyone*, before I do . . . I pretend to be upset about it, but only to stiffen her resolve to go through with it . . . As for me, no, I never want to marry anyone, never, I have zero interest in becoming a count palatine's wife. Yes," she said, "in another life I might have been quite happy as a clockmaker, I rather like mechanical objects, no one knows that about me . . ." And so, she went on, beneath her expression of wonder for the miraculous moving wheel of Balthasar von Ulm was a tone of contempt, but beneath the contempt was wonder. At first. For after a dozen revolutions of the wheel, a dozen hoistings of the weight, she started to smell a smell coming from the contraption, the distinctive smell of human sweat. And she asked von Ulm: "Is there not someone inside it?" And von Ulm replied: "No one inside! The wheel turns of its own accord." And her father cried: "Of its own accord!" Then she began to hear sounds coming from the wheel: breathing, gasping, wheezing, panting, even what sounded like someone muttering *Mein Gott, mein Gott . . .* And she said: "There's someone in there, Herr von Ulm," but he said: "There's no one," and her father said: "The wheel is a *perpetuum mobile.*" It felt now as if that colossal clattering wheel were revolving inside her head, slicing and slashing her fragile mental tissues as it turned. All signs pointed to there being a small person in the wheel, just as all signs pointed to there being an unbearable pain in her head, but in both cases her father overruled the testimony of his senses, *for* von Ulm, *against* her. She wondered: Why does he give von Ulm, a blatant charlatan, the benefit of the doubt, while to me, from the moment he made me, he has never once extended the benefit of the doubt? Why make me only to refuse to extend me the benefit of the doubt? "Make me or don't, but don't drag me into existence only to refuse to extend me the benefit of the doubt! cried Margaretha, chewing on a piece of tongue," said the astronomer, who added: "I am paraphrasing." Gottfried said: "We contravene reason when we hold our fork with our whole hand, like a stick." Margaretha said: "At last I spotted, through a tear in the canvas, a small person pedaling feverishly on a mechanical device installed in the center of the hollow wheel. Herr von Ulm was already slinking toward the door. The presence of the small person inside this big wheel was now undeniable. What more could my father say? There he was, the small person, pedaling madly! I thought: At last I have my father cornered, due to this indubitable small person! Yet when this small person was pointed out to him, what my father said was: This person is actually much *too* small to turn the wheel entirely on his own. Whatever his own contribution it must be in *addition* to the dazzling self-moving properties of this astonishing wheel..." At that instant, Margaretha said, her headache reached a point of unparalleled painfulness, never before or after had it hurt so much, and she mumbled, My head, and stumbled and collapsed and hit her head on the floor of the Great Hall. And because she bled there in front of everyone, before not only her family but also a horde of courtiers, because they could all *see* the blood pouring out of her head, her father, although he probably assumed she had fallen on purpose, relented at last and promised to send a new doctor, a chemical physician as she wished.

Unfortunately, this turned out to be the quack Thurneysser, who obtained a sample of her urine, heated it up, and concluded on the basis of this heated-up urine sample that her headaches were not real, and neither was the itching in her bones.

Never again was Princess Margaretha allowed to utter the word "headaches" in the Emperor's presence, nor the phrase "the incessant itching in my bones," nor was she permitted to refer to "the enlarged nodes in my neck."

"There was nothing else I wished to discuss with him, so over the course of the decade since we spoke less and less, and nowadays we hardly speak at all," the Princess told the astronomer as dessert was placed before her.

"What is doubtful," Leibniz comments, quoting Descartes, in a reference it is tempting to read as ironic, that is, sympathetic to Princess Margaretha, though there is evidence, in his *Hypothesis physica nova* (1671) among other places, that Leibniz in his youth was a faithful Cartesian, "should be considered false."

Only by the grace of God did her head gradually begin to ache less, did her bones become less itchy . . .

"Of course, I still itch, I still ache, but I keep it to myself, I don't complain. If you asked my sisters they would probably say I'm a happy, healthy person, but of course they have absolutely no idea the amount of stoicism required to give off that impression." She added: "The inner resources."

Gottfried said: "It is not proper to spit the pit of a fruit into the palm of the hand."

"Now what, you may wonder," said Margaretha, "has all of this to do with the glockenspiels?"

"And what," added the astronomer, peering into his telescope, "has all of *that* to do with my eyes?"

Not long after Margaretha collapsed on the floor of the Great Hall, her brother began to complain of a certain sound echoing faintly in his head. It was, as he described it, very, very faint, so faint indeed it verged on not being there at all, and caused him no pain whatsoever, it was even rather melodious, it was not the Devil's Tritone or any such discordant thing, just a single pleasant note, yet the mere fact of hearing a note no one else could hear, and which moreover he could not reproduce for anyone, his efforts at whistling or humming producing, at best, something slightly different from what he heard inside his head, was, he insisted, indescribably frustrating. Margaretha said: "You can see where this is going." She remembered lying in bed—her head swaddled in bandages, her bones itching, the nodes in her neck hugely enlarged—hearing her brother in her father's throne room humming and whistling note after note while interjecting at intervals: "*Like* that, but *not* that. *Like* that, but *not* that."

Gottfried said: "Rather, as in the Garden, we pluck it from our mouth with two fingers."

"So," said Margaretha, "our father sent for the Imperial Physician, the Imperial Physician examined Heinrich, concluded that the note he heard did not really exist, not really really, Father took his word for it, and that was that, right?" She bit into a peach. "Ha! Hilarious! No." No, it never even occurred to her father to doubt his son's putative pain, and he turned his realm upside down in an effort to assuage it, this pain so subtle and delicate and ethereal that Heinrich had great difficulty just describing it, "for the sound itself, he wanted us to know, *needed* us to know, was not unpleasant, that was not the problem at all, he'd often scream at us that we didn't understand the nature of the problem at all." (Once, Margaretha remembered, Heinrich tried to explain to her—her head still swathed in bandages apart from two eyeholes—that his inability to articulate *why* the inability to share with others the sound he heard *was* a pain, was itself a *second* kind of pain, a sort of metapain, or metadiscomfort: "I am afflicted not only by descriptive difficulties but also by the difficulty of describing those descriptive difficulties, and so on and so on. Against my will I find myself in perfect solitude.") "Perhaps," she said, biting into the peach, "Father respected the abstruse nature of his complaint, perhaps my pains were just too *obvious* for him, too much the pains of common folk, not kings, not to mention, of course"—she laughed—"too much the pains of a woman." Whatever the case: When it came to the faint note echoing uncomfortably in her brother's head, His Majesty spared no expense. First he summoned back to Prague the orchestral ensemble that had played at her mother's birthday party, and which subsequently had crossed the Alps; they performed the same piece of music they had performed then, but the sound in question, according to Heinrich, did not appear in it, so evidently the concert was not the cause.

Margaretha said: "That alone cost eight thousand eight hundred thalers."

A tattered notebook, which appeared to record in considerable detail the various expenditures her father had made on her brother's behalf, had suddenly materialized, he knew not from where, perhaps from within the folds of her very voluminous skirt, the astronomer told Leibniz.

Gottfried said: "The stone fruits Adam and Eve ate unthinkingly and in all innocence, yet whose pits they plucked from their mouths properly, can no longer be eaten rightly, their pits disposed of rightly (such is our depraved state) without reflection."

Then the Emperor issued a proclamation: Whoever could produce, for all to hear, the note that Prince Heinrich heard in his head, would be rewarded with riches beyond measure. Pilgrims poured into Prague, thousands of them, tens of thousands! They came bearing zithers and lutes and flutes and fiddles and horns. From the East came strange men lugging by oxcart gargantuan drums stretched with the skins of unfamiliar creatures, celebrated castrati risked the wrath of the chorus master of the Sistine Chapel Choir to make the journey from Rome, Jews came from every corner of Europe with ram's horns in their hands, and from the Siberian steppe three men and three women conveyed on a plank of wood an old man of exceptional frailty, perhaps their father, who to all appearances was near death by the time they arrived in Bohemia and no longer among the living by the hour he was brought into the Great Hall, and yet still generated, without opening his eyes, an unfathomable sound from deep in his throat.

And Heinrich said: That isn't it.

Scholars at the University of Leiden conducted a huge study of Heinrich's head, the most extensive head study yet conducted, which, if we believe Leibniz's account of the astronomer's account of Margaretha's account of it, might even be termed, at the risk of anachronism, a *psychological* study, and theorized the type of sound that was likely to lodge itself in such a head, and produced a newfangled instrument, partway between a church organ, a heavily modified hurdy-gurdy, and an early oboe, which, when a key was pressed, and a crank turned, and a tube blown into, generated a noise never before heard on Earth.

And the Emperor peered over at Heinrich, and Heinrich said: That isn't it.

Over and over their father peered anxiously at Heinrich and over and over Heinrich said: That isn't it. That isn't it. That isn't it.

And the drummers whipped their oxen eastward, and the castrati returned to Rome, and the Jews went home with their ram's horns, and the old Tatar was buried by his children on the outskirts of Prague, and the Leiden scholars took up once again their traditional disciplines.

Gottfried: "After the Fall no one dines rightly save by means of reflection."

"Imagine," said Margaretha, riffling through her notebook, "just the cost of administering all this! I'm not even referring to the reward, I'm just talking about the administrative costs—the administrative costs alone!"

114

You can think about the solitude in her father's eyes, or you can examine the record of his expenditures, "They tell the same tale," she said.

Wilhelmina tiptoed hastily past the door, pinching in each hand a piece of her gown, "which really did fit her well," Leibniz quotes the astronomer as saying, in such a tone, Leibniz notes, that a man with eyelids might have winked.

Gottfried: "It is no longer possible to eat a stone fruit properly without the *concept* of a stone fruit."

One day, while tramping around town terrorizing the local maidens—"For, as you shall see, sir, my brother, even at the height of his supposed mental illness, and notwithstanding how esoteric and how refined he wished this illness to seem, how profound, was never too ill or too profound to exploit the powers of his office to obtain for himself the pleasures of the flesh"—the Prince cried suddenly: That's it! That's it! That's the sound! And he pointed at a little bell that hung round the neck of a gaunt goat being driven to the butcher by its equally gaunt goatherd and his three skeletal sons, who in bafflement and distress trailed the royal retinue up the steep stairs to the Castle, begging the men who had seized their animal to give it back. Imagine how their grief turned to joy when the goatherd was told that the sound of his goat's bell matched the ringing in the Prince's head, and that this entitled him to unimaginable wealth! Sacks of gold were hauled out one after another; the old goatherd trembled and wept; his sons laughed and danced. Margaretha noticed, however, that her brother, who had blissfully been ringing that goat bell into one of his ears, had now cocked his head. And then he said: "Wait—it's actually slightly different.

It's *like* this, but it's *not* this." And the sacks of gold were hauled back into the Castle and the gaunt goat was thrust back at the old man and before he and his sons understood what was happening the gate had clanged shut in their faces. Margaretha said: "And I remember saying to Heinrich: Shouldn't we give them *something*, at least? And Heinrich said: Who? And I said: The goatherd and his sons. And Heinrich asked, in complete sincerity, and I shall never forget this, it is echt Heinrich: Why would we give them anything? It wasn't quite the right sound." She added: "Not quite the right sound, why give them anything: This is also our father's philosophy toward me, I point out to Katharina, and she runs off to the Music-Making Room." As Margaretha slipped out to press a few thalers into the palm of the poor goatherd, she heard Heinrich exclaim: "But at least we know it's in the *bell* family."

They came now with ringing things, with church bells and cowbells, with hand bells and sleigh bells, with wind chimes and triangles and cymbals and glockenspiels, and Heinrich narrowed it down to the last of these: what he heard in his head was the sound of a glockenspiel. "The moment he said that, Father set out to purchase every glockenspiel in Europe." Each one Heinrich would hit with his mallet once or twice or at most three times and then discard. Every day a new glockenspiel, a new very *expensive* glockenspiel, and since "the manufacturers of musical instruments aren't idiots," said Margaretha, the prices began going up like crazy, "May third," she read, "two hundred and thirty thalers, May fourth, four *thousand* thalers, May fifth, *eleven* thousand thalers," the sums her father shelled out per glockenspiel would have cured her a hundred times over, "body and soul." He was actually rapidly depleting the Imperial Treasury . . . Meanwhile, Protestants in the Palatinate were running amok . . . There were rumors, she recalled, that her uncle Matthias, Archduke of Austria, was amassing at his castle in Styria an army with which he planned to march on Prague and wrest the crown from his older brother . . . Also, incidentally, Heinrich received every day—and from the platter of fruit and pastries she disdainfully picked up and let fall a wrinkled little orange—a crate of these Seville oranges, the most expensive type of orange, and Heinrich's favorite orange . . . A sour orange, she said . . . "I prefer sweet oranges, so did my mother, she loathed sour oranges, I loathe them, too. We used to get lots of sweet oranges here but ever since she died Father has bought *only* sour oranges, Seville oranges" . . . That is to say, Heinrich's oranges . . . "I love oranges more than anything, but ever since Mother died I haven't eaten a single orange, too sour!" . . . The Turks, meanwhile, were, if various reports were to be believed, massing along the border with Transylvania . . . Protestants in Hesse-Kassel were running amok . . . Protestants in Baden-Durlach were running amok . . . Protestants in Brandenburg were running amok . . . Protestants in Hungary were running amok, too . . . Radical Anabaptists had seized the free imperial city of Schweinfurt . . . The Pope, she said, was rumored to be extremely unhappy . . . The Papal Nuncio to the Kingdom of Portugal was said to have said that it'd be a good thing for Heinrich and Christendom both if someone were to strangle the bastard in his sleep . . . "Even Willa was grumbling, although it occurs to me now she probably already had her future wedding in mind" . . . The Empire was actually on the verge of collapse due to the ringing in Heinrich's head . . . Still, every day, a new expensive glockenspiel . . . And another crate of Seville oranges . . . "Ah, the beauty of a father's blind devotion!" cried Margaretha, and she burst into laughter, and plucked from her mouth with two fingers the pit of her peach. Gottfried: "Yet just as the pit lies within the stone fruit, at its center, so the concept of the pit, the stone, lies within the concept of the stone fruit, at the center of it. Though we are left in dining as in dancing as in polite discourse at the mercy of our reason, God in his goodness has ordered the world such that our reason is sufficient—precisely sufficient! Yes, our reason is but a dim light yet the world is fashioned so as to shine quite luminously in it!" Margaretha: "Who knows what might have happened to the Habsburg Empire had not Heinrich declared one morning without a trace of shame that the ringing in his head had disappeared overnight."

Gottfried: "This, My Lady, is a gift from the Heavenly Father. It cannot be anything else."

Leibniz: "Referring, I think, to the harmony between words and things, not to the sudden cessation of Heinrich's malady."

"Perhaps," said Margaretha, "you can now understand why, a few months ago, when my brother, in a jealous rage, butchered a young lady and flung her mutilated body to his hogs, our father, besides shielding little Katharina from the truth of what her beloved big brother had done, shielded him from the judicial authorities, as well, and locked him up in his turret instead. Father still holds out hope that he'll get well again. That he'll get, I mean, *sane* again. Father still holds out hope for Heinrich's sanity! That is why you're here, you know: not to tally up the stars, but to make Heinrich sane again. The previous Imperial Astronomer wasn't able to make Heinrich sane again, but maybe you with that magical tube of yours will return him to his senses, my father must be thinking!" And she burst into laughter.

"There has been no justice," she added.

She said: "His only punishment for murdering that poor girl has been a halt on his supply of Seville oranges . . . An amazing mismatch between punishment and crime . . . Citrus . . . Murder . . . Taking a life . . . The things he did to the body . . . Of a girl he claimed to love . . . Mutilation . . . Versus no more oranges . . . When he actually still gets daily grapefruits . . . And daily tangerines . . . You'll find the floor of his turret strewn with citrus rinds . . . Still," she said, "the freeze on Seville oranges, probably because it is the first time Father, or else the Chamberlain under whose sway Father has fallen, has imposed *any* constraint on him whatsoever, has perturbed my brother a great deal . . ."

"And she picked up that wrinkled little orange again and handed it to me," the astronomer told Leibniz.

"The remarkable thing," she said, "is that Father still intends to be *succeeded* by Heinrich."

When the astronomer tried to teach her a bit of algebra, using the numbers in the notebook in which she tabulated Heinrich's expenses, she laughed and told him not to bother. "Father doesn't actually care whether I learn mathematics, just whether Heinrich does. If you were told to teach *me* mathematics, too, well, that's just my mother nudging him with her knee from beyond the grave." Suddenly she emitted a sob. "I miss my mother! She loved me!" For a moment, according to the astronomer, tears ran down her cheeks. Then Princess Margaretha laughed at her own outburst, flicked away a tear, smoothed her skirt, and said: "I want you to know, by the way, that I'm actually happy in spite of everything. Deep down, none of this affects me."

Wilhelmina in her wedding gown tiptoed past the open door.

"It is very improper," Gottfried was saying as the astronomer left the Small Dining Room, "to eat a pastry with one's hands."

)

HE TUTORED PRINCESS WILHELMINA in one of her two fitting rooms until the evening star twinkled in the sky.

)

THEN, EN ROUTE to the Imperial Observatory, the astronomer, armed now with a Seville orange, and mindful of those old fairy tales his mother used to tell him in which things always occur in threes, stopped for a third time by the south turret, where, feeling not a little foolish, he declared to the darkness that he'd brought a gift, "a certain *sour* gift, I said," the astronomer told Leibniz, and then tossed the orange between the iron bars. The next page has a sketch of the scene as Leibniz conceived it, above the caption: "The astronomer tossed a Seville orange into the south turret." The astronomer said: "It rolled into the gloom like a head from the chopping block." He put his ear through the bars. Perhaps (said the astronomer) he expected to hear an animalistic scurrying followed by the depraved devouring of that entire fruit, peel and all. But he heard nothing of the sort, nothing but the muted thud of the orange coming to rest against, presumably, the rear wall of the turret, followed by silence. He thought: So, then, I am not in one of my mother's tales. And he had turned on his heels and made his way halfway back down the hallway by which he'd come, convinced now that the guards over whom he had to step, for they would not interrupt their card game, were guarding, whether they knew it or not, nothing at all, and concerned that he himself might be losing his grip on reality, if he was tossing oranges into turrets, and expecting something to come of it, when he heard what sounded like the striking of a match and saw, when he turned once again on his heels, a faint flickering light emanating from the aperture.

He ran back, wrapped his hands around the iron bars, and peered in.

The astronomer pressed an eye socket to his telescope.

He said: "I invite you to imagine my state of mind—and at this remove I shall have to imagine it, too—when I saw, sitting on a silver platter on the floor, all of its toothed wheels taken out and replaced by a single candle, the light of which shone through the holes where the lenses had gone, my father's mechanical head, corroded only slightly from its spell in the river."

He picked up his quill and wrote something down.

Evidently, he said, the head had been salvaged from the bottom of the Vltava—but at whose behest, Emperor Rudolf's or Prince Heinrich's, and to what end? Was this a gift from father to son or an undertaking of the son's own initiative? Why, in short, salvage this head? The astronomer noted the return of a familiar question: Had he underestimated his father's head? Misunderstood it? Yet if it was worth salvaging, why empty it of its innards, leaving only its inert lead skull? And had whoever had ordered the salvaging of it ordered also the salvaging of the body of its maker, which presumably lay beside it on the riverbed?

Was, in other words, his father's corpse in that turret, too?

Then he realized:

Obviously, Prince Heinrich was trying, for whatever reason, to horrify him. And given what he knew about the Prince, and what he would learn subsequently, he *should*, in fact, have been horrified. The truth is I *ought* to have been horrified, the astronomer told Leibniz: "What I saw through that little iron-grated aperture *should* have horrified me." But it did not horrify him. On the contrary—it amused him. He began to laugh; and not simply to titter like the virtuosi in the Great Hall or to burst into Margaretha's scornful laughter but really to chortle, to laugh from the belly, to produce, that is, belly laughter. ("Have you noticed, Herr Leibniz, how our most celebrated scientists of the sentiments always possess the crudest understanding of laughter? I have seen laughter taxonomies that bundle together the giggle, the chortle, and the titter, or the chortle, the titter, the snicker, and the hoot. Even in Delft, where they have a superb understanding of tears, they do not distinguish between the whoop, the cackle, the guffaw, the hoot, and the hee-haw. Of course, the hee-haw has nothing to do with the hoot, and the whoop is not even a species of laughter at all! A man who confuses whimpering and weeping is rightly excluded from the circle of learned men, we demand very fine distinctions on the tragic side of life, yet someone who considers a hee-haw a hoot may still be regarded as an eminent authority on the nature of the world.") At the time, and for a long time afterward, the astronomer could not figure out why the sight of his father's gutted mechanical head sitting there aglow on a silver platter provoked in him this outburst of uncontrollable belly laughter. Maybe I am finally grieving, he thought, and the thought pleased him, he was actually relieved to find himself racked with grief, his grief hitherto had been all too controlled, too lucid, "I am always in my own head," he welcomed this spasm of grief even if it happened to express itself as belly laughter. But in truth his laughter had little to do with grief. This he realized only recently. His laughter, he realized at last, decades after the fact, was merely "the laughter invariably provoked by exceptionally bad art." The theatricality of the tableau Prince Heinrich had arranged, the utter artificiality of it, the melodramatic lighting, the (probably completely meaningless) allusion via the silver platter to the head of John the Baptist, all of which was meant to instill terror in the astronomer, for reasons he would begin to fathom shortly, provoked, instead, laughter. "He wanted I think to *seem* mad, but each of these aspects, and in particular the John the Baptist aspect, suggested, in fact, a surplus of sanity, of control, of *intention*, you see. There was something ineluctably sane about what I was seeing. The thought: I am seeing something so sane right now! That is what I thought as I peered through those iron bars, even if I didn't know at the time that that's what I was thinking. He wants me to see something insane, but I am seeing something sane! Sane, sane, I thought. The truly mad constantly try to make art, but they make only madness, the truly artful constantly try to make madness, but they make only art. He wants to seem insane, but in arranging in this pitch-black turret a tableau centered on my dead father's salvaged and repurposed lead head, lit from within, probably in emulation of Caravaggio's histrionic lighting techniques, if not in fact in direct imitation of Caravaggio's *Salome with the Head of John the Baptist*, which hung as I knew in the North Wing, he shows himself to be sane, I thought, though I only realized that this was the thought I was thinking many years after the fact," he told Leibniz. "He wishes to seem insane, he intends to come across as mad in my eyes, but the very wish, the very intention, and more than that the ability to execute his intention by means of a coherent set of artistic techniques, even entirely derivative ones, even wholly Caravaggesque ones, down to the absurd and probably meaningless John the Baptist reference, shows him to be sane, completely sane! *Intention*, Herr Leibniz, I am drawing your attention to the presence here of intention, intentionality, of reasoning about means and ends, and therefore of reason full stop. He wanted his artwork to *do* something to me! Peering through those iron bars, or rather peering between those iron bars, I probably thought: Merely by intending to make something horrific, he has made something ridiculous. He aims for the horror of the madman, but in so aiming he has achieved only the ridiculousness of the artist," the astronomer said. "The ridiculousness of the visual artist."

He added: "Hence, I laughed."

His laughter evidently perturbed the Prince, for a body came bounding out of the blackness . . .

To demonstrate the ensuing action the astronomer had to evict Linus from his lap. The cat meowed. "None of that," the astronomer said. To Leibniz: "Watch, he'll now sashay off with a show of indifference and begin licking himself zealously beneath the armillary sphere." Leibniz: "A minor prophecy, perhaps, but an accurate one."

Then, with difficulty, the astronomer stood up from his stool.

"A body, you see, bounded toward me out of the blackness," the astronomer said, and with his own bent, shrunken body he mimed what he was describing. "Yes, a body emerged from the blackness: from nothing, suddenly, a body! The body obviously of the Prince. Somehow he had an obviously *princely* comportment despite being naked top to bottom and streaked here and there with some sort of dark and foul matter, such is the power of upbringing. At first I thought, He's covered in mud from the river bottom, but from its texture and stink I realized it was more likely blood or feces, that is, matter of his own making. And probably I realized: It is too simple to say that he is sane. And all this time he is bounding toward me, bounding toward me so fast that the door separating him from me, however thick it was, seemed hardly sufficient, and I thought: He will splinter this thick door into a million pieces and I shall join my father in oblivion."

But instead the Prince came to a halt on the far side of the door. "Like so." And the Prince placed his hands on top of the astronomer's and gripped them as firmly as they were gripping the iron bars. "Like so," the astronomer said, and he found Leibniz's hands, tightened them into fists, and gripped them with what Leibniz reported was startling strength. Then the Prince spat in the astronomer's face. "Like so, *ptew!*" the astronomer said, and though he added, "I won't actually spit in your face, of course," Leibniz noted that the astronomer had, actually, spat in his face, when he had said "*ptew*" he had spat in his face. The astronomer tried to run away but could not, tried at least to wipe his face but could not do that either: the Prince's grip was preternaturally strong. And so, wrote Leibniz, for his age, was the astronomer's.

Then, quite calmly, while his saliva trickled down the astronomer's cheek, Prince Heinrich said:

"I shan't learn mathematics, sir. I shall not learn it. My father wants me to learn mathematics but I cannot and I shall not learn it. I have no interest in mathematics and I have no aptitude for it, sir. No mathematical aptitude, do you understand? My father puts far too much faith in mathematics, too much faith in it and too much emphasis on it, my father has altogether too much mathematical faith, sir, and if he expects that we will one day communicate mathematically, he is mistaken. I shall not learn mathematics. Perhaps at one time I could have learned it, I used to be clever, I used to be a clever person, but now I cannot learn it, now I am a stupid person, now I am a crazy person, my mind no longer functions as it ought to. My sisters have much more mathematical aptitude than me, they should have been me and I should have been them, yes, *I should have been my sisters!* That I should've been my sisters and my sisters me is a thought that often recurs to me. Father must not make me do mathematics, Father must allow me to be mad. Please inform my father of this, that if a mathematics tutor, in his capacity *as* a tutor, were to step foot in this turret, that tutor, in this turret, even before he attempts to impart to me the most elementary theorem, the most intuitive axiom, would be straightaway torn apart at the joints, a message for my father. I would pluck out the tutor's eyes, I would cut off the tutor's ears, I would tear out that tutor's tongue also. I thank you for the orange, sir, but I shan't learn mathematics. No, no, I shall not learn it."

And with that Prince Heinrich withdrew to the farthest and darkest corner of his turret.

)

THE ASTRONOMER PEERED into his telescope.

"The bodies are aligning exactly as they should," he said, according to Leibniz. There were eighty minutes till the predicted eclipse. Through the warped slat the sliver of sky was still bright and blue. The astronomer said: "The darkness will be very brief but it will be *very* dark, so dark that of the three of us only Linus will be able to see. The domestic cat is capable of seeing in conditions of considerable darkness."

And he picked up his quill and wrote something down.

)

HE HAD, NATURALLY, no intention of ever returning to that turret, much less stepping foot inside it.

Nothing, he felt, could make him do that, not even a commandment from the mouth of the Emperor.

Yet the following day would find him on his knees before its door begging for entrance.

Leibniz: And what could compel you to do such a thing?

"The stars compelled me," the astronomer said, peering into his telescope. "Listen."

That night, the third night of his stellar observations, a few minutes before the Sun absorbed in its rays every other entity in the heavens, the astronomer, his ears plugged with wax to block the sound of the maddening Benedictine bells, his eye fixed to his nineteen-inch, fourfold-magnifying silver telescope, surpassed the 1,164 stars enumerated in Bayer's *Uranometria*.

And he thought euphorically: I have now seen more stars than Johann Bayer, who saw more than Tycho, who saw more than Piccolomini, who saw more than Ptolemy and the Greeks.

He thought: At this moment I have seen more than *anyone*.

Then, however, he thought: At *this* moment I have seen more than anyone.

In the next moment someone else would see more than him.

What Piccolomini was to the Greeks, and Tycho to Piccolomini, and Bayer to Tycho, and he to Bayer, someone else would be to him. To come after someone, to come before someone: ridiculous! the astronomer said. "The pointlessness," he said, "of seeing more than Bayer. The emptiness of seeing more than Bayer." How important seeing more than Bayer had once been, and how little it now amounted to!

Short of seeing *all* the stars, an absurdity, there was no point in seeing *any* of them.

He would die, the stars would stay put, and someone else would see more of them.

He would be buried in that series of scientific surnames, beside Bayer, two down from Tycho, three away from Piccolomini.

Will everything, he wondered, amount to as little as this?

He tore out the wax from his ears, it had done nothing to stop the ringing of the bells, and he ran to the Benedictine monastery, and he kicked the stone wall with his feet, and he beat the wall bloody with his fists, and with his tongue he vilified those who lived within it, whose perpetual bell-ringing was inimical to the thinking of thoughts. The ringing of a bell enters the thinking head, proceeds straightaway to the thought-thinking part of the head, locates there the incipient thought, and destroys it: "Your bells have destroyed my thoughts!" Ringing bells and thinking heads cannot coexist (he cried) and since their monastery was filled with huge numbers of ringing bells, he could only conclude that it did not contain a single thinking head. By now a handful of white-haired monks had materialized on top of the stone wall where side by side they peered down at him with curiosity and compassion, that spiritual compassion which is commingled with bemusement over our investment in the things of this world. This needless to say only enraged the astronomer further, and he told the Benedictine monks what he would do to them, and what they ought to do to each other, and what they, the Benedictine monks, could do to their mothers, each monk to his own mother and each to each other's mothers, and finally what all of the Benedictine monks could do to a single Benedictine monk's mother. One by one the wizened old men shook their heads in sorrow and vanished from atop the wall. Only the last of them spoke: "Think, my child," he murmured as he, too, departed from the parapet, "of eternity."

Leibniz: At that moment, way down at the foot of the wall, the astronomer thought: "Why, actually, is it absurd to think of seeing all the stars?"

Leibniz writes: What had struck him as a matter of logic plunged now into the realm of the empirical.

He would need no doubt a long tube, maybe a very long tube, and possibly even an absurdly long tube, but between an absurdly long tube and an impossibly long tube there was, "contra Descartes, who would have seen two equally dubious tubes," Leibniz comments, all the difference in the world, the astronomer thought as he stood at the foot of the wall of the monastery.

And there was all the difference in the world between a star catalogue that was prodigious and one that was complete.

The astronomer had the sense that a complete star catalogue, an exhaustive star catalogue, the star catalogue God Himself were He to survey His creation would compose, a record in writing of *every*thing above—"In this very ledger!" he said, holding above his head the ledger in which he'd been writing all morning—would, aside from expiating completely his own guilt, mean something momentous for man's place in the cosmos.

What it would mean, momentous how, not to mention, he added, whom he thought he meant by man: all of this he did not yet know.

Now the Sun had risen. From the monastery the astronomer went straight to the Castle Workshop and demanded of his craftsmen a tube no less than three feet in length, forged of solid gold, and with the power to magnify things ninefold. But for the first time his metallurgists said: We cannot do that. So the astronomer said: Fine, then, make it of silver, as before, the tactile qualities of the tubes while significant are still secondary to the optical. But his metallurgists said: We cannot make it of silver either. And the astronomer shouted: Then of bronze, or brass, or iron, or lead, just so long as it magnifies objects nine times! And the metallurgists said: Not of bronze nor of brass, nor of iron nor lead. And the master lens-grinder from Nuremberg stepped forward and said: The Emperor has ordered us to make no more tubes for you. And his Augsburger apprentice said: I fear that you have not calculated the true cost of your celestial observations. If you have a place to go, go there, sir, I beg you, forget the stars, leave Prague.

He returned posthaste to the Imperial Observatory but found it padlocked. His own house he found padlocked, too. A note nailed to the door and stamped in red wax with the two-headed Habsburg eagle requested his presence in the North Wing "to discuss your future here, and the future of your tubes."

The astronomer peered into his telescope, picked up his quill, and wrote something down.

What if he had not gone? What if—"and nothing would have been easier!"—he had taken the stairs that wound down Hradčany Hill, crossed the Old Stone Bridge, left Prague, left Bohemia, left the Holy Roman Empire, left Europe? What if he had not gone? *What if he had not gone!* Again and again he demanded *What if he had not gone?* until it dawned on Leibniz that the old man was actually waiting for an answer, and Leibniz proposed: "You would still have your eyes?" And the old man smiled. "I would still," he said, "have my eyes."

)

THE ASTRONOMER TOLD LEIBNIZ: In one hand the Emperor held the horn of a unicorn and in the other he held a stone bowl into which the blood of Christ had once flowed. The Emperor whispered into the ear of the Court Chamberlain, and the Court

Chamberlain said: "Your horoscopes spoke of the Emperor's im-minent demise." And before the astronomer, in confusion and consternation, could object vociferously that this was not so, that he had spoken nothing of death, that he had foreseen for the Emperor only health and life, the Court Chamberlain said: "And in foreseeing that you have demonstrated your acumen in deciphering the stars." Under his breath the Emperor murmured: "I *know* that I am dead and damned."

And he gazed in contemplation at the horn in his hand.

The Court Chamberlain leaned toward the astronomer and whispered: "He is now in his fiftieth year, the very year that claimed his father."

The Emperor looked up from the horn, whispered into the ear of the Court Chamberlain, and the Chamberlain said: "He will die, as you have foreseen, either as his father did, of a weak-ness of the walls of the chambers of his heart"—and the Emperor whispered in his ear—"or (exactly as you wrote) as did Henri III, the last of the House of Valois, stabbed in the abdomen by a Catholic fanatic attired in the vestments of his Royal Confes-sor." He added: "As you wrote." Under his breath the Emperor murmured: "In the gut! In the gut! As you wrote."

And he gazed in contemplation at the bowl.

The Court Chamberlain leaned toward the astronomer and whispered: "He perused your horoscopes with admiration. The most brilliant prognostications he has ever seen! he said. And this is a man whose nativity was cast by Nostradamus himself."

Leibniz: The astronomer thought: Have my words been al-tered before they reached the Emperor's eyes? Or has he in his lunacy seen in them prophecies that weren't there?

The Emperor gazed in contemplation at the horn.

"And so," said the Court Chamberlain, "even before the New Star appeared, His Majesty was preoccupied by the question of succession. And now that the New Star has appeared he is possessed by it." The Emperor murmured: "The New Star is Heinrich, Heinrich the New Star." The Court Chamberlain: "As his last act, His Majesty wishes to ensure that the crown, upon his death, goes to his son. That it goes to Prince Heinrich." The Emperor murmured: "They are flimflamming me in Frankfurt!" The Court Chamberlain sighed: "Yes, it is true, the Emperor's three perfidious brothers are as we speak conducting a meeting in Frankfurt, ostensibly on the Protestant threat but in actuality on the subject of succession. The Electors have gone to Frankfurt, too . . ." The Emperor contemplated the bowl. The bowl, he murmured, is a microcosm of creation, every aspect of creation corresponds to an element of the bowl and every element of the bowl to an aspect of creation. "Same with the horn," he said, turning his head toward the horn. He added: "I *know* that I am dead and damned." "Neither His Majesty's three little brothers nor the seven Electors of the Holy Roman Empire hold Heinrich in high esteem, I am sorry to say, and that was the case long before the transient lunacy that led him to commit his unfortunate act," the Chamberlain said. "They still, for instance, call him a bastard, even though the Emperor legitimized him by edict a long time ago." "The Edict of Legitimation," said the Emperor. He put down the horn and the bowl and pounded his fists on the arms of his throne: "All of my children were legitimized by the Edict of Legitimation that I signed long ago in the spa town of Karlsbad!" "Though of course, as a gesture of moderation, you do not enforce it as it pertains to your daughters," said the Chamberlain, and the Emperor said: "To placate the forces of conservatism I do not enforce the edict as it pertains to my daughters of course." He picked up again the horn and the bowl and gazed in contemplation at the bowl. The Chamberlain said: "And in fact one of your daughters does not even agree with the edict in the first place! How many times has Margaretha tried to sign an edict revoking the Edict of Legitimation?" The Emperor murmured: "She does not have the authority to do that." "*Of course* she doesn't have the authority to do that," said the Chamberlain, "but does that stop her from going to Karls-bad and writing up her malicious Revocations of the Edict of Legitimation and forcing her ladies-in-waiting to sign it?" "I do not recognize her Karlsbad Revocations. They carry no legal weight." "It is not a matter of legality or the law, My Lord, it is a matter of mockery." The Emperor scrutinized the horn. "Why," he muttered, "is she so keen to revoke an edict that in any case I do not enforce as it pertains to her?" "As I say, it is a matter of mockery, My Lord. She is mocking your authority. A dreadful thing for any daughter to do to her father even were he not the King of the Romans." Still gazing in contemplation at the horn, the Emperor muttered: "I failed with Margaretha, I don't know why. She was such a pretty child, she looked just like her mother. When she was little she'd always take my hand and lead me over to the glass jars of pickled monstrosities you see yonder, she loved those jars more than I did even, loved and was afraid of them. There was one jar containing three unborn babies joined at the skulls that she could stare at for hours, but only if I stayed and stared with her, holding her hand—which I was happy to do, very! She would always ask, Daddy, does the baby *like* being in that jar? Always: Daddy, daddy, does the baby *like* being in that jar? I remember that. And I would explain, Greta, dear, the baby is *dead*, it is beyond the liking of things. She thought it was one baby with three faces, not three babies with basically one very big seriously deformed head, I remember that. She asked me once if the baby had eyes, so I had my anatomist sew them open for her, all six, after that she was even more spellbound by it and even more afraid of it. We spent *days* in here together! Until she was three, four, five she never left my *wunderkammer* or let me leave it. Then one day she lost all interest in it . . ." He gazed at the bowl. "She was so pretty, I thought she would marry and be happy. I've never understood Margaretha, that one's an enigma to me," he murmured, gazing at the horn.

"With respect, My Lord, she is mad, there is nothing to understand, and no enigma either," the Chamberlain said. "And it is precisely *because* she is mad that Matthias has seized upon her as the solution to his Heinrich problem. That's what he's plotting in Frankfurt as we speak, My Lord. In defiance of you." The Emperor suddenly flung the horn, and then the bowl; they clattered across the floor. "Fiend!" he cried. "Scoundrel!" And then: "Bring me the bowl! Bring me the horn!" Attendants returned the items to his hands and the Emperor contemplated them in turn. The Chamberlain turned to the astronomer: "You see, His Majesty's most treacherous and power-hungry brother has the most to lose if a man of Heinrich's fortitude and intellectual autonomy were to take the throne. Archduke Matthias knows full well that the Emperor's son is positively uninfluenceable, his cranium a keep." "A keep for a cranium—a kind of cranial keep," the Emperor murmured, adding: "An *uninfluenceable* son. Against Matthias's ideas pertaining to the Protestants?" "Just so, My Lord, very astute," said the Chamberlain. "Archduke Matthias wants an emperor into whose vulnerable head he can insert his own ideas regarding the Protestants, he cannot be emperor himself but he can put his poisonously anti-Protestant ideas into an emperor's head, if that head is sufficiently porous. But is Heinrich's head porous, My Lord? Is it vulnerable?" The Emperor raised both horn and bowl and cried: "No!" "No, Heinrich's head is exceedingly well fortified, you raised him right, My Lord, an *impregnable* head, walls thirty feet thick, forty feet, fifty feet! A fortified head that another man's sentences cannot hope to penetrate, much less inhabit. And Matthias knows that." The Emperor: "Yes, I raised Heinrich to be an independent thinker, basically I was continually fortifying his head against the world, for Matthias that's a catastrophe, he knows that Heinrich's head's walls are thirty to fifty feet thick and can't be penetrated or inhabited by his anti-Protestant sentences, Matthias *knows* that!" The Court Chamberlain: "But Matthias also knows that Margaretha's head is as vulnerable as Heinrich's head is impregnable, our sources in Frankfurt tell us that to Albert and Ernst and the seven Electors Matthias makes much of her hardheadedness, of her *supposed* hardheadedness that is, but our sources in Styria tell us that at home he speaks of nothing but her invented headaches, the phantom itch in her bones, the outrageous size to which she inflates in her mind the nodes in her neck, he speaks of nothing in short but the signs of her lunacy, of the traffic streaming from inside her head to outside it, and presumably also—what interests Matthias more—

from outside to inside. In private he meditates on his niece's useful *soft*headedness, but in public he expounds on her supposed *hard*headedness, not to mention of course her convenient status as your eldest child, and hence what he insists is her fitness in these troubled times for the office of Holy Roman Empress. In doing so Matthias not only flouts the Golden Bull promulgated in 1356 at the Diet of Metz in which Charles IV unambiguously restricted the elective dignity of Holy Roman Emperor to men but also directly defies Your Majesty's own express wishes." The horn and the bowl clattered across the floor. The Emperor cried: "Bring me the horn! Bring me the bowl!" He contemplated them in turn and then murmured: "I know that I am dead and damned, and demons move my muscles."

The astronomer put an eye socket to his telescope. He told Leibniz: "That instant kinship I had felt with the Emperor upon first gazing at his face, and which I thought far more profound than any kinship I had ever felt with my own father, had now, retrospectively, to be called into question, I thought." He picked up his quill. "We begin to see the virtues of our birth fathers only after the fathers we thought would replace them have disappointed us in turn. By then of course it is too late, our birth fathers are dead, the little playlets of repentance, forgiveness, and reconciliation we stage with them in our heads are performed entirely for our own gratification." And he wrote down a long string of numbers.

The Emperor, gesturing to one eye: "For two months the Devil himself has tugged at my left eyelid. A two-month eyelid twitch, inflicted by the Devil himself, at my brother Matthias's bidding."

The Chamberlain turned to the astronomer and said: "Now what, you may be asking, has all this palace intrigue to do with you?"

And the astronomer had replied: "Indeed, I was wondering."

"You who are no diplomat but are rather a hunter of the secrets of nature. One of those very valiant truth-seekers who intends to put nature on the rack till she reveals to you in her screams what she has so cunningly concealed from your eyes, right? Whose head belongs not in parlor rooms but among the stars, right? You, the Imperial Astronomer—what has all of this to do with *you*?"

"What indeed," said the astronomer, he told Leibniz. "And with my tubes."

The Court Chamberlain said: "That is the question you are asking yourself. The question *we* are asking *ourselves* is: Why has our new mathematics tutor not so much as stepped foot in Prince Heinrich's turret? Despite our explicit directive that the mathematical edification of the Prince ranked among the most important of his duties? Why instead has this purported mathematics tutor spent hour upon hour in the privacy of the Small Dining Room conferring in hushed tones with the very lady whom Archduke Matthias conspires to install on the throne? If an agent of Matthias's had infiltrated our Castle armed with a gadget stolen from the pages of a Neapolitan sage"—and he flung at the astronomer's feet a copy of Giambattista della Porta's *Magia naturalis*, which, with a smack, landed open to a diagram of a tube—"and under the pretense of creating a star catalogue had sought to inform the Princess of her uncle's plot, would that agent have acted any differently than you did, any differently at all? That's the question *we* are asking *ourselves*."

"An absurd allegation," sputtered the astronomer, so astonished that he was not yet alarmed, and the Court Chamberlain said, "Absurd, not impossible," and the astronomer took a step forward, intending to pick up Della Porta's book so he could illustrate the countless ways in which his own tube differed from the tube pictured within, but the imperial guards evidently interpreted his motion in another way for he swiftly found himself restrained by three of them.

The Emperor gazed in contemplation at the horn. "The horn," he muttered under his breath, "is *everything*, everything is the horn, and everything is also the bowl."

Now the Court Chamberlain ambled over to the astronomer, who was still held fast by the guards, and said: "I told His Majesty: Your brother has sent us this sham mathematician, let us cut off his sham mathematical organ, that is, his head, and send it back to your brother in a box. And His Majesty, who is far more sensitive than I to the subtleties of the distinctions of the disciplines, replied: Not a mathematician, an astronomer." The Emperor, scrutinizing the bowl, muttered: "Astronomy concerns appearances, not that which can be thought but that which can be seen." The astronomer to Leibniz: "True." The Court Chamberlain said: "So I said: Then let us pluck out his sham astronomical organs, his eyes, and send them back to your brother in a box. Basically I wanted to send the Emperor's brother some ironical organ of yours, in a box. But do you know what His Majesty said? He said: No sham astronomer could perceive in the stars what this man has perceived in them." The Emperor murmured: "In the gut, as you wrote. Disguised in the black robes of my Father Confessor." The Court Chamberlain: "In short, my dear sir"—and with the lightest tap of his hands on theirs he freed the astronomer from the grip of the guards and then fussily smoothed the creases they had left on his sleeves—"you have His Majesty's faith in you to thank for your life. And this is not a man who believes in just anyone! No, the Emperor is a skeptical soul, a true son of Pyrrho." "In the fiftieth year, the crumbling of the walls of the chambers of the heart," murmured the Emperor. "All things emanate from the One— the horn, the bowl, everything else, the jars, and so on." To the *Philosophical Transactions*, Leibniz remarks parenthetically: "An echo not of course of Pyrrho but of Plotinus."

The Court Chamberlain told the astronomer: "Perhaps you wish to express your gratitude . . ."

And the astronomer, who by now had probably gone pale, bowed at once to the waist and said: "Thank you, Your Majesty."

Raising his eyes briefly from the bowl, the Emperor nodded solemnly.

And the Court Chamberlain said: "But perhaps you feel, and I don't blame you, that this merely verbal expression of gratitude is insufficient recompense for all that the Emperor has given you: not only your life, but your house, your salary, your stewardship of the Imperial Observatory . . ." And the Court Chamberlain said he would now suggest how I might discharge my ostensible debt of gratitude, how I could, as he put it, "pay it off in full," the astronomer recalled. And the Chamberlain leaned over to him and whispered: "Listen carefully, for though you may feel that there is an element of theater in all this, the theater, too, can frighten, you know," and the Emperor evidently overheard this, for he murmured: "When the actors talk I am always afraid that I will suddenly stop understanding what they are talking *about* . . ." and the astronomer told Leibniz: "Although all this *had* seemed theatrical, it nevertheless *had* frightened me, so I *did* listen carefully. And as I did, it began to dawn on me how I might turn what he was telling me to my advantage."

Now, it seems, according to the Court Chamberlain, who repeated several times that he was only passing along what he had been told by his sources in Frankfurt, that Archduke Matthias's primary stratagem for persuading the seven Electors that upon His Majesty's death the crown ought to go to Margaretha, his eldest, instead of Heinrich, his firstborn son, had little to do with the latter's alleged illegitimacy, as that line of argument, even if it overcame the challenge of His Majesty's Edict of Legitimation, which is doubtful, would of course disqualify not only Heinrich but Margaretha as well. "Matthias is more clever than that!" No, his case rested not on Prince Heinrich's alleged illegitimacy but on his alleged insanity, for which the Archduke's main piece of evidence, and in fact his sole piece of evidence, was the unfortunate act that took place in Heinrich's turret in the middle of November, two Sundays before the start of Advent. The Court Chamberlain's sources in Frankfurt said that Archduke Matthias could not go two sentences without referring to "the things Heinrich did to the barber-surgeon's daughter." A devilishly clever politician, Archduke Matthias deployed the phrases "the things Heinrich did to the barber-surgeon's daughter" or "the unspeakable atrocities Heinrich committed on the evening of

November fourteenth" to imply, without ever explicitly asserting it, that Prince Heinrich was not of sound mind. Through shrewd repetition Matthias invested the words "Heinrich's behavior on the night of November fourteenth" with the meaning of the unsaid words "Heinrich's madness," or even—and it seemed to the astronomer that the Chamberlain shot him a pointed glance—"Heinrich's inherited madness." "From our earliest youth," muttered the Emperor, gazing at the horn, "Matthias has always called me mad. My gentleness he took for madness. My inwardness—madness. That I am soft-spoken makes me, for Matthias, mad . . . My interest in gems, madness, my interest in trompe l'oeil, in tapestries featuring elements of trompe l'oeil, madness, my interest in mechanics, madness, in emblems, madness." The Chamberlain: "But it was always a *political* maneuver to call you mad, from the time you were boys," and the Emperor, with, as the astronomer told Leibniz, sudden startling cogency, bellowed: "No, my dear Chamberlain, it is not always about politics! He *truly* thinks me mad, he truly thinks me *truly* mad, imagine being told by your little brother that you speak too close to other people's faces, and realizing that he is *right*! What he and everyone else knew how to do naturally I had to learn. Why? Conversations he could follow I could not. Why could he follow them? Why could I not? Our father used to bring farces to the Hofburg, French farces in private productions, he and my brothers adored those French farces but for me they were private nightmares. They used to laugh and laugh at them, our father would laugh, so would Matthias, so would Albert, and so would Ernst, and so so would I, laugh and laugh I mean, but all the time I was laughing I was wondering:

Can everyone tell that I don't know *why* I am laughing? Watching Father's face to know when to start laughing and when to stop . . . Sometimes I had an inkling why I was laughing but usually that inkling was wrong, it was actually something else that was funny, the thing that *I* thought was funny was usually really *serious*. A horrible thing, my dear Chamberlain, to laugh and laugh yet not know *why* you are laughing . . . when everyone else in your family seems to know . . . To not have inherited the family sense of humor: horrible . . . It is horrible, and it's not politics when Matthias yells: Crazy Rudolf doesn't know why he's laughing! This happened once, I forgot to keep an eye on my father's face and I kept laughing long after everyone else stopped laughing. And Matthias stood up, mid-farce, and pointed at me, and shouted: Look, Crazy Rudolf doesn't know why he's laughing, he's laughing and he doesn't know why!" The Emperor gazed at the bowl. "And I am the eldest, remember, I should know why I'm laughing. So I said: I know exactly why I'm laughing. And our father said: Let him be, Matthias. And I said: No, it's fine, I *know* why I am laughing! And Matthias said: Good, then tell us what's so funny, Crazy Rudolf. And I said something, and obviously whatever I said *wasn't* the funny thing because suddenly everyone *else* was laughing, roaring with laughter, my whole family and even the actors. And Albert, obviously feeling guilty, or maybe it was Ernst actually, said, You've got to brush up on your French, Rudolf! And Matthias cried: He understands French perfectly, it's not the *French* he doesn't understand! Meaning I suppose that it was the human affairs. None of this, so far as I can tell, my dear Chamberlain, touches on imperial politics rather than simple, straightforward brotherly cruelty, save insofar as I know that Father always lamented that the son of his who inherited his melancholy was next in line for the throne while the son who inherited his sense of humor, plus his equestrian prowess, was not . . . I have never been comfortable on a horse, by the way, Matthias has always been comfortable on horses, he belongs on a horse, I don't, I do not see what that has to do with politics . . ." The Court Chamberlain begged His Majesty's forgiveness. "I only meant that as long as *I* have known him, I've always understood the Archduke best when I understand him as a wholly rational, wholly political being, as political reason incarnate." The Emperor, satisfied, gazed intensely at the horn, the astronomer told Leibniz. The Court Chamberlain went on: "And it is part of his political genius to refer in Frankfurt only to Heinrich's behavior, never once to his soul or state of mind. Here Matthias was a step ahead of us. While we suspected, rightly, that he would make the case for Heinrich's being mad, we assumed, wrongly, that he would do so *in those terms* . . . And we assumed that the moment he turned the Frankfurt conclave into a referendum on the state of Heinrich's mind, or soul, it would—like all symposia that seek to settle a matter incapable of being settled, for it is well known that the state of one's soul is opaque to others, murky also to oneself, and seen clearly only by God—descend into an anarchy of opinion and interpretation, an anarchy without end. And if, as happens often enough, the disputants decided to truncate their otherwise infinite deliberations and solve the insoluble by appealing to the most prestigious man of science in their vicinity, whose expert judgment all would agree to abide by . . . well, in case of that, we had briefed fourteen of Frankfurt's most eminent physicians, each of whom, if summoned, was prepared to testify, firstly, that Prince Heinrich's mania on the night in question was consistent only with a blockage of the so-called pineal net, a membrane the many holes of which ordinarily allow the spirit to ascend and descend as it wishes, but which when blocked will induce the tics, perverse temptations, and sad thoughts that led to the unfortunate death and defenestration on November fourteenth of the barbersurgeon's daughter; secondly, that Prince Heinrich's mood from the morning of November fifteenth to the present day indicates beyond doubt that his pineal net holes have cleared up considerably, possibly completely; and thirdly, that these holes could be kept permanently clear (and so Heinrich permanently sane) simply by the ingestion once a week between his bloodletting and his bath of an electuary composed of pearls, amber, violets, verbena, barley, lettuce seed, the cordial powder *aromaticum rosarum*, and three droplets of human breast milk, as well as liberal quantities of saffron, honey, and sweet clover."

In short, the Chamberlain explained, a battle over the state of Heinrich's mind, or soul, was a battle on favorable terrain. "As soon as Archduke Matthias uttered the words 'Heinrich's mind' or 'Heinrich's soul' or 'Heinrich's madness,' or 'Heinrich's hereditary madness,' the battle was won."

He added: "And Matthias must have known that, for he never once uttered those words."

Rather than planting his flag inside Heinrich's head, Matthias has planted it outside it, on the grounds of Heinrich's behavior on the night of November fourteenth, his observed and mutually agreed upon behavior, his indubitable and incontrovertible behavior, his well-witnessed crime, the magnitude, iniquity, and oddity of which, regardless of what was going through his mind as he perpetrated it, ought to disqualify him, so argued the Archduke, from the office of Holy Roman Emperor. That was the extent of the Archduke's argument, and despite its apparent simplicity, in seeming to reason simply that a prince who has dismembered and defenestrated the daughter of a tradesman ought not ascend to the throne, it was in fact terrifically subtle. "*An emperor cannot behave this way*: That's been Matthias's constant refrain in Frankfurt," said the Court Chamberlain, and, leaning toward the astronomer, he whispered: "I doubt whether His Majesty appreciates his brother's cunning in selecting that verb. Like all world-class politicians, the Archduke is, above all, a world-class wordsmith. An emperor," he repeated, enunciating each word, eyes alight at the Archduke's artfulness, "cannot *behave* this way.

"And so," the Chamberlain continued, "our strategy has changed accordingly."

The astronomer put an eye socket to his telescope, picked up his quill, and wrote down a string of numbers. There was, he declared, pulling his pocket watch from his rags, little more than an hour now till the solar eclipse.

Leibniz asked him: What exactly did the Prince do to the barber-surgeon's daughter? And why?

"Those were my questions, also!" cried the astronomer. "Yes, what did he do, and why did he do it? Was there, in other words, a reason? What of the jealous rage Margaretha had mentioned?

My questions also. But I suspected I would not get the truth from these two."

"Yes," the Chamberlain had said, the astronomer continued, "our strategy has changed accordingly—and here is where you come in. Since Matthias has brought the battle to the shores of Heinrich's behavior, we must engage him there. We must prove what we know to be true, that the night of November fourteenth was a bizarre aberration, that Heinrich's behavior now is behavior befitting a Holy Roman Emperor. We must prove by his behavior that he is sane."

The astronomer: "I suddenly wondered what kind of minuets Gottfried had been instructed to teach Margaretha . . . In retrospect, the way he was teaching her to eat seemed completely insane. I remembered what he'd said about soup, about serving tongs, about stone fruit. Gottfried was intentionally inculcating in her the manners of a madwoman, I realized. He was not there to help her wed . . ."

The Court Chamberlain continued: "Now, among the seven Electors, there is one who is friendly to our cause. For his sake I shall not name him but suffice it to say it is neither the Archbishop of Trier nor the Archbishop of Cologne, papal zealots both." The Emperor: "I want to say who it is." He raised both the horn and the bowl and cried: "It is the Duke of Saxony!" The Court Chamberlain: "It is. And the Duke is well positioned, for though he is a Lutheran he is a lukewarm one and has steadfastly refused to join the Union of Auhausen, a fact that has led Matthias to believe that the Duke wishes to curry favor with the Catholic states, and has even led Matthias to dream—rather madly— that he might coax Saxony to join the Catholic League."

Leibniz, parenthetically: "This incidentally supports a theory of mine that events which the astronomer narrated as taking place over three or four days actually took place, if they took place at all, over three or four years, for the Protestant Union was not formed at Auhausen until 1608, four years after the supernova, and the Catholic League was not formed until July of the following year . . ."

The Emperor pressed the horn and the bowl together and scrutinized them that way. Then he put the horn into the bowl, held the bowl aloft in the palm of one hand, and scrutinized that.

The Court Chamberlain said: "So we were in the fortunate position that the very person whom we wanted to gain Matthias's confidence was being sought out *by* Matthias, who wanted to gain *his*, the Duke's, confidence . . . Instead of the Duke approaching the Archduke, we could wait for the Archduke to approach the Duke." The Emperor murmured: "Archduke, archduke, duke, duke, very astute." The Chamberlain: "And that's what happened. Matthias midway through the Frankfurt conclave sidled up to the Duke of Saxony and said, sotto voce, So, how do we settle our little Heinrich problem once and for all? This happened just a few days ago. How, in short, Matthias asked the Duke, do we put the bastard to bed? And the Duke of Saxony, as we had rehearsed, said: We ought to let my fellow Electors see the boy's behavior for themselves . . . If they have some suspicions of what you say, especially our friend from the Palatinate, it is because they know you aren't impartial, you do after all have an interest in the matter, they fear that it aligns too well with the interests of Rome. But let my colleagues see the poor Prince for themselves, let them assess his sanity, or

I should say his insanity, with their own eyes, and their doubts will be put to bed—and with their doubts the bastard himself. Let them *see* him, I say! He is said to be interested in the stars, let us pose him one or two simple questions, which one is the Dog Star, which one is the New Star, how far away do you suppose they are from us, he will respond in his disturbed and disordered way, and that will be that. And Matthias thought this very crafty, a sanity assessment the boy was bound to fail. How far is the New Star, do you suppose? we will ask him, said Matthias, probably smirking, a most innocent question, and the boy will utter something unutterably mad, and that will be the end of it! Of course," the Court Chamberlain told the astronomer, "what he does not know is that Prince Heinrich, in the meantime, will have mastered, under your tutelage, the principles of trigonometry . . ."

"*You must teach my son about triangles!*" cried the Emperor, lifting his eyes for the first time from the bowl and the unicorn horn and staring wildly at the astronomer. "The relations of their sides, the relations of their inner angles and their outer ones!"

The Chamberlain said: "Matthias will ask, How far is the New Star? And the Prince will proceed calmly to his scientific cabinet, procure from within it one of your state-of-the-art tubes, aim it at the star, and then perform for the Electors a dazzling calculation of its remoteness based upon the principles of trigonometry you shall have taught him. And since mathematical reason is or is regarded as the queen of reason, his sanity will be demonstrated beyond all doubt." The Emperor whispered into the ear of the Chamberlain, and the Chamberlain said: "You must go *into* his turret and teach him all about triangles!" And the Emperor whispered in his ear again, and the Chamberlain said: "All about *all* triangles. How the sides relate to the sides and the angles to the angles, and the sides to the angles and the angles to the sides." The Emperor whispered in the Chamberlain's ear and the Chamberlain said: "This cannot be done through the door of the turret, it must be done *in* the turret, inside the turret, face-to-face interaction is vital for truly teaching someone trigonometry." The Emperor, gazing at the bowl, murmured: "For Pythagoras, the triangle lay at the root of all things, beneath the circle, beneath the square. For Pythagoras the square was really nothing but two right triangles, pressed together. When you see a square, you are actually seeing triangles, two of them, pressed tightly together, the diagonal line of their union erased, Pythagoras taught, and for this he was killed."

The Chamberlain said: "Now, Matthias and the Electors depart from Frankfurt this afternoon. They will arrive in Prague in a week. Between now and the moment at which they cross the Old Stone Bridge, you shall teach the Prince enough trigonometry for him to produce a reasonable estimate of the distance of the New Star."

And the astronomer, who by now had concocted a ploy of his own, replied: "It cannot be done."

And he recounted to the Emperor the pitiable state in which he had found his son, how he had looked and how he had smelled and the threats he had made, and the bowl and the unicorn horn fell to the floor as the Emperor buried his face in his hands. "Then Matthias is right," he moaned between his fingers, "my madness has reached full flower in him, my boy is beyond redemption! He, too, is dead and damned, we're all dead and damned in this family." And scurrying to return to the Emperor the bowl and the horn, the Court Chamberlain insisted, with some desperation, that Matthias was wrong, that the Prince was much less mad than he appeared, that in his nakedness and agitation, in his smearing on his own body of his own effluence—"a *calculated* smearing!"—the Prince was obviously playacting the role of a madman, to secure for himself the solitude he had always sought, for he had never *wanted* to be emperor and that's what would make him such a good one. It is a performance, he insisted, a cliché albeit quasi-convincing performance of a mad prince! And the Emperor kept moaning: "A dead and damned family, full of dead and damned family members!" And the astronomer, in order to intensify the chaos which, so he claimed to Leibniz, he had instigated intentionally, chimed in intermittently with: "Not suited for a trigonometry tutorial." And the Emperor howled: "Dead and damned!" And the Chamberlain insisted: "An act! A pantomime! A performance!"

Only when the havoc had reached its highest pitch did the astronomer put forward the proposal he had formulated.

There is, he said, one condition under which he might consider risking life and limb to enter Prince Heinrich's turret and teach him the mathematics of triangles.

And peering through his fingers the Emperor murmured: "What is it?"

And the Court Chamberlain hissed: "Speak, man!"

The condition, the astronomer declared, was this: he required a written guarantee that, if he succeeded, he would receive carte blanche funding from the Imperial Treasury for the production of his tubes—not within reason, so to speak, but without, not bound by common sense but unbound by it, funding constrained by nothing but the demands of his own eyes. "That is my condition," the astronomer said, and no sooner had he said it than the Emperor had drawn up an edict to this effect and signed it.

"A historic document, with historic consequences," the astronomer said, flipping through his ledger. "Eventually it pitted the Habsburg Empire against the exigencies of the infinite. Here it is, I am not inventing it, I am not making it up!" And he thrust under Leibniz's nose a torn scrap of paper on which was written in faded ink: "Tube funding without reason if Heinrich learns about triangles, Rudolf." Leibniz: "I cannot tell you the provenance of that paper, but those were the words on it." The astronomer: "Some, with some reason, as you will see, Herr Leibniz, have blamed the so-called Edict of the Tubes for the wars that ravaged these lands a few years later. They pile millions of Germans at my feet, millions of dead Germans, and my father besides! But if not for this edict I would never have seen what I have seen, I would not know about the night sky what I know about it now. In science as they pile millions and millions of corpses at your feet you must keep your eyes fixed on the firmament, you must proceed as if everyone is already dead, your own family and everyone else also. The most modern scientific methods call for considering everyone in the world to be dead already. Not *really* dead, science is a social act, if everyone were *really* dead you would just laze about, but not really alive either. One must always proceed as if everyone is alive and dead, a little dead, a little alive, I think I learned that philosophy from Heinrich, actually," the astronomer said. And he peered into the telescope, picked up his quill, and wrote down a long string of numbers.

"HER NAME, FATHER," said Prince Heinrich at last from the spot where he lay on the cold stone floor of his turret, and from which spot he had for some time stared in placid silence at the black-robed astronomer, "was Ludmila. She was the daughter, the only daughter, the only *child*, of the bloodletter Zikmund who came once a week to open my veins and bleed me into my father's beloved agate bowl, a procedure intended to relieve my nervousness, Father, for I am a nervous person, I am a known nervous person, that is not meant as an excuse. From the moment I laid eyes on her I said to myself, You mustn't touch her, Heinrich, no touching, no touching, this one is not to be touched! Even if she *wants* to be touched, you must not touch her, no touching, I said to myself. And for a long time, Father, I actually did not touch her." The astronomer told Leibniz: "Meanwhile I am thinking, Does he actually believe I'm a priest? Perhaps he does, I hope he does, but it would also be quite in keeping with what little I know of Prince Heinrich's character for him to be playing games with me, calling me Father, confessing to me some contrived and sordid tale, even asking me for absolution, all while knowing precisely who I am and lying in wait for the right time to reveal it. Do not forget," the astronomer told himself, he told Leibniz, "that you might not be the only person here putting on a performance . . ." He, the astronomer, inspired by the prediction he'd allegedly made in his horoscope but which had probably been inserted by the Court Chamberlain, had returned to the Prince's turret disguised in the vestments of a confessor, with a hood over his head, and he had knelt before the thick wooden door and rapped on the iron bars with the splendid gilded staff lent to him at the Emperor's behest by the deacon of the Cathedral of Saint Vitus, and with the attitude of bemused compassion with which the Benedictine monks had gazed upon him he had asked the Prince to open the door so that he might hear his confession and provide to him the sacrament of reconciliation. His pleas were met, once again, with silence. This time, however, the four guards in the corridor leapt to their feet, as reverent of his religious regalia as they'd been scornful of his scientific paraphernalia, and as three of them genuflected before him the fourth took out a set of keys and said: "We can let you in if you wish, Father, but I'd advise you to minister to the Prince through the door, the last servant to go *in* the turret was stabbed five times in the legs with the Prince's penknife and once in the head, and only by the grace of God did he come out again with his life." And the astronomer said: "Let me in." And as the other three readied their pikes, the tips of which could be seen to quiver, the fourth guard unlocked the door, bowed his head and mouthed a prayer as the astronomer entered, and then promptly clanged the door shut again and bolted it twice.

"It took a long time for my eyes to adjust to the darkness," the astronomer remembered, peering into the telescope, picking up his quill, and writing down a long string of numbers. At last he saw the outline of a bed, but the Prince was not lying on it. He saw a three-legged stool, but the Prince was not sitting on it. Where, then, was the Prince? You should leave! he thought, and it was only by summoning the countervailing thought, The world, as you've established, is entirely pointless save possibly for the composition of a star catalogue that is genuinely complete, that he was able to prevent himself from fleeing. His eyes, meanwhile, continued to adjust. He stepped on something that crunched delicately underfoot like a dead bird, the phrase "a dead songbird" popped into his head as soon as he stepped on it, though it was obviously unlikely, he realized, to *be* a dead bird; and he remembered Margaretha's forewarning that he would find citrus peels littering the turret floor; but when he squatted down to inspect what he'd stepped on he saw that it really *was* a dead bird, a dead songbird, not the desiccated rind of a tangerine. The floor of the turret was littered, as he saw now, not with citrus peels but with these dead birds, as well as with large shards of glass. "Soon enough," Leibniz quotes him as saying, "I would learn what the dead birds had to do with the shards of glass, and what the birds and the glass had to do with the various bits of brass tubing that also (as I now saw as my eyes continued to adjust) littered the floor, and what the birds and glass and bits of brass had to do with Ludmila, the young doomed only child of Zikmund the Imperial Bloodletter." As the astronomer's eyes adjusted still further they alighted on his father's mechanical head, which lay toppled over onto one side just a few feet away and appeared ("through its two mournful eyeholes") to be peering at him queerly. And when his eyes adjusted fully he saw that Prince Heinrich lay right behind it, also on his side, one ear to the floor, also peering at him queerly. Heinrich did not blink, and it occurred to the astronomer that he, "and therefore my dream of a complete star catalogue," was dead. Then, however, he blinked, he wasn't dead. He wore breeches now, and white stockings, possibly a positive sign, as against his past nudity, though "I knew I could deduce nothing very definite about the state of his mind from the fact of his breeches, the fact of his stockings." Tugging on his hood to better hide his face and adopting again the tenor that had struck him so at the foot of the wall of the monastery, of sympathy as infinite as it is indifferent, the astronomer asked the Prince whether there were any sins he wished to confess. The Prince was silent. And for several minutes he remained silent, his two glassy eyes fixed almost unblinkingly on the astronomer's face, which he, the astronomer, had to hope was sufficiently hidden by the hood. What is he seeing when he stares at my face, under this hood, in this light? the astronomer had to wonder, wrote Leibniz. Then ("Did I observe a slight smirk or did I invent it?") the Prince pulled the mechanical head into an embrace, shot out his legs in a "curiously catlike" stretch, and said: "Forgive me, Father, for I have sinned. It has been thirteen years since my last confession." And then: "Her name, Father, was Ludmila."

She came to the Castle every Wednesday with her father, to whom she was apprenticed, a tiny, solemn girl who participated in the task of bleeding the Prince with, although she was only a few years older than Katharina, an astonishing lack of squeamishness. On Tuesdays his nervousness reached its peak, Tuesday nights he never slept a wink but skulked around the Castle observing his sisters sleeping ("My sisters have always been good sleepers, superb sleepers, even Greta, with all her ailments, has never had any trouble falling asleep or staying asleep, whereas I cannot fall asleep or, if I do fall asleep, stay asleep"), and on Wednesdays Ludmila came with her father to bleed him. "My father believes that we share the same form of madness, that mine is merely a heightened version of his, a quantitatively greater madness, yet *he is a sleeper!*, he is a sleeper, I've even seen him fall asleep on his throne while a supplicant is addressing him, he is a sleeper, our madnesses are qualitatively different. He and Greta are superb sleepers, they think they have nothing in common but they have this in common: They sleep, they fall asleep and they actually stay asleep . . . Wilhelmina, as perhaps you yourself know, is a sleeper, too . . . Perhaps you've even seen her sleep . . . Whereas my mother had insomnia, like me, Father . . ." Katharina liked to pretend she had insomnia as well, oftentimes staying up late with Heinrich in his turret, complaining that she couldn't sleep, but he could tell she was exhausted, she *wanted* to sleep, "she was only staying up for my sake," so sooner or later he'd shut his eyes and pretend to sleep and she would fall asleep in a flash. He, however, did not sleep. Only on Wednesdays, after being bled by Ludmila and her father, and then taking a warm bath, was the Prince able to sleep, sometimes continuously for up to three or four or even five hours.

"And so before I knew anything about her, Father," said Heinrich, peering at the astronomer, who adjusted his hood, he recalled to Leibniz, peering into the telescope, "Ludmila signified sleep. You must not touch her, no touching, this one is not to be touched, I would tell myself, but also: When Ludmila comes, you shall finally get some sleep."

When some procedure gives an insomniac some sleep, some rest, a respite from perception, a respite from intellection, he cannot resist sentimentalizing that procedure, no matter how straightforwardly scientific that procedure may, in reality, be, Heinrich said. Hence he probably transfigured in his mind Ludmila into an angel who bestowed upon him the blessing of sleep.

In fact, everything about Ludmila seemed as far as possible from the world to which he was accustomed, and to which he had grown—"far worse than merely hostile"—chillingly indifferent. His days of hostility toward the world were behind him. "That was what frightened me.

"But Ludmila was different, Father, she wasn't of that world," Heinrich told the astronomer, who, as he told Leibniz, had begun to worry about how upon the conclusion of the Prince's murder confession he would suddenly turn the topic of conversation toward the mathematics of triangles.

Yes, Heinrich said, "Ludmila was different." Her father would open one of Heinrich's veins and she would silently hold the stone bowl and watch his blood rise in it, her eyes held level with its rim—possibly, the astronomer surmised, "to avoid the illusions of parallax." Prince Heinrich: "I was squeamish, I couldn't bear to look at my blood in that bowl, I got nauseous, it was pure princely squeamishness, but she wasn't squeamish at all, she kept her eyes fixed on the bowl, on my blood, and when it had reached a certain level she'd say something softly in Czech to her father, who would close up the wound." The Prince was mesmerized by her facility with his blood, her comfort with it. "Her upbringing had inculcated in her an entirely different attitude toward blood than mine had in me, and this astonished me, captivated me, and consoled me." At the time he could not understand why it provided consolation. Now he understood. His malaise in those days, Heinrich explained to the astronomer, issued from his "horrific suspicion" that "everything everywhere was more or less the same." He felt in all things and in all people, and even in all animals, a "creeping sameness."

Everything, in short, was the same, he felt, Heinrich told the astronomer/confessor, reported Leibniz. This suspicion, forged in the formalities of diplomatic ceremonies and the eerie regimentation of imperial dinners, had vexed him from his earliest childhood, but it had seeped far beyond its initial ambit, first from the public chambers of the Castle to the private ones, then to the animal kingdom and even to the stars, and it had now congealed into a "scary conviction" concerning "all things." From the sameness of Castle life he was led inexorably to the sameness of life life, and from the absolute sameness of life life, seen from a strictly scientific perspective, he would be led, he feared, to "a bad conclusion!" "Even my sisters, apparently so different from one another, and from me, were actually more or less the same as one another and the same as me," he realized. The distinctions the Prince had drawn between Margaretha and Katharina, and Katharina and Wilhelmina, and Wilhelmina and Margaretha, and between the three of them and himself, and him and his mother, and him and his father, and his father and his father's father, and the Austrian Habsburgs and the Spanish Habsburgs, were all artificial, "These distinctions did not carve nature at its joints, Father, for nature, I thought, in horror, *has* no joints, I had the horrible image in my head of a jointless nature, a giant jointless nature." Every distinction and thus every thought was contrived: "The world is an undifferentiated manifold, a giant everywhere-identical tapestry." There were of course slight variations here and there, "variations in the stitching," some things were things and some were people, some people were princes and some were pig farmers, some princes—and probably most pig farmers—were sleepers and some did *not* sleep well, but "more or less everything was the same, I felt, Father," Heinrich told the astronomer. The Emperor saw in the novelties he collected in the North Wing evidence of different worlds, tears in the world-tapestry through which perhaps one could peep at God, but the Prince saw everywhere the same world, with no tears in it, and considered his father's novelties to be the mere detritus of that sameness, "identical elements which my father was making even more indistinguishable by collecting them together in the same place, jarring them in the same sort of jars, subjecting them to the same principles of acquisition, restoration, and display. My father's fabled cabinet of curiosities only contributes, I thought, Father," the astronomer quoted Prince Heinrich as saying, "to the catastrophic sameness of the world." It was catastrophic because if everything was more or less the same, then nothing could any longer surprise him, "and I am someone who has always taken great pleasure in being surprised."

Heinrich added: "It is only in this context that you can understand why the fact of Ludmila's being different, her being an obviously different kind of being, affected me so."

The astronomer tugged on his hood and held up his staff. "Go on, my son."

To Leibniz he noted: "Soon I must begin to pay more attention to the sky."

Leibniz wrote: "There were fifty minutes until the eclipse he had predicted. Through the slightly warped slat the sky looked the same as it had all morning." He had the (*nonscientific*) sense that he would see *something* at noon, but he did not know what. "That it should in fact be an eclipse of the Sun: this I now felt increasingly to be doubtful."

Now, having seen with what lack of squeamishness little Ludmila watched his blood gather in the stone bowl, Heinrich resolved one Wednesday not to look away from the bowl but to look directly into it. He wanted to see how blood looked to her, for blood obviously did not look to her as it did to him, or to the royalty by whom he was perpetually surrounded, all of whom shared his aristocratic blood squeamishness. "Blood actually *looked* different to her. It wasn't that she *thought* of blood differently, if she had merely thought of blood differently she would have been squeamish, too, and have had to pit, as I did, her squeamishness against her thoughts, against her will, in the hope that her thoughts and will would overcome her squeamishness instead of her squeamishness her thoughts and will. But there was in Ludmila's head no such battle of thoughts-and-will versus squeamishness, there was simply no squeamishness for her thoughts and will to overcome. When she looked at blood she *saw* something different. What did she see? This question possessed me, Father." Again and again he thought: "Not the Emperor's son but a bloodletter's daughter ... How the Empire appears to the Emperor's son, how blood appears to a bloodletter's daughter ..." And he thought: "Which of us is seeing how the Empire *actually* looks? Which of us is seeing how blood *actually* looks?" And he thought: "You mustn't touch her, Heinrich, no touching, no, no, this one's not to be touched!" So, on that particular Wednesday, in his endeavor to see how blood looked to her, he looked right into instead of away from the stone bowl she was holding, but fainted immediately. He was awoken by Ludmila crouching over him, gently slapping his cheek, he recalled. You mustn't touch her, Heinrich, he told himself, no, not yet. "From that angle, Father, she actually did look a little like Katharina, as Greta liked to tease me by saying." To tease him, Heinrich added, Margaretha, the moment she saw the way he gazed at the bloodletter's daughter, had taken to calling her "the Czech Katharina," she claimed to see a "remarkable resemblance" between the two and used this resemblance to torment him. Greta, of course, had teased him this way before, he had never taken a lover whom Margaretha had not insisted looked exactly like Katharina, "typical sibling ribbing!," there had already been an Italian Katharina, a French Katharina, a Portuguese Katharina, and a Big Swedish Katharina, not one of whom resembled Katharina "in the slightest" except insofar as they were all brown-haired, sweet-tempered, finely featured, and, apart from the big Swede, small, Heinrich said. "I suppose," he said, and he burst into laughter, "it was a funny joke, Margaretha can be very funny, she's the funniest of all of us, we always say we have no idea where Greta got her sense of humor from, certainly it wasn't from Father! She makes wonderful jokes, though most of them I admit I don't *totally* understand, such as this one about my mistresses all resembling Katharina, since anyone who looks at them can see they look nothing like her." The likeness if there was any did not go beyond hair color, affect, bone structure, and size: perhaps they shared certain accidental properties "but they did not share her essence." Standing above him gently slapping him, Ludmila did perhaps resemble Katharina standing above him gently tickling him, but the semblance was physical, not metaphysical, Ludmila had no *meta*physical semblance to anyone in the Prince's world, she was different, different. Katharina for example "is the single most squeamish person I know, Father."

As she stood above him Heinrich resolved to make Ludmila his concubine.

Less and less did he find himself saying to himself, "You mustn't touch her, Heinrich, no, no, she is not to be touched."

There remained however the difficulty of language, for she spoke hardly a word of German, and he not one word of Czech.

The next Wednesday, after Zikmund had opened and closed one of his veins, the Prince looked at Ludmila, pointed to the contents of the bowl she was holding, and said with a warm smile the Czech word for "blood." He'd rehearsed that all week, the astronomer told Leibniz that Heinrich had told him. "His pronunciation was perfect." Zikmund was delighted; ever since the Emperor had moved to Prague it had been a source of some tension that neither he nor his family spoke the language of the locals; now, the Prince had spoken his first word in their noble Slavic tongue, not only (as Prince Heinrich speculated that Zikmund must have felt) in Zikmund's presence and in reference to his trade, but directed at his daughter. "She for her part did not know how to react," the Prince said. "In the whites of the eyes which she cast frantically at her father one saw an entirely charming and wholly endearing social anxiety. Blood was nothing to her, but never before had Ludmila been addressed by royalty, and she had not the slightest idea how to respond! She had no fear of blood but a tremendous fear of repartee." Her father uttered a few firm words to her and she turned back to the Prince, curtsied, and repeated the Czech for "blood." "I said it again, and she said it again, blood, blood, blood, blood, back and forth, blood and blood, blood and blood, blood and blood, in Czech, Father," Heinrich said. "What was interesting to me was that though we were saying the same word in the same language we obviously meant something quite different by it. Blood for *me* meant dynastic lineages, inheritances, and controversies of succession, it meant physical abnormalities and psychical irregularities, warfare and territorial losses, it meant this huge Habsburg jaw of mine (the fact that it is hard for me even to chew!) and this debilitating Habsburg madness of mine, the fact that it is hard for me even to think straight, it meant my mother's inability to sleep and my father's mechanical preoccupations, it meant what I share with my family and what I don't share with them, what I share with my father and what I do *not* share with him, what I share with my sisters and what I don't, what I can *never* share with them . . . That's what *I* meant by blood. What I can't share with Wilhelmina, what I can never, ever share with Katharina. How my sisters avoided inheriting our father's madness and also avoided inheriting his jaw, except I suppose for Margaretha, who did get the jaw, yes, true, *Greta got the jaw*, she got Father's jaw but not his madness, no, I do not think his madness. Ina and Willa, no madness no jaw, Greta, no madness *yes* jaw, I, yes madness yes jaw. When I say blood I mean my father's madness, I mean my father's jaw, I mean his crown and my head. That's what blood meant for me. For Ludmila, however," Prince Heinrich went on from the floor of the turret, cradling in his arms the astronomer's father's emptied-out automaton head, "blood was labor, blood was money, blood was shelter, blood was one's livelihood, blood was just a substance that one handled in that family from the time one emerged from the womb, blood was what one worked with, what one dealt with, blood was what one did, a life lived in blood, around blood, with blood, a life bathed in blood. Blood was almost too ubiquitous in her life to mean anything at all, it's just what life was, what the world was, the whole thing was blood! To ask Ludmila what blood meant would be like asking her what the world meant . . . What a goat is for a goatherd and salt for a salt miner, what the water is for fish and the sky for birds, so blood is for a bloodletter, a barber-surgeon. And doubly so for his children, Father."

For the following Wednesday, Heinrich learned the Czech word for "bowl." "I said bowl, she said bowl, I said bowl, she said bowl." It meant something different to each of them.

Next Wednesday it was the word "sleep."

The following Wednesday it was "castle."

The Wednesday after that it was "tonight."

And the Wednesday after that Heinrich haltingly stitched together his first complete Czech sentence, an invitation he whispered into her ear: "Ludmila sleep castle tonight." Her reaction was not what he had hoped. What had he done wrong? Brooding upon it afterward, Heinrich realized—"Like my father I have no talent for languages!"—that he had conjugated "sleep" in the imperative rather than the interrogative. The sentence had emerged as an injunction rather than an invitation. The following Wednesday, Heinrich once again whispered into her ear "Ludmila sleep castle tonight," but so fretfully did he concentrate on conjugating "sleep" in the interrogative mood that instead of the word "castle" he accidentally said the words "blood bowl." Her reaction was not what he had hoped. The Wednesday after that, however, Heinrich said the sentence flawlessly, at last, and just loud enough, evidently, for Zikmund to overhear, for though

Ludmila, whose daughterly devotion was unequaled in the world, wrapped her arms round one of her father's legs and gave every indication that she did not wish to be separated from him, Zikmund, who it must be said was an ambitious man who must have foreseen the benefits that would accrue to the father of the mistress of the heir apparent to the imperial throne, walked with stiff clownish steps over to the Prince, one leg heavy with the weight of his weeping daughter. Heinrich: "I ask you, Father, does a man like this *deserve* his daughter's devotion? She binds herself to him, to his leg, and he strides over and offers her up to me. What kind of father is this? Was it merely self-justification to ask myself, as I playfully pried little Ludmila off her father's leg, if she would not actually be *happier* with me in the Castle?" That playful prying of Ludmila off her father's leg was the first time he had ever touched her. Zikmund left, Ludmila's wails dwindled in time into whimpers and snorts, Heinrich told her that she had nothing to fear, nothing at all to be afraid of, they would have fun, "We shall become family!" Of course he said this all in German and she understood none of it. He tried to soothe her with a comforting remark in her own tongue but the words that came spontaneously to his lips unfortunately were the words "blood bowl."

Thereafter Ludmila lived at the Castle.

The astronomer tugged on his hood and held up his staff. "Go on, my son."

"For the first three days, Father, she did not rise from that bed," said Prince Heinrich, pointing through the astronomer's chest to the bed that stood in the darkness behind him. Even on the evening of the third day, when, through a stonemason employed in the Castle Workshop who spoke both of their languages fluently, Prince Heinrich suggested to Ludmila as sweetly and discreetly as he could that she repair to Margaretha's boudoir to cleanse herself and dress herself, in preparation for the act he had in mind for that night and which could—"forgive me, Father!"—be postponed no longer, she refused, so that he had to have Greta's ladies-in-waiting cleanse and clothe her in the bed. As they did so she whimpered continually for the man who had abandoned her, "a whimpering which began to infuriate me," the Prince told the astronomer, "for what apart from begetting her had he done to warrant such unremitting devotion? Would she ever be as devoted to me as she was to him? Is not the unremittingness of the devotion of a daughter to her father even in the face of the father's iniquity a sign that it is something *less* than love, something more mechanistic than love, something more deterministic?" Naturally Heinrich thought of the unremitting nature of the clocks he dismantled, how they ticked and tocked unflaggingly till the moment he took out their innermost gear. Mustn't a feeling be *able* to flag to be love, indeed to be a feeling? Heinrich mused, the astronomer quoted him as saying, and the act that ensued once Ludmila had been scrubbed and scoured was consumed, on his end, by such ruminations on the quirks, oddities, and clocklike qualities of the filial bond. This did not, Heinrich noted, lessen the pleasure they took in it.

That night the Prince slept *six* hours. And in the morning, another miracle: although the Sun, by design, had not penetrated his turret in years, he awoke in a beam of light. Propping himself up on an elbow he saw that Ludmila had not only risen at last, she had also torn down the dark Flemish tapestries he had hung over the windows three, four, even five thick to stop natural light from interfering with his "investigations into the mechanism or mechanisms of nature and man." In the fur-lined nightgown Margaretha's ladies-in-waiting had lent her from Katharina's wardrobe, Ludmila stood there staring at one such investigation. In her primitive German she demanded: What is this? And he, elated, leapt out of bed, summoned the stonemason, and through him explained that this was a clock in an early stage of being dismantled. That seemed to please her. She said: And this? This, replied Heinrich, by way of the stonemason, is a clock in a late stage of being dismantled. That, too, seemed to please her. She said: And this? This, he replied, is a clock that has been completely dismantled. "Please tell her," he told the stonemason, "that I am someone who likes to take clocks apart, please tell her *completely* apart, I like to take clocks completely apart to see how they work. You cannot understand how something works until you take it apart, say that. To know something, tell her this verbatim, is to have taken it apart, completely." This seemed to please her also. Later there occurred to him a different explanation of her pleasure, namely relief at learning that these perhaps frightful-looking apparatuses were instruments of science and not, as he realized the poor thing might have feared, as though he were an agent of the Inquisition, instruments of torture; and later still he realized that her pleasure sprang from another source altogether; but that sunny morning he took it as a sign of her interest in the properties of time, of duration, or if not her interest in the properties themselves, then of her interest in his interest in them. He took it as an overture. The first sign that their worlds "might be made to merge on a plane higher than that of mere matter, Father."

There followed the happiest days of his life. "Perhaps," Heinrich said, "the only truly happy days of it."

Hand in hand they strolled through the Imperial Arboretum and the Imperial Rose Garden, through the Imperial Menagerie and the Imperial Portrait Gallery, the route he sometimes walked with Katharina when he sought to inform her about the ways of the world. In the arboretum he taught Ludmila about trees, first their nature, that is, their leaves and trunks, the range of their root systems, how they jostle with one another for sunlight, and then their meaning, the melancholy thoughts trees inspired in his head, thoughts that had their origins in his childhood experiences with trees, the way trees figured in his adolescence and in his early adulthood, the connotations of trees, their associations, gnarled knots that called to mind his mother's father's bent bulging fist gripping the knob of his cane, the gorgeous springtime flowering of a particular tree that reminded him of the dreadful, very drawn-out and very depressing springtime death of his beloved paternal grandmother long ago. Heinrich said: "I wanted to be transparent to her, Father—I wished Ludmila to know *exactly* what I was thinking when I looked at a tree." The thought that a tree might put in his head a thought which she remained unaware of was actually painful to him; he felt the strange sensation that his head (which just a few weeks ago had been empty, continuous with everything else and the same as it) was teeming with personal arboreal associations which, if he didn't want his head to shatter from the pressure, he had to reveal to Ludmila at *once*. In the rose garden he taught her about roses, first their nature, the purpose of their thorns and scents, and then their meaning, his own personal rose associations, of which, like his tree associations, Heinrich felt an urgent need to unburden himself, to share with her, lest his head shatter from the pressure of them. In the Imperial Menagerie he explained how the animals worked, how the hog worked, its nature, and what the animals, and particularly the hog, meant to him, what and whom he associated with them. Same with the portraits in the Imperial Portrait Gallery. He came to realize that the pressure he felt in his head, which was not unpleasant but which could only be relieved by disclosing to Ludmila with perfect precision what everything—hogs, trees, people, paintings, and everything else—evoked in him, in his head, was love. It was what love was. The feeling of being in love is the feeling, Heinrich realized, of one's head being no longer equilibrated with the cosmos but being instead perilously albeit pleasurably out of equilibrium with it, overinflated with private associations that must at all costs be discharged, or pumped, into the head of the loved one. One's head never feels more private, more cloistered, more one's own, than when one is in love, love seals us in our head and our lover in our lover's head, "Every single poet from Homer till now has got this backward, poets think love joins heads, fuses them together, when in fact it sequesters them." This head sequestration was by no means an unpleasant phenomenon. The fervid urge to share one's thoughts, in conversation, is the mental counterpart of the material urge to share one's seed, in the carnal act, Heinrich observed, and how often after sharing with Ludmila that, say, the knot of this tree reminded him of his departed grandfather's arthritic fist, darkened here and there by blood pooling beneath the skin, did he take her by the hand, dismiss the stonemason who'd been translating for them, and draw her down into the dirt.

Now and then Margaretha teased: "How goes your edification of our little Czech Katharina?"

But of course he had never drawn Katharina down into the dirt with him, except of course to tickle her, and of course to be tickled by her.

Strolling with Ludmila around the Castle complex, articulating to her each and every one of his innermost thoughts and copulating with her there in the dirt beneath the big windows of the North Wing, with his father's eyes possibly on his back, or hers, the Prince felt that no one had ever seemed more real to him than she did, a "wonderful, wonderful feeling." Prince Heinrich said: "I cannot express to you, Father, how *real* she seemed to me in those days, how really real, what a really real person Ludmila seemed to me to be! A real person, a real *other* person, not me, with another person's head." She even learned to speak excellent German, far better, actually, than she let on at first, and upon discovering this he was able to dismiss the stonemason permanently and commune with her directly in his mother tongue.

Every night he fell asleep.

During the night he stayed asleep.

And every morning he awoke in natural light.

"Never had I dared dream of such happiness, Father." Heinrich added: "Of course, it did not last."

One day, the inventor Balthasar von Ulm came to the Great Hall to exhibit his latest invention, a smallish thing concealed theatrically beneath a white sheet.

"Ten years ago, Your Majesty, My Lords and Ladies," proclaimed Herr von Ulm, Prince Heinrich told the astronomer, "you saw with your very own eyes that the law prohibiting the indefinite motion of bodies—the *alleged* law, legislated to us by the logicians—has no basis in fact, it is an artifact of their reason, a whim of their madness, the logicians inscribe their proscriptions of the perpetuum mobile in a thousand thousand books but Nature does not read their books and she need not heed their laws. With your own eyes you saw how my wondrous wheel moved of its own accord, your own eyes proved it to you! I daresay Your Majesty's own eyes refuted the logicians." Margaretha scoffed. She of course had not believed in that wheel, and she now signaled this disbelief to their father with the scoffing sound that remained for him (Heinrich) her most salient trait. After months of his being confined to his turret, Greta's face, her jaw aside, was already growing blurry to him, but the scoffing sound she produced often in her throat remained clear as a bell. Prince Heinrich told the astronomer: "Wilhelmina and I, too, of course, had had doubts about von Ulm's wheel, but only Margaretha took our father *seriously* enough to signal to him with her constant scoffing sound that she thought he was wrong, that there was a small person turning the wheel from the inside, et cetera. Of the three of us, not counting Ina, Willa once said to me, possibly ironically, only Greta truly respects Father, only Greta reveres Father, it is because she loves him so much (like a god even! Willa said) that as long as they live a friendly word will never pass between them. She told me: You and I were happy to leave him his delusions about the wheel, if it made him happy to think it revolved on its own we were happy to let him think that, but not Margaretha! Greta *had* to make him see the person pedaling inside it, for her everything depended on Father's seeing that person pedaling and *admitting* that he saw him, whereas for you and me Father's seeing that person pedaling away in there was a matter of indifference. You might say: You and I have given him up for mad, whereas Greta has never given him up. I'm tempted, Willa said, to say that of us three, not counting Ina, only Margaretha is a good child, only her devotion is undying, only she loves Father the way a child should love her father . . . To which," Heinrich went on, "I replied: Maybe, maybe . . . I was thinking: *Maybe* she's onto something—but maybe she's overthinking things, maybe Greta just hates Father, maybe Greta's apparent hatred for him, which it is tempting to see, paradoxically, as love, is simply hatred, straight, scathing hatred, Father, expressed incessantly by her scoffing sound. And I thought: And I *do* love him, I *do*—in my own way—respect him, I *did* care if he saw the man in the wheel dripping with sweat turning it from the inside, maybe not as much as Margaretha cared if he saw him but more than Wilhelmina did. I do take him seriously, I do, I thought . . ." the Prince told the astronomer, who now peered into his telescope and murmured: "Everything is darkening now, it is getting darker and darker, can you see that, Herr Leibniz? How everything's getting gradually darker out there?" And Leibniz said that he did see it, everything was getting darker, and the astronomer said, "And a bit gloomier, yes?," and Leibniz said yes, it was all a bit gloomier, and to the *Philosophical*

Transactions he reported that the sky through the askew slat did in fact seem slightly darker, slightly gloomier, though he did not know of course if this was just a matter of suggestion, if he just was seeing what the astronomer wanted him to see. He wrote: "There was now hardly more than a half hour until the promised eclipse, yet the astronomer, in his tale, still had his eyes. How, I thought, will he have *time* to lose his eyes, to narrate, that is, the losing of his eyes, in the next thirty-some minutes, when we seem, in his tale, and in the Prince's tale within his tale, no closer than when we began to a juncture at which they might suddenly be gouged out?"

Now, ten years later, Balthasar von Ulm had gone on, he had returned with a new and even more stupendous invention, one with which, if His Majesty and His Lords and Ladies would lend him their eyes, he would refute another alleged law, a law that since antiquity has been held even more sacrosanct by those bookish thinkers who presume to hand down natural law without ever looking up from their texts to cast a single glance at the outside world: namely, the scholastic doctrine of horror vacui, the law prohibiting the possibility of the void. "Yes," cried von Ulm, "the void exists, it exists, you shall see it yourselves!" With that he yanked off the white sheet to reveal a peculiar apparatus consisting of a glass globe about the size of an adult human head mounted on a wooden frame and into the bottom of which was inserted a brass tube that ran toward the floor, where it tapered and terminated beside a sort of foot treadle such as one might find on a loom or lathe. "With this machine," von Ulm said, pulling over a stool and pedaling the treadle, "I shall evacuate the globe of everything inside it, producing the very vacuum that no less an authority than Aristotle assures us cannot be found in any corner of the cosmos. Yet we shall find it right here, in the Great Hall!" Margaretha scoffed, the Emperor leaned forward on his throne, and Herr von Ulm treadled away, thereby opening and closing a certain valve, and drawing a piston up and down the length of the tube, so the Prince explained to the astronomer and the astronomer in turn enlightened Leibniz, who noted parenthetically to the *Philosophical Transactions* that if it indeed existed, which he had doubts that it did, then that machine would appear to be an early "but of course quite crude" antecedent of the "very exquisite pneumatical engine" devised in recent times by the "Honorable Mr. Boyle, expert explorer of nature, who in this very journal" (to which Robert Boyle was already a prolific contributor, which made doubly delicate this suggestion by young Leibniz that he had found a possible forerunner to Boyle's famous invention and thus cast into doubt the latter's priority over it) "has brought such admirable clarity to the concept of coldness, and has related the interesting account of the monstrous calf discovered of late in its mother's womb, whose hind legs lacked joints, and whose tongue was split into three parts . . ." For some time the Great Hall was silent apart from the rocking back and forth of the foot treadle, the shuttling up and down of the piston, the periodic bulletins ("A quarter empty! Half-empty!") Herr von Ulm broadcast with monumental fanfare, and the scoffing sounds Margaretha produced at intervals deep in her throat, which, "although Wilhelmina and I were completely inured to them, still had the capacity to perturb Father, not to mention Katharina," said Heinrich, and after each of which the Court Chamberlain whispered something into His Majesty's ear.

Finally Balthasar von Ulm leapt up from his stool, indicated with a flourish the glass globe, and proclaimed: "My Lords, My Ladies: the void."

Heinrich said: "My father fell to his knees before the glass globe. Remarkable, he murmured. Miraculous. And here on Earth, right here on Earth! Children, come look, come see, Heinrich, Wilhelmina, Katharina, come look, the void, come see. Margaretha, come see. The scoffing sound my sister produced in response must have come from very deep in her throat, very deep indeed, Father! To express skepticism of that magnitude one must will the walls of one's throat to bleed. And she said: There is no void, there is no vacuum, that sphere is filled with our atmosphere just as it was before. Tell me, Father, she said slowly, in a singsong, as one would address not a god," said the Prince, "but a child, or a simpleton, what *sensible* distinction do you note? How exactly does the nothingness in that sphere make itself known, she asked, to your organs of sense?"

Their father, who now cocked his head and stared more quizzically into the glass globe, said nothing.

Herr von Ulm did not, however, as Margaretha (the astronomer surmised) must have expected that he would, and as he had done a decade ago, slink toward the door.

No, Princess Margaretha's doubt had evidently been anticipated—and not merely anticipated, but actually *incorporated* into the performance, for von Ulm began now to pace dramatically back and forth, mumbling to himself *The senses!, the senses!,* his hands gripped behind his back, a frown on his face as ludicrously pronounced as that on the mask of a tragic figure in an Italian commedia. At last, he came to a halt. He snapped his fingers. "A bird!" he cried. And he brought one hand to his lips and behind it in a stage whisper he hissed at his son, who was also his assistant: "Hans, bring me a bird!" And turning to the audience he clasped his hands before him and said: "Lady Margaretha is quite right. Why should you take my word for it? That would not be in the spirit of our times. Why should you take this globe to be empty simply because I say it is, when perhaps it is filled with air? Perhaps the globe leaks where it meets the tube, or perhaps the pump is a sham, and I a charlatan! Ah, excellent, here is Hans with a bird." Enter Hans with a pretty little bird on his finger, singing (the bird) a pretty little song, said the Prince, and from where he lay on the floor he sang me "snippets" of the song the bird had sung, the astronomer told Leibniz. "I am mad enough to sing you a snippet of that song, Father, perhaps even several snippets, but I'm not so mad as to sing you the whole birdsong, Father!" said the Prince, laughing. "Snippets only, snippets only! In a world such as mine—for this is my world, not yours, although of course that sentence makes no sense at all aloud, when I *say* it it sounds stupid—one must come up with one's own measures of true madness (not the entire birdsong, Heinrich, sing him only snippets thereof! I actually told myself that) and measure oneself, which is to say myself, by them. All nonsense of course. Today, Heinrich, you shall dress him, which is to say yourself, up as a confessor and regale him, which is to say yourself, with your tale, which is to say your murder tale, and when you reach the birdsong part you shall sing him (yourself!) only snippets not the entire thing, *that* is a sign of your sanity, yes, not singing yourself the entire birdsong is today's sign of your sanity!"

He laughed.

"I believe the bird, incidentally, was a lark."

And though it struck him now that Prince Heinrich knew he was no confessor, the astronomer nevertheless tugged on his hood, held up his staff, and intoned: "Go on, my son."

To Leibniz the astronomer added: "If you are wondering about the point of all this, rest assured that what the Prince told me would have major ramifications for my ultimate interpretation of the tube, my ultimate understanding of what the tube, or telescope, *is*—what it actually is. Everything I am telling you, everything I have already told you, and especially everything I am still to tell you: it all touches the problem of the true nature of the astral tube."

Hans held his hand beside Herr von Ulm's hand and the little bird hopped from the one to the other. Herr von Ulm stroked the bird's head. "If, Your Majesty," he said, "the globe remains full of air even after I have pumped it, as your daughter suggests, then she should have no qualms about my repeating that operation with a little bird inside. God only knows what would happen to a bird in a vacuum, but if it is indeed a plenum, as your daughter suspects, then a bird should continue to sing in it quite contentedly! So, shall I put the bird in the globe, Your Majesty?"

And Katharina cried: "Father, no!" And Margaretha laughed and waved her hand and said: "Why not, go ahead, put it in." And the Emperor looked at the Prince and said: "What do you think?" And Margaretha said: "Why are you asking *Heinrich* that?" And the Emperor said: "I'm asking all of you, I'm canvassing all of your thoughts." And Margaretha said: "No, Father, you're asking Heinrich, you are obviously only asking Heinrich, and in terms of the canvassing of people's thoughts it's obvious you're canvassing only *his* thoughts, do you really not see that? Really? Is that not obvious to you, Father? Am I going crazy? Obviously there is only one opinion about the bird that matters here, what the rest of us have to say about what to do with the bird is immaterial." Heinrich told the astronomer: "On my father's face I saw the expression I often saw there after she had spoken to him, an expression of solemnity, perplexity, and woe." The Court Chamberlain whispered something into the Emperor's ear. The astronomer peered into the telescope, picked up his quill, and wrote something down. He said that Prince Heinrich had told him: "My concern for the bird was overridden by my desire for family harmony, by the fear my older sister could still instill in me. So I said: I agree with Margaretha, put the bird in the globe." Katharina ran over to the Emperor where he was kneeling before the pump and wrapped her arms around him and cried: "No, Father, please, no! You can't let him do it, it doesn't *matter* what's in there, and it's going to hurt that bird!" And Margaretha burst into laughter and said: "It does matter, of course it matters, the truth always matters, silly child, the fact is that nothing matters *except* the truth, nothing *else* matters, you will learn that sooner or later—at least I hope! And of course it is not going to hurt the bird, it's a *trick*, an illusion, nothing more, you know nothing about this man, he's a magician, an illusionist, nothing more, the last time he came here you didn't even exist yet, you were still sloshing around in Mother's belly, Mother was still here and you were still in her belly, yet you *talk* as if you know what's going on here! It is the funniest thing, really. Have you not noticed that Heinrich and I, your oldest siblings, who actually *know* something about this magician, have both said: Sure, go ahead, put the bird in the globe? Honestly, Katharina, it amazes me sometimes how *confidently* you talk about things that came along a long time before you did, such an attitude may serve a person well in politics, but in circumstances like this it just makes you look a little ridiculous. Come here, come here, come here, come sit on my lap." Katharina, who, noted Heinrich, had begun rubbing her eyes, shot a quick glance at Wilhelmina (who, probably fearful of Margaretha, did not return it) and then shuffled over to Margaretha and climbed up onto her lap. "It's just, I don't want him to hurt the bird," Katharina managed to say between sobs, and Margaretha, smoothing down her hair, said: "You are the sweetest thing, and you have the softest hair I've ever felt in my entire life, and a big wonderful heart besides, but you know nothing about anything happening here, the meaning of all this is flying over your head, and the bird, I promise you, is not going to get hurt." And she kissed the top of Katharina's head.

At a gesture from the Emperor, von Ulm unscrewed a portion of the globe, lowered the bird into it on one finger, and screwed the globe shut again. The bird hopped to its left, hopped to its right, cocked its head, and sang its song. Von Ulm began to work the foot treadle, and the bird, according to the Prince, continued to sing. "You see, you silly child!" said Margaretha, bouncing Katharina on her knee, and Katharina laughed through her tears. Soon thereafter however the bird began to suffer. First it ceased to sing. Next it started to wither and droop, and after that to convulse. Now Katharina began to scream. But not only she, for "what surprised me more, Father," Heinrich told the astronomer, "is that Ludmila—who before our walks in the menagerie had shown no affinity for animals, for she, like so many of her class, for whom privation instrumentalizes the relationship with animals, had seen animals as potential *resources* rather than potential *friends*—had also begun to scream, and to scream, moreover, the same scream Katharina was screaming. I thought: The sound coming out of them is the same! Katharina was shaking me, I think she wanted me to stop von Ulm's experiment, and Ludmila was shaking me, too, for the same reason, but I was too consumed by their startling similitude, not only externally—for Ludmila was wearing, as she had been from her third evening in the Castle, one of Katharina's gowns—but also internally, to intervene. And then I realized: The scream they are screaming about the bird is the scream I, too, would have screamed about the bird had I not been able to achieve, via thought, a philosophical distance from the bird. The scream they're screaming is *my* scream, the emotions inducing it are my emotions, I taught them this scream, I inculcated in them these emotions, one is not *born* feeling bad for a bird."

Von Ulm, smiling, being pummeled now by Katharina's little fists: "As you can plainly see, Your Majesty, the little bird, who cannot live in the absence of air, has been deprived of it. That the globe now contains nothing, a void, is beyond all doubt, I am sure even Lady Margaretha would agree! Shall I now open it up again and rejuvenate our little ornithological colleague here so we can thank her for her contribution to science?"

Margaretha scoffed. "It is no bird, this bird is no bird, it's a mechanism, an automaton, a clever facsimile. He takes you for a fool, Father."

Von Ulm, nervous: "Your Majesty, may I open the globe? If I do not open it now the bird will surely die."

Margaretha: "Look at him squirm, he knows that thing won't die, he knows it cannot die, something that does not live cannot die!"

"Father," whispered Katharina, recalled the Prince, having reached beyond her delirium a mad sort of stillness, "please save the bird."

But the Emperor, kneeling with his nose to the glass, just behind which the bird twitched and convulsed, simply said: "This bird is dead and damned." It died half a minute later, its yellow breast pointed upward at the fine ribbed vaults of the Great Hall, its head twisted weirdly to one side.

Margaretha's headaches had not visited her in years, said Prince Heinrich, but a moment later she was apparently struck by one, for she mumbled, My head, and pitched forward headfirst onto the floor. And when, between the courtiers who gathered around Margaretha to attend to her, Ludmila and Katharina caught a glimpse of the gash on her head, and the blood that spurted from it, they gasped identically, went identically pale, and ran identically from the room.

"They were squeamish," Prince Heinrich told the astronomer.

A disturbing hypothesis began to form in Heinrich's head.

His nervousness returned. He stopped sleeping also.

He now undertook to observe Katharina and Ludmila—"with as much rigor, precision, and systematicity as you, Father, when I incarnate you as an astronomer rather than a confessor," said Heinrich, "must observe the stars, the only difference being this, that when you observe the stars it is of no consequence whether or not the stars watch you in return, whereas in observing Katharina and Ludmila it was important that they not observe me observing them, at the risk of perverting what I observed of them."

To that end he tried to move in darkness. Once again Prince Heinrich hung over his windows his tapestries.

At nightfall, instead of sleeping—"Impossible!"—and without, as yet, quite knowing why, Heinrich turned his attention to the putting together of air pumps, no longer the taking apart of clocks but now the putting together of air pumps, of bigger and bigger air pumps, the integrity of which he tested with more and more songbirds, as well as a few other animals. "I find it interesting, Father," the Prince said, "how, over the course of centuries, we breed dogs to love us, we fashion dogs precisely such that they love us, with each new generation dogs love us, by design, more and more, a dog breed is not finished until it loves us, we do not really call it a dog at all until it loves us, before that point we call it a *wolf*—and yet when, after all that, a dog does, tautologically, love us, we are nevertheless moved."

Come dawn, he put aside his pumps and returned to his observations. And before long these observations validated the theory he feared, that Katharina and Ludmila, his little sister and his lover, once so different, were now the same, "and the conclusion

could not be avoided, Father, that I had *made* them the same."
On the floor of the Music-Making Room he observed Ina singing to herself amidst his old glockenspiels, singing herself songs
he had taught her, and between songs she spoke to herself,
words he had taught her, thoughts he had taught her, everything she sang or said was his, and even the motions of her
body as she sang and as she spoke "were mine, Father, motions
I myself had taught her, even if I'd taught her them tacitly, un-
intentionally." He recognized her swaying of her shoulders as *his*
swaying of *his* shoulders. The subtlest things had imprinted
themselves upon her. What she had learned on our walks went
well beyond what I'd deliberately taught her. From the Music-
Making Room I went to the Stonemason's Workshop. There
I saw the same thing, that is, myself . . . Though Ludmila spoke
not to herself but to another person, and not in German but in
Czech, Heinrich said, one nevertheless caught my own cadences,
nothing but my own cadences, and my own gestures, or gesticulations, and presumably my own thoughts, and basically my own
being, or at least my own behavior, which of course was also
Katharina's being or behavior. Heinrich: "The uncanny sensation of observing *oneself*, hearing *oneself*, albeit as a woman,
albeit in Czech . . ." Before their walks she was different, after
their walks she was the same; his mind had taken something
different, evacuated it somehow of itself, and made it all the
same. Heinrich said: "I thought: By collecting them in the same
place and subjecting them to the same principles I have made
Katharina and Ludmila indistinguishable from each other."

And since, in nature, no two things are identical, whenever
we come upon two indistinguishable things we always suspect

them of being unnatural, artificial, "in other words, man-made," said Prince Heinrich, "which is to say, not organisms but mechanisms, containing neither mind nor soul but gears engaging gears . . ."

How, thought Heinrich, can we tell an organism apart from a mechanism?

Ludmila had begun to seem profoundly unreal to him, "as unreal, perhaps, as she's seemed to you the whole time I've been telling you this tale, Father. You would not be wrong if you've been thinking that Ludmila hardly seems to exist in and of herself (outside my telling) at all." But her seeming unreal to him was no proof that she was unreal, that she was a mechanism, since after all, Heinrich noted, *he* might be mad, he might be quite mad and she quite real, organismic—"something *seeming* some way to me is no proof of anything."

Her reality or unreality had to be demonstrated out *there*, he said: "On the outside of my head."

How, Heinrich thought, as he told the astronomer, can we tell an organism from a mechanism, objectively, outside our head, when that mechanism might be very fine, very, very delicate, as precise as you like, and engineered by a craftsman of genius?

For six days and six nights Heinrich brooded upon the conundrum in vain. At dawn on the seventh day, a Sunday, November fourteenth, "what should have been a day of rest," the solution came to him, as blindingly obvious as such solutions tend to be: "You put her in the pump! You put her in the pump." He understood now why he had been building pump after pump, and such big pumps to boot, "the man of science like the artist will sometimes find that his materials lead him to where his thoughts ought to go, though perhaps they fear to go there," he had been building bigger and bigger air pumps in order to be able to put a person in one of them—or better to say, so as not to beg the question, something the size of a person, and the shape of one.

Life cannot subsist in the void, the Prince remarked, but a mechanism can. In the absence of the atmosphere a soul will grind to a halt but cogs will continue to turn.

On the Sunday in question, the Sun had risen, but the turret on account of the tapestries over the windows was still dark and Ludmila in Katharina's nightgown was still asleep. Heinrich picked her up and put her in the pump. She had slipped into bed late the night before so even this did not wake her. But when he began to pedal the treadle and thereby to remove the air from the globe in which she found herself trapped she awoke and started to scream. Heinrich: "Her screams touched me, I'm human after all, it's hard to hear such a human scream without imputing the scream to a human being. I almost stopped the experiment then and there, and I might have done so had I not remembered this mechanical head"—he indicated with his head the Head of Phalaris in his arms—"which, rudimentary as it was, mimicked nevertheless the sound of a man. Your father's head gave me the courage to continue, Father." Of course, the astronomer told Leibniz, peering into his telescope, such an assertion lay bare the disordered nature of Heinrich's head, as he'd had the astronomer's father's mechanical head in his possession no longer than a few days—although as we've seen, Leibniz noted to the *Philosophical Transactions*, the disorder may have been in the astronomer's head instead, or in addition, for those few days were likely a few years. Feeling ridiculous now in his costume, and unnerved by the Prince's willingness to play along with his farce, but not wishing to disrupt the tale, the astronomer tugged on his hood, held up his staff, and intoned: "Go on, my son." Heinrich said: "I continued to treadle, the pump continued to evacuate the air, Ludmila continued in the motions of her body and the color of her face to give outward signs that she like the bird was suffering, but obviously none of these motions and none of these colors were effects that could not have been generated by a craftsman of sufficient genius." Then, all of a sudden, her behavior changed: between gasps, she began to apologize. "Yes, Father," Heinrich said. "*She* apologized to *me*!" This baffled him. He thought: What in God's name does she have to apologize for, when really *I* should be apologizing to *her*, for developing doubts about her actuality, and then putting her in this pump! It emerged, however, that she *did* have reason to apologize. She confessed—"and this, she must have assumed, was why I was doing this to her!" the Prince cried—to an affair with her compatriot the stonemason, she loved him and he her and their love had long ago been consummated, she was sorry to have hurt Heinrich but he after all had hurt her far worse, and the truth is—she could barely breathe now—she hated Heinrich, she detested him, he repulsed her, and she was certain he would go straight to hell, the stonemason was everything Heinrich was not, mentally of course, "mentally, she said, and this of course was absurd, he was a million times my superior," the Prince recalled, and he told the astronomer that this was so ludicrous that it did not wound him, but physically, too, yes, and somehow she summoned the energy to laugh, a mocking laugh he had never heard from her before, physically, too, My Lord, she said, there's no comparison between you and the stonemason, no comparison at all—not in how you *think*, not in how you *fuck*. And in the gargantuan glass globe she collapsed and lost consciousness. "Now, it is true," Prince Heinrich told the astronomer, "that the affair was news to me. And it's true, as you may have heard Greta claim, for I know she likes to ascribe Ludmila's passing to *this*, to something very base, rather than something very philosophical, that I went into a jealous rage. Yes, Father, I went into a jealous rage—true. But it is *not* true that that jealous rage of mine killed her. Quite on the contrary, it saved her life!" In his rage he despised her, he said, and in despising her she became real to him again, a being again, a different being from him, a *despised* being, of course, but a being nevertheless, a mechanism never elicits such fervor pro or contra. The Prince shattered the glass globe with an elbow and on his knees in the shards of it he held Ludmila's limp body and wept over her and prayed over her and breathed into her mouth. Whatever he did did the trick; she came back to life, gasping for the air he was giving her. "We underestimate pneumatics," the astronomer said to Leibniz. Heinrich told the astronomer: "All day long we stayed intertwined, talking and copulating, copulating and talking, and in our talking and copulating both we felt for the first time that we were getting to the bottom of the other person, I told her about my father and my sisters, how I *really* felt about them, I told her things about them I have not even told you, Father, intimate and complicated things, the truth, the truth! And she told me about her father, i.e., about Zikmund, whom she loved like no one else in the world yet who had more or less abandoned her to me, and all of the complicated feelings that entailed, she shared thoughts

and feelings of remarkable intimacy and astounding complicat-
edness, and she even told me at my urging about the stonemason, every single thing about him, even at my urging how he
made love, at my urging she told me what he looked like, everywhere, and what they had done, in detail, and in return I told
her about my demons and doubts, how I had come to question
her inner life, she was a quick study on this and soon wielded
the same thought process against me, how do I know *you* think,
how do I know *you* have a mind, how do I know *you're* not a machine, she cried cleverly, et cetera, and in this way we peered all
the way down into each other's depths, never in my life had
I peered into someone so deeply or let them peer so deeply into
me, deep, deep, *unbelievably* deep! Yet at bottom there was between us a substrate of mutual loathing that safeguarded for
each of us the autonomy and actuality of the other. The perverse
pleasure of a jealous rage . . . The *salubriousness* of jealousy," he
said, per the astronomer, "which is nothing else but resistance . . .
And it is good for a prince to feel such resistance, so rarely does
the world resist him, something is only real to you when it re-
sists you, and so makes you *rage*." (Is it fanciful to discern in such
sentiments the seed of Leibniz's later contention that "the nature
of body does not consist in extension alone," as the Cartesians
liked to insist, but also in the solidity of bodies, in their impen-
etrability, in their exclusion of other bodies, in their ability, in
short, to resist things?) Heinrich: "That day she seemed so real
to me, so real, more real than ever before." That night, however,
as she slept, and he did not, and he watched her sleep, her body
rising and falling with each breath, Ludmila sank back into a
profound and, as he could plainly see, irreversible unreality, and

he was assailed once again by his former suspicion that her head was hollow and void or else filled like a clock with gears upon gears, and it was then ("I confess!") that he inflicted such injuries upon her head in his effort to open it up and look inside, cutting off her ears, plucking out one eye, shattering her teeth, and finally splitting open her skull. The severity of her maiming should not imply, he noted, that it was done in violence, no, it was done with equanimity, in a philosophical mood, it is just not as easy as one might think to open a human head. Upon doing so, and finding that her head was neither hollow nor filled with gears, he flung her corpse in Ina's gown to his hogs in the menagerie down below, and he'd put one foot on the sill to fling himself after her before it dawned on him that he had not been wrong, what had appeared organic to *him* would not appear so to someone much smaller, or to someone equipped with a magnifying glass of sufficient power, "or a tube like yours, Father"; seen by such a small person, or under such a powerful glass, or through a long enough tube, what appeared to be organic, pinkly, soggily, squeamishly organic, would show itself to be mechanical through and through, little but toothed wheels turning one another in vast empty silent spaces.

Then Heinrich said: "For these and all my sins I am very sorry." He added: "It sounds stupid when I say it. When I say anything." Since the world was his the Prince was obviously doing something completely crazy, truly stupid, and entirely contradictory whenever he opened his mouth to say anything to anyone, Heinrich noted. "And in any case I haven't infiltrated my own turret disguised as a priest in order to forgive myself my sins such as they are but in order to teach myself about triangles, yes, triangles! So, then, Father," said Prince Heinrich, and he burst into laughter, then looked frightened, and at last went still: "Speak. Teach me. I am all yours."

And the astronomer took off his hood and set down his staff and taught the Prince about triangles.

And he found—"and this tells us something about the nature of mathematics"—that despite his being clearly completely crazy Heinrich's aptitude for trigonometry was undiminished.

And when the delegation of the Electors arrived a few days later the Prince with extraordinary skill and the ardor of a genuine pursuer of truth estimated the distance from Earth of the New Star, and when the Electors departed each for his own dominion all seven were persuaded beyond doubt of the young man's sanity, and thus his fitness for his father's office, the astronomer told Leibniz, putting an empty eye socket to the eyepiece of his telescope, picking up his quill, and writing down a long string of numbers. And even though Prince Heinrich was found dead the next day in the privy protruding from his turret, slain, it seemed, by his own hand, it could not be denied that he had learned about triangles, and the grief-stricken Emperor assured his Imperial Astronomer that he intended to honor the edict he had signed.

FOUR

*T*HE REST OF THE STORY spans half a century, but is swiftly told—and must be swiftly told, said the astronomer, according to Leibniz, for the Moon will interpose herself between us and the Sun exactly twenty-four minutes from now, "neither more nor less."

)

WITHIN A WEEK the astronomer had his three-foot-long nine-fold-magnifying tube, within a month he had ordered and obtained a telescope four and a half feet in length that magnified objects thirteen times, and before the year gave out the astral tube which he trained at the heavens was as long as the astronomer himself was tall, enlarged the world some sixteen times, and disclosed to the eye no fewer than 1,202 stars. Matters might well have continued in this fashion, "and my eyes, my dear Leibniz, have remained right here in my head," were it not for the fact that Wilhelmina—only eight months after her nuptials to the decadent scion of the House of Wittelsbach, in a small, sullen ceremony at which a decrepit factotum of the Castle scattered the flower petals to which Katharina had once laid claim, and during which no one in the chapel beamed more strenuously than Margaretha—gave birth in Zweibrücken to a baby boy who appeared to have been carried to term. The suspicions of the Count Palatine, who besides bathing nude in the Vltava was known mainly for his zest for masques, falconry, drink, poetry, old foreign coinage, and decor, as well as for his academic interest in the art of war, were stoked by one or another of the astronomer's corruptible colleagues, who for a presumably trivial sum informed the irate aristocrat that the Princess's mathematics tutor had on at least one occasion emerged from her fitting room in a state of dishevelment. The old man apparently grinned, and then peered into his telescope; a note of diffidence here enters Leibniz's text; the conjecture of one contemporary Leibnizian, having scoured his archives, is perhaps relevant in this regard, that Leibniz in his long life never loved, and was never loved. In any case, as the Count Palatine in his finery and with his sash of white and blue galloped eastward from the Rhineland with a hundred cavalrymen, intending to demand satisfaction from the astronomer, the latter, with the forbearance of the Emperor, absconded from Prague, first by carriage, then by horse, and lastly by foot, concluding with a frenzied ascent of this very mountain, an ascent during which he was very nearly driven mad with visions, around every bend, behind each tree, at first of the Count Palatine, but then of his mother, of his father, his father in his prized plumed cap holding out his many-mirrored box— "he had fixed it, he cried, he had fixed it!" said the astronomer to Leibniz—but even in a state delirious enough to confuse the visions of my father for the real thing I knew nevertheless that he had *not* fixed it, he had by no means fixed it, what do you even mean fixed it, fixed it how, with more mirrors? Meanwhile his mother or his vision thereof said not a word, she did not even look at me, the astronomer told Leibniz, she was fixated on the velvet cap on my father's head, it was dusty, incredibly dusty, she was wondering how it had got so dusty, and how she would ever dust it. As my father bore down upon me I wanted her to look at me, just my mother looking at me I felt would save me from him, but she was wondering how to dust his cap, it had got so dusty, and the dust showed up so clearly against the black. "I remember thinking, vis-à-vis my father and his box, You'll never fix it, and vis-à-vis my mother and that cap, You'll never dust it." Then he saw that his visions of his father had a mechanical rather than a corporeal head on his shoulders and his mother, too, had a mechanical instead of a corporeal head, and he recalled that both of them were dead—Leibniz observes that the astronomer hadn't mentioned his mother's death—and it occurred to him at that moment that he had actually ascended the entire mountain and stood now on the peak of it, "right here, right where we now sit, my dear Herr Leibniz," and the final vision he had before fainting was of an astronomical observatory, seemingly perfectly circular but, for reasons touching on the workings of the senses, actually departing from perfect circularity at an infinite number of points, "a polygon, not a circle," which the Emperor duly constructed for him and equipped as he wished with a tube nine feet long, with the power to make objects seem twenty-five times larger than they actually are, and with which the astronomer brought the number of entries in his star catalogue to 1,277.

"Twenty-two minutes," said the astronomer, peering into his telescope, according to Leibniz. "It is getting darker and darker." And he picked up his quill and wrote something down.

)

TWELVE FEET, FOURTEEN FEET, seventeen, nineteen—then an astral tube no less than twenty-two feet long, borne with care from the capital on the backs of half as many men. Having long since dismissed his assistants, whose clock and quadrant measurements he could never wholly trust, the astronomer now wielded the clock and quadrant himself, in addition to the tube, and although as a consequence his stellar data were a great deal slower and more laborious to record they were more perfect, too; and so here in this observatory far away from the social as well as the visual distractions of Prague, from the people in other words and the lanterns, he saw farther and clearer than ever before, his increasingly long tubes were piercing through the cosmos, and sooner or later one tube or another would pierce through the cosmos in its entirety and his star catalogue would be complete. One day, however, when a dozen men hauled to his observatory a new tube twenty-four feet in length, there came with them a thirteenth man who instead of helping with the hauling identified himself as an imperial envoy and handed the astronomer a letter from Rudolf sealed with the two-headed eagle. It said, I paraphrase, Leibniz quotes the astronomer as saying, that the Emperor now found himself in a perilous situation, the Holy Father and the Estates of Bohemia having abandoned him at the very moment when he most needed the subsidies of the former and the tributes of the latter in order to pay the soldiers of fortune he had hired to protect Prague from his disloyal brother and who no doubt would plunder the city if their salaries were not paid. The astronomer would be doing the Empire a service if for the time being he would conduct his valuable investigations with the present tube and not request a new one until the current crisis with God's help has passed. The astronomer, indignant, wrote back straightaway. Even if what the Emperor wrote was true and not simply a sly attempt to evade his responsibilities, these affairs of state and of man were nevertheless not the astronomer's concern; his own empire lay on another plane. Pursuant to the terms of the Edict of the Tubes, and here he quoted it in full, tube funding *without reason* if Heinrich learns about triangles, he demanded a tube thirty feet in length, with a magnifying power of forty. Three weeks later an astral tube of those specifications was delivered to his observatory with a warm note wishing the astronomer well in his researches, signed by Matthias, Archduke of Austria, King of Hungary and Croatia, King of Bohemia, and Holy Roman Emperor.

"Twenty minutes," declared the astronomer, Leibniz reported. "Darker and darker."

)

PRINCE HEINRICH WAS DEAD, Princess Margaretha after her brother's death went no less mad than he had gone, Princess Wilhelmina was held captive by her husband the wary Count Palatine in his meticulously maintained but petite castle on the banks of the Schwarzbach at Zweibrücken, and as for Princess Katharina, musical Katharina, who, as you recall, the astronomer told Leibniz, had, according to the Court Chamberlain, been sent to Spain to visit her cousins at the court in Madrid of Philip III, the astronomer—after years of keeping an ear out for the opus he knew her capable of composing—learned at last that she *had* been sent to Spain, that much was true, but not to Madrid, and not to the court there, but rather to Toledo, where she took her vows, how willingly we do not know, and joined the silent Carmelite sisters of the Convent of Our Lady of Light. The astronomer said: "The world has not heard a peep from her since."

Hence the field was cleared for the devout Matthias, and after Matthias for the fanatical Ferdinand II. Each of them, however, with that peculiar comical strut of constitutionality that marked German politics even in the depths of the war to come, when peasants feasted on human corpses, and imperial soldiers raped the daughters of respected burghers, and Swedes fed filth into the mouths of Bavarians until their bellies burst from the pressure, agreed, according to the astronomer, to abide by their predecessor's Edict of the Tubes—"though you will see momentarily that this was less than forthright!"—and professed each of them an interest in the natural world.

Thus there was a forty-foot tube, and then a fifty-foot tube, and then a sixty-foot tube, the last of which conveyed to the astronomer's eye 1,436 glittering stars.

He peered into his telescope and picked up his quill. "Nineteen minutes, darker and darker," he said, and wrote something down.

)

ONE MORNING A BOY knocked on the door of the observatory. From one look at his face, "which was my face, Herr Leibniz," the astronomer concluded that the boy was his own son. He gathered from what the boy told him, after he embraced him and brought him in and warmed him by the fire, that the Count Palatine had concluded this, also. For as long as the boy could remember he'd often caught his father staring at his nose, he didn't know why, the boy told the astronomer. When he had been drinking and thought the boy was sleeping the Count Palatine would sometimes steal into his bedroom and measure the boy's nose between his thumb and his forefinger. Then, taking care to preserve the space between them, he would bring those two fingers to his own nose. "How many times had the boy awoken in the night to find this decadent drunk Wittelsbach Count hovering over him in the dark, comparing with his fingers the sizes of their noses," the astronomer said. Of course when it dawned on him eventually that his father dreaded for some reason the growth of his nose, the boy tried everything in his power to stop his nose from growing, squeezing and squashing it, lashing it to his face with string, sleeping on his stomach with it pressed to his bed. "Basically the boy bound that nose in every conceivable way." But no matter what he did, his nose continued to grow. Finally it could no longer be denied—not even by the Count Palatine, who, as the astronomer discerned from what the boy told him, although the boy did not seem to realize it, loved the boy deeply—that the boy's nose wasn't the Count Palatine's nose, and so the boy was not the Count Palatine's. The latter had no choice but to turn the boy out from his castle at Zweibrücken and let fall the portcullis behind him, which is what he did, with the brusque counsel through the iron grating that he find his true father, his father by blood, whom as far as the Count Palatine knew was a lunatic Jew bleeding the Empire fiscally dry by staring directly at the Sun through ever longer and ever costlier tubes somewhere in the mountains of Bohemia, near Schwarzenberg.

And now here the boy was.

The astronomer was overjoyed. In his absorption in the firmament he had forgotten his wish years earlier, at the instant Princess Katharina had struck with her mallet what she believed to be her father's glockenspiel, for a child of his own. The mere sight of this face, a face he had not seen anywhere but in his own mirror since his last glimpse of his father in the Great Hall, caused him to tremble. Yes, he was overjoyed, at first! Very quickly, however, the astronomer realized that beneath the familiar face lurked an alien essence.

Only outwardly was his son his son. "Inwardly he was a Wittelsbach."

The boy showed little interest in the quadrant, none at all in the clock, hardly any even in the extremely long tube. No sooner on that first night had they begun their astronomical investigations than the boy declared that he was bored, and asked to be taken to the aviary to see the astronomer's falcons. The revelation that the astronomer had no aviary and kept no falcons shocked the boy silent. He recorded the coordinates of another three stars before looking up from the ledger and demanding to see the single oldest and most foreign coin in the astronomer's entire coin collection; when the astronomer reached into a pocket and tossed him a thaler minted the year before in Joachimsthal the boy burst into tears and could not be consoled. He had spent too much of his brief life in that small castle on the Schwarzbach at Zweibrücken. He was a fop like his foster father. The astronomer: "He had come to me too late." The astronomer thought of Prince Heinrich's walks with Princess Katharina and reflected: "A young person is an astoundingly pliable thing. A personality unlike a nose can in its infancy be bound and shaped." Beneath the surface of this seven- or eight-year-old boy beat the heart of a jaded and dissipated middle-aged dynast and aesthete.

Now perhaps—thought the astronomer optimistically—the boy was pliable still, he was still, after all, fairly young! And he put reading material into the boy's hands, books that would teach him how he, his father, saw things, what he took for real and what for illusory, what for the causes of our torment on Earth and what if anything for the consolations; but though the boy tried to feign an interest in them these books "obviously bored him half to death." Euclid bored him, Campanella bored him, Grosseteste bored him, Friar Bacon bored him. Even if he didn't take an interest in optics, the astronomer thought he might take an interest in his *father's* interest in it, but he did not, though of course he said that he did. When the astronomer seemed engrossed in the tube the boy probably forlornly scanned the spines on his shelf for military histories, dynastic panegyrics, old volumes of light Latin verse. "The question of the fundamental nature of things did not grip him." How many stars there were, how they were distributed, and how they were constituted— what the stars *were*—held no fascination at all for the boy in spite of the astronomer's unflagging efforts over months and then years to interest him in such elemental questions; no, whatever allure the stars had for the boy lay only in their aesthetic potentialities, their vulnerability to versification, their more or less inexhaustible metaphorical application ("their ability," the astronomer explained, "to mean *anything*"), and the decorative charm they possessed when shimmering above the landscapes the boy sketched of the surrounding mountains and valleys. In sonnet after sonnet he extolled the virtues of heavenly entities of whose nature he was wholly ignorant; in sketch after sketch their light was exploited to illumine one or another alpine scene. The astronomer responded coolly to such poems and drawings and the boy did not know why. "How could he have understood that the lordly way he put the world to his own artistic use was his Wittelsbach birthright? That though my blood ran in his veins his head had been formed by a Wittelsbach upbringing? That from that dissolute Bavarian dynasty he had inherited the chutzpah to transform the world at his will into aristocratic amateur art? That that which licensed his foster father the Count Palatine to bathe nude in the Vltava River before all the plebs and the potentates of Prague licensed also his own aloof aestheticization of the world?" It must have seemed cruel when he dismissed the boy's sonnets as Wittelsbach doggerel, his landscapes as Wittelsbach doodles, when he cut short the boy's attempts to converse with him about the stars on the grounds that what each of them meant by that word was too different for them to conduct a conversation; but although he must have seemed cruel, the astronomer was grieving. Often, like the Count Palatine, he observed the boy sleeping, though unlike the Count there was nothing he could measure with two fingers to quantify their divergence.

He told Leibniz: "He was a stranger wearing my face."

One winter night, years into a cohabitation that had long since turned taciturn and cold, the astronomer, having combed every inch of the heavens with his seventy-five-foot tube and found only three stars that he had not seen through his previous tube, of seventy feet, and who, in consequence, was suffused with the ecstatic awareness that he was finally approaching the goal toward which everything had been directed, dreamily let the tube drift, and it drifted toward the portion of the heavens known to the Greeks as the Milky Way and to the Germans as the Way to the Shrine of Saint Jacob, and there he saw something he did not expect.

He roused the boy and ordered him to look through the tube. "What do you see? Tell me what you see!"

The boy looked through the tube. And after a moment he murmured: "It is beautiful."

"I am not asking you if it's beautiful," the astronomer said. "That you find it beautiful is absolutely immaterial to me. I am asking you what it *is*."

And the boy, who by now was a young man, replied: "What it is, Father, is a rather beautiful illustration of the futility, the farcicality, and the senselessness of your life. That is what I see through the tube." And he put on his boots and his coat and walked out of the observatory into the deep snow, and he did not return that day, or the next, or any of the days that followed. The astronomer said: "And he was not wrong, Herr Leibniz. For what we saw through the tube was that the nebulous substance that composes the Way to the Shrine of Saint Jacob consists of nothing but innumerable stars crowded close together." Between his catalogue and the sky itself there was now almost as great a difference as there'd been when he began; and between an absurdly long tube and one that was infinitely long there was, he thought as he contemplated throwing himself out of a window of his observatory, perhaps less of a difference than he'd hoped.

"Fifteen minutes, darker and darker," the astronomer added, peering into his telescope. Leibniz noted that whatever slight darkening he had formerly assented to had long since passed, and through the askew slat it was now as bright outside, and as blue, as it had ever been, or more so.

)

INSTEAD OF KILLING HIMSELF—"which would have been exceptionally foolish to do *then*, before I knew what the stars actually *were*, and where they actually came from!"—he catalogued the stars in the Way to the Shrine of Saint Jacob, nearly three thousand of them, and requested from Emperor Ferdinand a new tube ninety feet long, after that a tube one hundred feet long, and

shortly after that a tube not less than a hundred and fifteen feet
in length, with the power to magnify things ninety times, and
which required, per the astronomer, a whole battalion of Wallenstein's men, fresh from their victory over Mansfield at Dessau,
on the Elbe, to haul up the hillside. Through each new tube
something that had appeared in the prior one to be a nebulosity
or a cloud of dust was revealed to be another multitude of stars,
necessitating the tube to follow. "Until the sky looked the same
through two tubes of different lengths the star catalogue was in-
complete." The tubes, it is true, now became enormously long.
But so long as Wallenstein struck fear into the hearts of the Protestant princes, the Emperor with his veneer of constitutionality
was if not delighted to supply them at least prompt in doing so,
in accordance with the edict issued by his predecessor by two.
Years passed in this way, the tubes getting longer and longer, and
resolving more and more nebulosities into clusters of stars. What
is interesting, noted the astronomer, per Leibniz, is that his inner technology kept pace with his outer technology; as his outer
technology, the tubes, grew longer and longer outward, his inner
technology, the introspective mechanism, grew longer and longer inward, and became more and more powerful, and as he resolved the nebulosities into vast multitudes of stars, he also
simultaneously resolved himself and his mother and his father
and his son into vast multitudes of motivations; "The tale I am
now telling you—minus of course the last and most crucial part,
wherein I lost my eyes—began in those days to arrange itself in
my head, as I peered at my life through my longer and longer
introspective mechanism and broke myself and my family
members into smaller and smaller (rearrangeable) bits and

pieces," said the astronomer. This was not entirely a good thing, he felt, and in fact as he resolved the nebulous portions of his life into discrete and indistinguishable bits and pieces, just as he resolved the nebulous portions of the skies into discrete and indistinguishable stars, he felt it was entirely a bad thing. With his longer and longer and more and more powerful inner technology he resolved his mother into smaller and smaller and hence less and less nebulous and interesting bits, chopped her basically into hundreds of tiny bits and pieces, and then did likewise to his father, then to his son, and then to himself, until they were all chopped into extremely small, entirely unmysterious, and completely uninteresting bits, bits of disposition, personality pieces, bits and pieces of belief and inclination and habit. And to the sky he did the same thing, or something similar.

There's actually nothing interesting above and actually nothing interesting within, the astronomer thought at that time. Prince Heinrich was right. "Everything everywhere is more or less the same."

For the first time in his life, the astronomer wanted to *stop* looking, to stop looking out at the sky, and to stop looking into himself.

But he could not stop. He felt he had a "compulsion to look," to look closer and closer, "a looking-closer-and-closer compulsion." What (he wondered) would it take to stop looking, "to look *this* closely, and no closer? Through such and such a magnification, and no higher?"

Now, these thoughts must have occurred to him around the year 1628, just after the imperial army failed at the siege of Stralsund to oust the King of Sweden from his foothold in Pomerania, for that was the moment at which an anonymous Munich pamphleteer, "as though reading my mind," charged the astronomer with a "Judaic looking-compulsion," which, by channeling toward his long nonsensical Judaic tubes funds required for the defense of Germany and Catholicism from the heretics and philistines of the north, sacrificed the fatherland to the singleminded "compulsion to look ever closer" common to all Jews but especially pronounced in this particular Jew, "who reserves for himself the right to look as closely as humanly possible at all things, though it means the devastation of our mother country, and the ruin of Christendom." As he read the pamphlet, and even as he recognized the danger it posed to his project, and to his person, the astronomer recalled thinking that no one on Earth understood him as well as did this pamphleteer, perhaps not even he himself, and certainly not his own son. Still, he would not let it deter him, "a compulsion leads a life quite independent of one's consciousness of it," and the afternoon of the morning he read it he wrote to Ferdinand demanding a new tube one hundred and sixty feet in length, with the power to magnify things a hundred and twenty times. The timing of this demand was inauspicious. It arrived at the Hofburg at the very instant that a breathless courier came with the ominous news that the Swedish Estates had voted with one voice to finance three years' worth of war with Germany. If Gustavus Adolphus had not already set sail from Stockholm with his forces he was surely soon to do so. Meanwhile the Imperial Treasury was in a lamentable state. Ferdinand had taken to selling his own land, first Lusatia in perpetuity to the Elector of Saxony, then Upper Austria as a pledge to Maximilian of Bavaria. In partial payment of a debt of some half a million gulden Wallenstein was granted the dukedom of Mecklenburg. And now this superannuated Imperial Astronomer, "having taught Prince Heinrich about triangles," as he prefaced each of his demands, was demanding a tube one hundred and sixty feet long, so fast on the heels of one that was one hundred and fifty feet? Ferdinand, moreover, was not deaf to the whispering among his Bavarian subjects, including Duke Maximilian himself, that he was held hostage to a Judaic looking-compulsion, that he was mortgaging the German lands in order to let a single Jew look more and more closely, indeed "pointlessly close," in the words of the Munich polemicist, at all things, in heaven, on Earth, "and in himself, as well: into his own repugnant and blaspheming soul," as the astronomer recalled one of the pamphlets alleging, "not wholly without justification," he told Leibniz. The Emperor therefore found himself in a bind. On the one hand he had to uphold at all costs the appearance of constitutionality, or else it was certain that Saxony would relinquish its neutrality and align itself with the Swedes; and no argument founded upon the reason of state, upon the identity of the reasonable with the necessary, would persuade the Elector of Saxony to do otherwise; if, on the other hand, he continued to tap the Imperial Treasury to pay for these longer and longer and now extraordinarily long tubes, he would lose the support of the good people of Munich, then of all Bavaria, after that he would lose Maximilian, and hence the army his Catholic League had put under the command of Count Tilly, and soon after that he would lose the war. "In either case my tubes seemed to spell the end of the Holy Roman Empire," the astronomer told Leibniz.

Emperor Ferdinand's solution was ingenious.

He would continue, he declared, to uphold the letter of the law of the Edict of the Tubes, but no longer would he bankroll these costly tubes exclusively out of his own pocket, not, in other words, out of the imperial pocket, not exclusively, so the astronomer told Leibniz; henceforth the cost of the tubes would be subsidized by a new and annually escalating tax, a so-called tube tax, levied on the goatherds and salt miners who populated the mountainous province at the highest and most visible point of which the observatory stood. At first the new policy seemed inane; the people who lived here were poor and there were not many of them; even if the Crown confiscated every last thaler in the whole province, the revenues would not come to a tenth of a single tube. Soon, however, it dawned on the astronomer that the policy had political aims, not economic ones. "With that tube tax, the Emperor turned those salt miners and goatherds against me." Across these hills there were thousands of manual laborers but only a single "laborer of the mind," in the astronomer's words; Emperor Ferdinand hoped, presumably, that the body would turn against the mind, so to speak, that it would reject the mind, attack the mind, and kill the mind. That is nearly what happened. It was, of course, no accident that the observatory itself was selected as the tube tax collection point, and as the goatherds and salt miners dropped off their in-kind payments of goats on the one hand and sacks of salt on the other they murmured imprecations at their aberrant neighbor with his arcane concerns. Some vowed violence against him. More than one tried to hack his tubes in two. When a goatherd's wife, whose six sons, she said, were off God-knows-where fighting God-knows-who, and whose starving daughter could not make enough milk to nourish her newborn, inquired of the astronomer, as she surrendered her last runtish goat, what wisdom he had gained from his observations of the stars, and he replied with a laugh that he had learned nothing, he had gained nothing at all in the way of wisdom, and he knew less now than he did when he began, she with a howl such as he had never heard took from within her cloak a vial containing some sort of acidic substance which she flung at the astronomer's face, and which might well have blinded him then and there had he not had the nimbleness to duck. One evening matters came to a head. Through the tube the astronomer observed a strange reddish glow emanating from the Earth that revealed itself when they had crested the hill to be four or five hundred of his neighbors bearing torches in one hand and weapons in the other, pickaxes for the salt miners and pitchforks for the goatherds. The astronomer told Leibniz: "These men had come to kill me." He took what he feared would be his final glance at the heavens and then went out to meet them. And he thought, per Leibniz: My father, who worked his whole life with his hands, would know how to address these men; I, who put all my faith in my eyes, not to mention my mind, do not, I do not know how to address them, I don't know how to speak to these manual laborers the way manual laborers like being spoken to. "For the first time in my life, I wanted to be *more* like my father." No longer did he pride himself on the esoteric metaphysical torment that he sensed and suffered and that his father did not; now the astronomer just wanted to be able to speak to manual laborers, like his father could. "In that moment, there seemed to me nothing more worthy than to know how to get one's meaning across to a man whose life is devoted to goats. But I knew I could not get my meaning across to him nor could I justify myself to those men with weathered hands whose coats glittered with crystals of salt." And so, with little hope that his words would save him, certain that his own inescapable erudition would only confirm for these earthy people his monstrousness, the astronomer took off his thick spectacles and opened his mouth to speak—yet what came out, he marveled to Leibniz, "but my father's words, my father's cadences! He was within me still, I do not know how deep within, it was as if in my boyhood I had without realizing it swallowed the man whole." He spoke to those manual laborers the way manual laborers like being spoken to, he made them laugh with the manual-laborer jokes his father had once told the men in his workshop, made them misty-eyed with his father's manual-laborer mawkishness, gesticulating all the while with his father's manual-laborer gesticulations. Though without his spectacles he could hardly see the crowd he could sense that his performance was winning them over. And he ended by justifying what he was doing there with his tubes in terms they understood innately.

And so, as the King of Sweden plunged deeper and deeper into the heart of Germany, from Brandenburg to Saxony, then headlong through Thuringia and on to Bavaria, the miners and herdsmen put their hands on their hearts and pledged their devotion to the astronomer, and he demanded from Vienna tubes a hundred eighty, a hundred ninety, two hundred feet long, and what choice did the Emperor have but to provide them? Ferdinand's gambit, however ingenious it was, had failed. He would have to formulate another.

Yet none of this made the astronomer happy. The tube now made sense to the goatherds, perhaps, "but it was making less and less sense to me." Thousands of the astronomer's tubes had flooded the continent ever since Galileo had popularized it with his fanciful tale about the Doge of Venice atop the Campanile di San Marco, but "no one, I thought, understands how it truly works, and neither do I." If he truly understood how the tube worked, he thought, he should be able, whenever he wished, *not* to look through it, to *stop* looking through it, to curb the compulsion to look through it, complete star catalogue or no, even for the rest of his life if he wished, and that was something he was manifestly unable to do.

And along with that thought, and linked to it in some obscure way he could not comprehend, came another: he wanted his son back.

How badly he wanted his son back!

And then one day, around the time Gustavus Adolphus traversed the Lech, and seized Augsburg, and conquered Munich, and threatened in fewer than three weeks to appear at the gates of Vienna with forty thousand men, the astronomer's son did come back.

"Ten minutes," said the astronomer, peering into his telescope, picking up his quill, and writing down a string of numbers. "Be ready, my friend! It is nearly upon us."

)

FOR YEARS HE HAD REHEARSED in his head the words with which he would beg for forgiveness if his son ever returned. As little blame as the boy bore for the nose that grew inexorably on his face, he bore even less—the astronomer intended to say—for the mind that formed inexorably in his head. How can anything that pops into existence from one moment to the next be held to blame for anything at all? The astronomer intended to say all this and much more besides. But when his son reappeared one morning at the astronomer's door, the boy, who was now a grown man, tall and strong, though unkempt, and oddly unsteady on his feet, and with a glimmer in his eye which his father took for sincere derangement, fell to his knees before his father could, and buried his face in his father's belly, and wept. "The perfect picture of the prodigal son," the astronomer told Leibniz, putting an eye socket to his telescope. The boy, or now the man rather, said: "O the things I have seen, the things I have seen, Father!" and over and over repeated the phrase: "My accursed Wittelsbach detachment!" And then he cried: "My *aloofness*, Father! My absolute aloofness, my unbearable aloofness!" He cried: "The aloofness I imbibed with my mother's milk, you tried to warn me, I know it, an aristocratic aloofness you tried to warn me about!" and he shrieked the words: "Breitenfeld! The bridge at Dessau! Magdeburg! Magdeburg! Magdeburg!"

It was some time before the man recovered his composure sufficiently to tell what had happened to him in the order in which it had happened.

Upon leaving the observatory that cold winter night those many years ago, the boy like little Lázaro de Tormes had served a series of masters, each of whom, he said, thrashed him more than the one before, and fed him less, though with his ancestral aloofness he "felt far from all this, and absolutely safe, and looked down on them all," until he met his final master, a tailor, in Münster, who thrashed him the most, and fed him the least—"I did not feel it!"—but taught him also the art of embroidery. He had a knack for it. When the boy surpassed the master in his skill with a needle, the master, who had no heir, seized the boy's hand between his and said in a voice wobbly with sentiment that he wished, upon his death, to bequeath him his business. The boy threw his arms around the old man and kissed his withered cheeks left and right and left and right but had no intention of spending his life in a Münster tailor shop letting out the waists of the trousers of burghers. No, his Wittelsbach breeding would not let him rest content as a Münster trouser alterer. That night, the old man, exhilarated by the thought that his establishment would live on after he himself had vanished from the mortal realm, drank himself into a delirium and had to be shepherded by the boy into bed, where, with a smile on his lips, he promptly began to snore, at which point the boy stole from beneath that selfsame bed the strongbox containing the old man's life savings, with which he traveled in high style to Antwerp. There and afterward in Brussels he perfected his art under the guidance of two tapestry-makers of genius. Though he was but a weaver in a workshop he lived on the old man's money like the son of a count—"I felt no qualms, nothing, nothing!"—and when that money ran out he continued to do so. He indebted himself to a moneylender who would accept no collateral from a young man he could plainly see was a fellow member of the faith, notwithstanding the borrower's own diatribes to the contrary (and contra his own pecuniary interests) that he descended from a distinguished line of German dukes and kings who had been taking communion for some six hundred years. "My friend," the money-lender cried with a wink, "the nose on your face is collateral enough!" When the loan came due he fled to Cologne, then Augsburg, and finally Salzburg, where he established his own workshop, the man told the astronomer. En route he saw horrible things. Near Mainz he saw a troop of dragoons looting a monastery, exhuming the tombs of the monks and cutting their fingers off to get at their rings. Before a farmhouse burning somewhere between Heidelberg and Stuttgart he saw seventeen putative thieves hanging by their necks from the only limb of a charred tree that could still bear any weight, two of them still in their boyhoods. In Frankfurt after a skirmish so many deserters and suspected spies were being publicly tortured by their imperial superiors that a representative of the citizenry was dispatched to request the army to stagger the punishments—now the strappado, now the wheel—so that the spectacle could be enjoyed less hectically. "We do not know where to look," he explained. The astronomer's son felt similarly. He remembered his "exultation" at the richness of the material with which God had seen fit to furnish him. No sooner had he finished sketching the avaricious amputation of the monks' fingers than his eyes were offered the mass execution of seventeen peasants, two of them children, on a visually interesting tree. And no sooner had he drawn the hanged peasants than he saw in Frankfurt on that day of depravity one hundred things worth drawing, all of them congregated in the main square as if for his own convenience, all of them set against the backdrop of the Fountain of Justice, which God seems to have placed there to provide the young artist with an ironic counterpoint to the barbarism in the foreground. "I felt nothing, nothing at all, except *gratitude* at being given so much inspiration for my work, at entering the art world so to speak at a moment of such widespread and visually interesting cruelty. I could not believe my good fortune, to see so many interesting atrocities so artfully composed, so many corpses in such colorful positions! Germany at the moment is basically a series of arresting tableaux, I thought. I could not look away, nor did I *want* to look away—I could not understand those people who tried to shield their eyes from it, or to look at it through their fingers, those people must not be artists, I thought, not one of those people looking at that tree through their fingers is going to turn the tree and the peasants hanging from it into a tapestry, or into a painting, or into a poem, or into a song, or into a dance, or into a dish, or even into an interesting anecdote, is what I probably thought, whereas I wanted to look *straight at* it, to look at *all of it*, and to turn all of it into *tapestries*." And although he added: "You are thinking: His wicked Wittelsbach aloofness!," the astronomer was actually thinking: "My Judaic looking-compulsion!," according to Leibniz. In his workshop in Salzburg he began weaving these sketches of brutality and inhumanity into colossal tapestries of wool and silk, which found many enthusiastic buyers among the wealthy, "though the poor, too, would have bought them, if they could afford them." Soon his patrons commissioned him to make more. One patron, whose complexion and accent seemed to mark him as a Spaniard and whose wealth seemed inexhaustible, surpassing many times over that of even the richest burghers, commissioned him more than anyone else, with instructions to give his imagination free rein, not to restrain himself in depicting the sadism of war. "Tell the truth!" said the Spaniard. "Tell the truth." Perhaps, he thought, this enigmatic Spaniard is a pacifist. Quite the contrary. Whatever he wove the Spaniard praised to the heavens but chided also in the same breath for being too restrained, "in terms of the sadism." (My translation. Though the word of course is an anachronism, it captures the Spaniard's meaning, at least as the Spaniard's meaning has come down to us through the weaver, the astronomer, and Leibniz.) "Tell the truth!" he would cry. "Tell the truth about the sadism of man." Over and over: "It is very pretty, but next time tell the truth! In terms of the sadism." Or: "You're withholding, my friend! Weave truthfully what you have seen." Yet no matter how truthfully he converted on his loom what he had seen with his own eyes, the Spaniard responded: "Where is the truth? Where's the sadism?" Or else: "You are being sentimental!" Or simply: "More sadistic." Finally the weaver realized that what that Spaniard meant by "truth" greatly exceeded even the most barbarous things he or anyone else had ever seen on Earth. For his next tapestry, his largest, ornamented lavishly with threads of gold, he magnified the anguish, doubling the height of the flames and doubling the number of the dead, tripling the number of carnal crimes, and making more intimate the relation between villain and victim; and when he saw it the Spaniard said: "Aha! The truth. Now *this* is how the world is." And stooping to kiss the artist's hand he introduced himself as an agent of Emperor Ferdinand and invited the tapestry-weaver to come to Vienna in the role of Imperial Embroiderer. He accepted and went. There in the Imperial Workshop he continued to weave into tapestries the consequences of Ferdinand's policies. "I was sent to witness and weave for the walls of the Hofburg the battles at Dessau, at Wolgast, at Lutter am Barenberge. Even of those battles where his own army was massacred, as at Breitenfeld, the Emperor wanted a largish wall hanging." It was, in fact, while watching Ferdinand linger pensively over a tapestry portraying the slaughter at Breitenfeld that the words of his father—"Your words!"—had first returned to him. Lordliness . . . Aloofness . . . The aestheticization of the world . . . Yes, I thought, Ferdinand with his Habsburg upbringing and I with my Wittelsbach one are aristocratically sequestered from the suffering of our fellow men. Look at him, solemnly fingering the needlework where a bayonet pierced the neck of one of his soldiers, I thought. I could actually remember seeing that man being run through, or a man like him, the blood spurting from the hole in his neck. I had felt nothing, more or less. Probably I thought: I should weave that. Remember, I probably told myself, how his neck looks right now, do not forget how that neck looks! Probably my central concern was that I would forget how the hole in his neck looked by the time I got back to my loom. But evidently I did not forget. I wove it, and it became beautiful. The Emperor admired it. From the moment he saw Emperor Ferdinand contemplatively fingering those red threads the weaver understood that there was something the matter with his own mind and therefore with his art. "From gazing at Ferdinand's face as he gazed at the depictions of the death of his men I realized how little I had penetrated into their pain, I *wanted* to be able to penetrate their pain, but I had stopped at the surface of things, just as you always said I did. You're interested, you used to tell me, in the sensuous only and the superficial, whereas I like to penetrate the essence of things, we have two different temperaments, we'll never understand each other, *never!* you used to say, I remember this well, *never, never!* I did not understand it then, but gazing at Ferdinand's face I understood it now, I understood how little I had penetrated into the pain of those men." But while he understood it intellectually he could not feel it viscerally. He understood that he ought to feel disgusted by his art, by his transfiguration of suffering which he could not feel into wall hangings for Emperor Ferdinand to admire, but he did not feel disgusted by it. As Emperor Ferdinand dispatched him to more and more battlefields, having politely declined the recommendation on the part of the Imperial Embroiderer to bring some variation to the walls of the Hofburg by means of a sequence of mythological tapestries, the weaver found that he *did* have a new attitude toward his art, one that he hoped was a kind of incipient disgust, but which he realized, to his dismay, was a kind of incipient boredom. At least, he thought, let me grow disgusted by what I'm seeing and doing before I grow bored of it, at least that! To become bored of this before I grow disgusted by it, he thought, standing amid the scorched ruins of Magdeburg, amid the stench of it, amid the wails of suffering and worse of pleasure, sketching everything he could see for a tapestry he knew would be his magnum opus, would be a sign of a genuinely irredeemable soul, he told the astronomer, and the astronomer Leibniz, who commented parenthetically that in fact Magdeburg was sacked months before Breitenfeld was lost. Please: not bored before disgusted, not bored before disgusted, he prayed, the tapestry-weaver told the astronomer, let me *at least* as a minimal sign of my humanity grow disgusted by all this before I grow bored of it!

Only a monster could stand in the old square of Magdeburg in the midst of its sacking and grow bored of all that he saw before growing disgusted. "All I wanted," said the tapestry-weaver from his knees, his face pressed against his father's belly, "was to feel a pang of disgust before I felt a pang of boredom, to become disgusted before becoming bored, but no, I became bored before I became disgusted." The pang he felt in Magdeburg was a pang of boredom, not of disgust. Of everyone who witnessed or committed or suffered the atrocities that occurred that day and night in Magdeburg, which only a sixth of the citizenry survived, the tapestry-weaver was probably the only person who experienced boredom. Only in retrospect, back in Vienna, long after he had grown bored of his material, did he finally grow disgusted by it, by everything he had seen there.

Upon finishing his Magdeburg tapestry, his finest, he resigned as Imperial Embroiderer, renounced the sensuous and the superficial, fled from Vienna, and came back here, to the mountains of Bohemia, where, if his father would forgive him for leaving the first time, he wanted to stay and help him pierce the heavens, the tapestry-weaver said, the astronomer told Leibniz.

And the astronomer did forgive him. And the tapestry-weaver stayed.

And that same night the astronomer peered through the tube, and his son wielded the quadrant, and kept an eye on the clock, and together they catalogued 9,137 stars.

And not long after that something seemingly miraculous took place.

"Five minutes," said the astronomer, peering into his telescope.

It required two regiments of Wallenstein's men and two of Count Tilly's to carry up the hillside the tube that arrived the next morning, this very instrument, the astronomer told Leibniz, patting the telescope, "two hundred and twenty-five feet long, per my specifications, and with the power to magnify objects that many times, a tube far longer and far more powerful than any of its predecessors." "Who knows," he had mused as the Sun went down, "how many stars we shall see tonight," and his son had replied: "Who knows?" But by the time the Sun came up again they had catalogued 9,137 stars—not a single star more than they'd seen through the previous tube. Through two tubes of vastly different lengths the sky looked exactly the same. "The star catalogue was complete," the astronomer told Leibniz. He added: "And how gratifying, how wonderful, how very *providential*, I thought, to complete my catalogue in my son's presence—the very opposite of my father never completing his box in mine." In case he had missed something up there, the astronomer did not stop in the weeks and months that followed to peer at the sky through his tube. But he had missed nothing; now and then he might see some celestial phenomenon he had not observed before, the tail, say, of a new comet, or the rings of Mars, which he was the first ("so I thought!") to discover, as well as the rings ("so I thought!") of Venus, but never again a new star, nor even a nebulosity that might be resolved into one. He felt less and less compelled to peer into his tube, until one day he ceased peering into it at all. Thereafter he and his son lived together in silence, just as they had when the boy was little, but it was now a different silence, a richer, warmer silence, actually an infinitely rich warm silence, there are two kinds of silence, this, the astronomer thought, was the other one. At Lützen, meanwhile, the King of Sweden was slain by a shot to the temple, Germany was saved, the war turned decisively in Ferdinand's favor. Then years passed, and then decades, the astronomer became an old man and then a very old man, first a little bit bent over and then bent over a lot. He was one of those old men who was bent but serene, content with how he'd lived his life and what he had done in it.

"Until one night . . ."

Although he had long since stopped conducting his nocturnal observations, the sleeplessness of old age gradually returned him to the schedule of his youth, and on the night in question he lay in bed wide awake as his son snored. He experienced, Leibniz wrote, an unusual urge: to see the night sky, but to see it as he had seen it in his childhood—not through the tube, in other words, but with the naked eye. "I wanted to see with my own two eyes the New Star with which I had once tied into knots the old Aristotelians of Prague," he told Leibniz. Quietly, without waking his son, he crept out of the observatory and gazed in stupefaction at the stars, in stupefaction and satisfaction, for those were *his* stars, he'd catalogued them completely, and he strolled here and there, and gazed every which way, and strolled and gazed and strolled and gazed until the moment ("Three minutes, darker and darker, it is almost upon us!") when, out of nowhere, he collided with something soft, "with something very soft and very *velvety*, Herr Leibniz." He asked Leibniz: "Do you understand?" He added: "I had to think: Am I crazy? And what was worse is I had to think: I am not crazy, there really *is* a bolt of very soft, very black velvet standing aloft here in the middle of the hills studded with twinkling bits of salt and quartz and other minerals!" How big, he wondered, naturally enough, is this bewildering bolt of soft black velvet? And after running his hands along it up and down and side to side he realized—"I had to think: Am I crazy?"—that it was very big indeed, that it soared high overhead and encircled the observatory completely. "This was a truly huge bolt of prettily ornamented black velvet which girdled my observatory hemispherically with a radius of precisely two hundred and thirty feet, so I determined." He asked Leibniz: "Now do you understand? *I* had not yet connected this mystifying bolt of black velvet to the Empire's victory over Gustavus Adolphus, *you* my dear Leibniz probably have, *you* probably see the link between the velvet and Lützen, you are a bright young man! Two minutes." While the astronomer was inspecting the velvet and wondering what it was doing there, he saw that his son had now awoken, and had emerged from the observatory, and was sprinting toward him as fast as he could, and crying something unintelligible, and it was only then ("I'm not crazy but I am *slow!*") that it dawned on him that his son was still the Imperial Embroiderer, had never ceased being it, that he was still Ferdinand's loyal subject, and that this enormous vault of black velvet into which the astronomer had been made to stare for ten, twenty, thirty years: *this* was his son's magnum opus, a tapestry not of the Sack of Magdeburg but of the night sky over Bohemia, rotated incrementally overhead minute by minute every night by a hidden crew of astronomically astute assistants. With a few exceptions—the rings of Venus!—the tapestry was remarkably accurate, his son must have had an intimate and sophisticated understanding of the astronomer's work in order to weave it, "it suggested to me a prolonged period of time during which he had done nothing but study my work, scrutinize it, live with it, *in* it. I would almost have been proud of him for what he had made, were it not for the purpose to which he had put it." That is what the astronomer was thinking when his son ran up to him, dug his fingers into his sockets, and tore out his eyes, so he could never again demand from the Emperor another tube. The astronomer burst into laughter: "Of course, when I came to and discovered that my eyes were gone, he tried to convince me that I like some latter-day Oedipus had plucked them out myself, with my own two hands! Sixty seconds."

Since that time he had lived alone apart from the company of cats, of Linus now—"Where are you, Linus, old friend, the world is drawing to a close," said the astronomer on his hands and knees beneath the armillary sphere, where he found Linus lazily sprawled out to maximal length and buried his face briefly in what he identified as "the softest part of the cat," his underbelly—and before Linus Linus's mother, Urania, in whose sensory organs, so different from his own, he developed a keen interest. "Forty-five seconds!" He in his newfound blindness had bumped into things all the time, she even at night never did, *she* smelled *him* all the time, *he* smelled *her* almost never. "It is the same with Linus: he is always smelling me, I almost never him." It was considerations such as these that moved him, one night, years after his son had torn out his eyes and torn down the enormous tapestry and returned to Vienna, to peer once again, without quite knowing why, into his tube. And what the astronomer saw there astonished him. For he saw not his usual blackness but actually the very same stars he had seen back before he'd been blinded. Through the tube, the night sky looked as it always had! The astronomer said: "And I realize: from deep down *inside* my head I am peering *out* at the *inner* surface of the *outer* wall of my head, if that makes sense. Of *my* head, I mean, not yours, and not anyone else's either. I realize: Aristotle was not wrong to posit his celestial spheres, it is true we are not in the infinite cosmos of Democritus, we are bound, it is true, by *something*, but in positing fifty-five spheres Aristotle posited fifty-four too many of them! In my much simpler system there is only one sphere. The curvature of the sky is the curvature of my skull. Ten seconds." He stood now beside his telescope with one arm resting upon it. He said: "And as for the stars in the sky, Herr Leibniz, basically I had blasted them up there myself, onto the inner wall of my own skull, *boom, boom,* if that makes sense. That is why in my heart of hearts I call this instrument of mine neither the telescope nor even the astral tube but actually the astral cannon . . ."

Then he cried: "Now! Now! Look! Look!"

It was noon.

)

AND THE ASTRONOMER ushered Leibniz onto the three-legged stool, and with a firm hand on the back of the young philosopher's skull he pressed Leibniz's eye to the eyepiece. And Leibniz looked through it. The astronomer cried: "It is dark, yes? Absolutely dark, yes? You see that, do you not? You confirm it?" And though Leibniz, who'd grown oddly fond of the lonely old lunatic, had decided to tell him ("What would be the harm?") that he saw the eclipse whether or not he did in fact see it, he was amazed to see that it really *was* dark, the Moon really *had* come between the Sun and the Earth, he would not have to lie. "I see it!" Leibniz exclaimed. "Yes, I see it, I see the eclipse, it is pitch-black! Oh, how strange it is, and how beautiful!" And very near his ear the astronomer said: "And just like that, it is over." But although the forecasted four seconds had indeed elapsed, and then five seconds, and then six, it was still dark through the telescope, absolutely dark. And Leibniz ("I am not crazy," he wrote, "but I am slow") now realized the obvious, which is that the telescope was broken. He lifted his eyes from it and looked at the sliver of sky visible through the warped slat of the window blind. It was bright and blue. Then he peered through the telescope again. There it was still dark, and absolutely so. "I decided to say nothing to the old man." But when Leibniz turned to the astronomer, he wasn't there. Then Leibniz noticed that the candle had gone out, smoke now rose from it, it had been snuffed out it seems by a breeze blowing through one of the little windows overlooking the void, which had been shut until now but which now was wide open, and through which, it was not hard to deduce, the astronomer had just flung himself. It seemed he had leapt with his ledger in hand, and for a moment Leibniz thought he had taken Linus with him also. But, as Leibniz illustrates in a final diagram on the final page, the cat lay under the armillary sphere still, in the same position as before, though he had lifted his head a little, "not to look at the window out of which his master had fallen" (so the caption reads) "but to sniff with interest at the smoke from the candle."

THAT SAME AFTERNOON Leibniz embarked on his return to Germany, first by foot, then by horse, and finally by carriage, wondering all the while if he had profited at all from lending his ear to a tale so mad or if he had merely squandered a part of his brief time on Earth. The incident must, however, have had some effect on him, for by the time he neared the gates of Leipzig he had resolved to abandon academia and to pursue his fortune as a man of letters, and he told the coachman not to stop there. Not long afterward he was appointed Privy Counselor of Justice in the court of the Archbishop-Elector of Mainz, where in autumn 1666 and winter 1667 he composed this account. He would not have written it, he informed the editor of the *Philosophical Transactions*, in my translation, were it not for the fact, which disquieted him at first but which he later found apt and even amusing, that in every town he passed through from Saxony to the Rhineland no one spoke of anything but the total eclipse that had occurred a few weeks earlier, at noon on the thirtieth of June, and which had plunged Germany for four seconds into darkness. "If we assume," Leibniz writes, "that Central Europe is not all in cahoots," then he himself, with his eye to a broken telescope, had been perhaps the only person on the continent not to see it.

A NOTE ABOUT THE AUTHOR

Adam Ehrlich Sachs is the author of the collection *Inherited Disorders: Stories, Parables & Problems*, which was a semifinalist for the Thurber Prize for American Humor and a finalist for the Sami Rohr Prize for Jewish Literature. His work has appeared in *The New Yorker*, *Harper's Magazine*, and *n+1*, among other publications, and he was named a 2018 NEA Literature Fellow. He has a degree in the history of science from Harvard, where he was a member of *The Harvard Lampoon*. He lives in Pittsburgh.